From a purely physical standpoint,

it was tough to say for sure whether Sara was his type. Swaddled in big gray sweats, she looked more like a shorter version of the guys he played basketball with than someone he'd face over a candle-lit table.

Still, Flynn didn't so much have a type he preferred as a type he avoided. The type with pianos and houseplants and sensible cars. The sort who lived life according to a Plan, with a space reserved for a Significant Other.

Sara McAllister was definitely a woman with a Plan. Hell, he'd bet she was so good at planning that she made regular deposits into her retirement account and kept a fire-escape ladder under her bed just to be on the safe side.

A waste, thought Flynn. What Sara didn't know was that there *was* no safe side in the sights of a master hunter....

D0051444

Dear Reader,

Welcome to Silhouette **Special Edition** . . . welcome to romance. Each month Silhouette **Special Edition** publishes six novels with you in mind—stories of love and life, tales that you can identify with . . . as well as dream about.

This month has some wonderful stories for you— after all, March comes in like a lion and goes out like a lamb! And in Lisa Jackson's new series, MAVERICKS, we meet three men who just won't be tamed! This month, don't miss *He's Just a Cowboy* by Lisa Jackson.

THAT SPECIAL WOMAN!, Silhouette **Special Edition**'s new series that salutes women, has a wonderful book this month from Patricia Coughlin. *The Awakening* is the tender story of Sara Marie McAllister—and her awakening to love when she meets bounty hunter John Flynn. It takes a very special man to win That Special Woman! And handsome Flynn is up for the challenge!

Rounding out this month are books from other favorite writers: Elizabeth Bevarly, Susan Mallery, Trisha Alexander and Carole Halston!

I hope that you enjoy this book, and all the stories to come! Have a wonderful March!

Sincerely,

Tara Gavin
Senior Editor
Silhouette Books

PATRICIA COUGHLIN

THE AWAKENING

Silhouette®

™

SPECIAL EDITION®

Published by Silhouette Books New York

America's Publisher of Contemporary Romance

For my son, Ryan, who has stories of his own to tell.

SILHOUETTE BOOKS
300 East 42nd St., New York, N.Y. 10017

THE AWAKENING

ISBN: 0-373-09804-9

First Silhouette Books printing March 1993

Printed in the U.S.A.

PATRICIA COUGHLIN

is also known to romance fans as Liz Grady and lives in Rhode Island with her husband and two sons. A former schoolteacher, she says she started writing to fill her hours at home after her second son was born. Having always read romances, she decided to try penning her own. Though she was duly astounded by the difficulty of her new hobby, her hard work paid off, and she accomplished the rare feat of having her very first manuscript published. For now, writing has replaced quilting, embroidery and other pastimes, and with more than a dozen published novels under her belt, the author hopes to be happily writing romances for a long time to come.

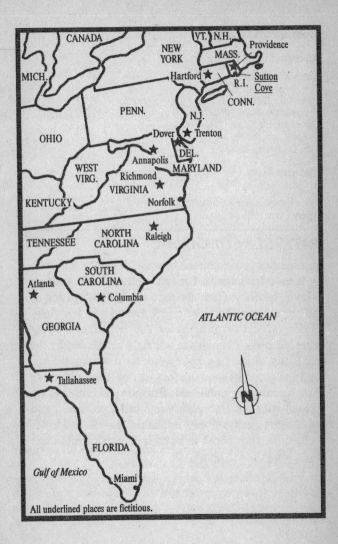

All underlined places are fictitious.

Chapter One

"I need a man. And I need him fast."

Sara waited for her best friend's reaction. When none was forthcoming, she frowned at her in the beauty shop mirror.

"What? No response?" she prodded.

"I'm thinking, I'm thinking," countered her friend, Nancy.

Sara sighed. "Some help you are. I should have gone home and consulted the goldfish."

"You don't have goldfish."

"I still would have gotten the same response."

Nancy chuckled. If the announcement about needing a man had come from someone—*anyone*—other than Sara, she would have reacted. She would have been startled, intrigued even. But she'd known Sara since grade school and understood that the words, edged with desperation though they were, were rooted in practical rather than lascivious concerns.

Sara Marie McAllister simply didn't have a lascivious bone in her body. Nancy knew because she'd expended a great deal of effort during her lifetime trying to uncover one. The cynic in her simply couldn't accept that anyone could be as nice and wholesome as "that nice McAllister girl," as so many of her elderly customers at The Cutting Edge referred to her friend. Never mind that Sara had left her twenties in the dust two years ago. Change came slowly in the small town of Sutton Cove, Rhode Island, and she would probably be "that nice McAllister girl" till the day she died. Unless she got lucky, thought Nancy.

Not that Nancy would change Sara too much even if she could. Sara was, after all, everything you could want in a best friend, which she had been practically since first grade. She was fun and generous and loyal and just all-around nice. Too damn nice for all the rotten luck that came her way.

"Why a man?" Nancy asked, focusing her attention on the problem at hand. She was glad Sara's visit to the shop had co-incided with a rare break between appointments. With business booming and the kids at an age where she spent every free moment chauffeuring them to or from someplace, it seemed they hardly ever had a chance to just sit and talk the way they used to. "Why can't you rent the room to a woman?"

"Because I still have the first room rented to Russell," Sara reminded her, idly swiveling the elevated chair she was sitting in. "And whoever rents the other one will have to share the bathroom with him."

"So?" countered Nancy.

"So what woman's going to want to share a bathroom with a strange man?"

"Lots of them. Remember, Sara, we are in the nineties." She twisted her mouth into an expression of distaste. "On the other hand, when you consider that the strange man in question is Russell LeFleur, you may have a point."

"Come on, Russell's not so bad."

"Compared to what?" Nancy returned pointedly. "He sort of reminds me of a shifty-eyed Don Ameche."

Sara had to laugh, agreeing with Nancy's assessment in spite of herself. "Don Ameche's evil twin."

"Complete with a soup-strainer mustache. You think he ever trims that thing?"

"How should I know? I certainly don't share a bathroom with him."

"A gruesome thought. Although," added Nancy, her expression contemplative, "it might be worth it just to find out if he does trim it. And what he uses. What do you figure, hedge clippers?"

"Truthfully, I try not to think about it. I just know that whenever he's around I shove my hands in my pockets real fast so he won't make a move to kiss them again. He doesn't say much about himself, but I think old Russell must have spent his formative years in Europe."

"Probably Transylvania."

They both laughed. Nancy was the only person in the world Sara felt comfortable enough with to talk this way, and still she felt a trifle guilty to be gossiping about her tenant or boarder or whatever the proper name for him was.

Tenant, she decided. The word *boarder* conjured up depressing pictures of rooming houses and spinster landladies that she'd rather not dwell on. The failing economy and rising expenses had forced her to convert the south wing of her family home into a pair of oversize rooms with an adjoining bath, and even though she'd done it a year and a half ago, she still hadn't grown comfortable with the notion of letting strangers live in her house in return for money.

Much-needed money, she reminded herself, although she hardly had to be reminded with the memory of her recent meeting at the bank like something sharp stuck dead center in her back.

"I have to admit, though," she said with a sigh, "right about now I'd be willing to let him kiss both hands if he'd just show up with this month's rent."

"He's still not back?" inquired Nancy.

Sara shook her head. "I'm beginning to think the guy is off somewhere minting coins instead of just buying and selling them."

"I still don't really get what it is he does."

"I'm not sure I do, either," Sara told her. "He said he locates rare coins for collectors. I know he keeps this little black book full of names and coins, a record of who's looking for what. He's like a numismatist matchmaker."

"Numismatist," echoed Nancy experimentally. She shrugged. "It sure sounds important, like it ought to pay him enough to cover the rent on one little old room."

"He doesn't seem to have trouble paying the rent . . . that is, when he's around. He paid the first two months in advance, then showed up two days late with the third. This time he's been gone two weeks, which means this month's rent is ten days overdue. Granted, that money won't change the fact that I'm two months behind on the mortgage, but it would have given me some ammunition when I faced Stuart today."

Nancy's dark eyes grew concerned. "You really think he'll foreclose on you?"

"In a minute," Sara replied. "It's no secret Corrine would love to get her hands on the place."

"The witch. How that man could have married her when he could have—"

"Enough," Sara said, cutting her off with a raised hand. "That was all over and done with a long time ago."

"Nothing is ever over until the score is settled," insisted Nancy. "Stuart Bowers is a—"

"I'm not interested in settling the score with Stuart," Sara interrupted. "Only in keeping my house."

"Maybe that's a mistake," her friend suggested gently and not for the first time. "Sara, you have to admit the place is too big for you. The taxes are outlandish, it's a bear to heat, and the constant upkeep on a place that old takes time you could be spending doing something fun."

"Such as?"

"Shopping," she replied without hesitation.

"I can't afford to go shopping."

"Ah, but you could if you sold that white elephant and bought one of those new condos. . . ." She gave up at the stubborn shaking of Sara's head.

"No. I know you don't understand, Nancy. On a practical level, I'm not sure even I understand. But that house has been in the McAllister family for almost a hundred years. I just can't stand the thought that I'm going to be the one to screw things up and lose it."

"You screw things up?" exclaimed Nancy, then immediately bit her tongue. It was true enough that it had been not Sara but her father who screwed things up so royally, and her mother hadn't helped any, either. But they were still Sara's parents, and they were both dead, and if Sara didn't hold them accountable for the mess she was in, it certainly wasn't Nancy's place to point out the obvious. She sighed and rested her chin on her upturned palm. "Too bad you didn't put in a second bath when you remodeled."

"No doubt about it. And a hot tub, while I was at it. A nice long soak would be so refreshing after a dip in the Olympic size pool or a run down the private ski slope I had built out back." She shook her head, exasperated. "Have you forgotten that I barely had enough money to pay the plumber to turn the water on in the one bathroom I have, never mind install another one?"

"Yeah, I had forgotten about that. And he was such a terrific looking plumber," added Nancy, eyes glazing over as she recalled the man. "All those great tools and that leather tool belt slung low on his hips. Lean hips, as I recollect. Tool belt . . . it even sounds sexy."

"Snap out of it," Sara ordered, laughing. "You're married, remember?"

"Yes, but you're not. If you'd followed my advice and tried to barter with that guy, you probably would have ended up having an extra bath *and* a good time."

"You're hopeless."

"Not at all. I have infinite hope that one of these days you're going to listen to me and let some man break through that cool, calm, collected shell of yours and discover that inside is a real, flesh and blood, horny as hell woman."

"I don't have time to be horny . . . unless it pays money."

"It does. You've heard of the oldest profession in the world, haven't you?"

Sara smiled and shrugged. "Sure, but unfortunately if it comes down to selling my body or my house, there'll probably be a lot more buyers interested in the house."

"Will you stop with that?" snapped Nancy. "You are a very pretty woman with great—"

"Potential," Sara finished along with her. This was familiar territory.

"Exactly," Nancy continued with satisfaction as she slipped from her seat and moved to stand behind Sara, spinning her chair so that it faced the wall of mirrors. The contrast between the two women was dramatic. Although both were average size, Nancy had short spiky dark hair and big brown eyes, and was every inch the spitfire her husband, Drew, accused her of being. Sara's long brown hair was closer to the color of gold than coffee and her demeanor reflected her quiet, purposeful personality.

Nancy studied her friend in the mirror. "You can't sit there and deny the fact that you have the most gorgeous blue..."

"Eyes," Sara said along with her.

"And," Nancy went on, refusing to be derailed from her self-appointed mission in life, the transformation of Sara Marie McAllister, "cheekbones I would kill for, and perfect teeth..."

"Number one on every man's list of things he looks for in a woman."

"You've got that, too, smart aleck," retorted Nancy, "you just haven't used it in so long you've forgotten it's there."

Sara laughed out loud, which she wouldn't have done if the comment had come from anyone else. She didn't have any sisters, or brothers, for that matter, but she couldn't imagine any sisters being closer than she and Nancy were. She knew that these pep talks were an honest attempt to help. A small part of her even thrilled to them, wanting to believe that all Nancy's compliments were true. The rest of her knew better.

"The problem," Nancy concluded, as she inevitably did, "is that all this raw potential is wasted if you don't use it. You have to meet Mother Nature halfway, hon."

"Unless Mother Nature is looking to rent a room *and* doesn't mind sharing a bath with Russell LeFleur, I don't have time to meet her."

"Sure you do, and as it so happens, so do I. I had a cancellation, which means I have nearly an hour before Gwen Maxwell shows up for her perm...probably even longer since she's always late because she stops by the garage on her way here to moon over Darrell Gates's brother, which is a waste of time, if you ask me. Of course, I'm not married to Evan Maxwell, either, so I suppose it's all relative, lust is in the eye of the beholder and all that. The fact remains that I have plenty of time," she concluded, snapping a fresh hot pink plastic cape from a nearby rack.

"Time for what?" Sara inquired, warding off the cape with one hand.

"To start developing your raw potential. Personally," she said, removing the plain gold barrette that held Sara's hair neatly at the back of her neck and lifting it off her shoulders, "I vote for the radical approach, maybe something short that will free your hair's natural wave."

"My hair is straight."

"You just think it's straight because it's so long and heavy. But if we do something like this," she said, puffing Sara's hair up around her ears, "it'll fall all tousled and loose."

Sara frowned into the mirror.

"Of course, there'll be something wispy here in front, too," Nancy added quickly. "Use your imagination."

"I don't have any. Besides, I like my hair long."

"How do you know you won't like it even better short? You've worn it this way for as long as I've known you, which is longer than I care to mention. All right," she hurried on, preempting Sara's refusal, "if you're not ready for short, how about a compromise? Shoulder length, like about here, with just a few shaggy bangs, and we'll do some highlighting to bring out all the blond buried in there."

"No."

"Why?"

"Because I don't feel blond. And I certainly don't feel in any state of mind to make a decision about lopping off twelve inches of my hair."

"Six."

"Even so. My hair's fine the way it is. It's the rest of my life that needs a make-over."

"Exactly, and you have to start somewhere. When you're down is precisely the time you need to shake things up. It'll give you a totally new perspective on everything."

"Thanks, Nancy," she said, slipping from the chair. "I know you're trying to help, but I don't think a haircut and some peroxide is going to make the prospect of foreclosure any prettier."

"Probably not." Sighing, Nancy folded her arms around the plastic cape. "Sara, you know that if Drew and I had the money to..."

"I know, Nancy, and I appreciate it. But you're helping just by listening, believe me. I'm going to find a way out of this thing, and if I don't..." She shrugged and forced a smile. "It's not the end of the world."

No, thought Sara after she'd left Nancy's shop and started walking toward home, *it wasn't the end of the world.* Exactly. But in a very real way, losing the rambling white clapboard house that occupied a place of honor in the center of Sutton Cove, overlooking the town green and the harbor beyond, would be the end of *her* world. The three-story house, with its high ceilings and brick fireplaces and intricate parquet floors, was the only home she'd ever known. Moreover, it was the McAllister legacy, a source of family pride for nearly a century, now entrusted to her care.

She used to dream of the time when she would live in the house with the man she married and raise her children there and how they would someday carry on the same time-honored tradition. Of course, that had turned out to be exactly that, a dream. Sara slammed a mental door on the disturbing image of Stuart Bowers that sprang to mind with thoughts of marriage. Recent studies showing the dismal odds of a woman over thirty marrying for the first time had cast a bleak shadow over the tatters of her old daydreams. These days she thought less about what would happen to the house after she was gone and more about just hanging onto it until then—an increasingly difficult task.

Almost as daunting was the process of simply keeping the old place standing. Vintage charm was all well and good, but Sara's current fantasies often centered on combination storm windows and no-wax floors. Her father hadn't been much of a handyman. Most of the repairs he got around to doing were patch-up jobs at best, and lately they all seemed to be coming unpatched at once. Armed with a home repair manual, Sara did her best, but the fact remained that the house needed a major influx of cash that she just didn't have.

For the same reason, she had no choice but to handle all the cleaning and yard work herself. Her current project was the annual spring ritual of removing the ancient metal storm windows and putting up the screens. So far, she'd completed the task in most of the upstairs rooms as well as the kitchen. This afternoon she planned to tackle the living room and the guest rooms, as she preferred to think of them.

With that in mind, she stopped by Mason's Hardware to pick up two screens she'd given up on after a lengthy and painful battle with a roll of wire screening and had resorted to paying to have repaired. Mason's was on the way home. Almost everything in Sutton Cove was. It was a typical small New England town, with the usual array of shops strung along a picturesque main street. You could buy a new outfit, have your hair done, pick up some perfume at the pharmacy and wear it all out to dinner at the fanciest restaurant in town without once getting into your car.

A few blocks farther along Weymouth Street was the town green, watched over by a statue of Jeremiah Sutton, the town founder, and surrounded on three sides by rambling historical homes that dated back to the turn of the century. Her own, Sara thought with steely pride that had been indelibly honed in her at an early age, was the grandest of them all.

If there was anything that set her hometown apart from hundreds of others, it was the picture postcard harbor across from the green. The boats that docked there were small and most of them locally owned. Located on the Sakonnet River rather than the Atlantic proper, the area didn't draw nearly as many tourists as did the towns along the state's southern shore, and that suited folks in Sutton Cove just fine. Not that people here weren't friendly; they were. But they were also Yankees, steeped in the tradition of minding their own business and tending to their own affairs.

Conservatively speaking, Sara guessed it took about twenty or thirty years to be accepted as a local. Once you were, Sutton Cove was as open and welcoming as the big old front porches on the houses along Weymouth Street, and its standards of what constituted proper and improper, success and failure, were as narrow and as rigidly defined as the lawns that lay in front of them. Fall short of the mark and you were fair game for the gossip mill that operated at peak efficiency in small towns everywhere, Sutton Cove included. You became the subject of dinner table conversations and, worse, the object of pity. Sara was never going to let that happen to her again.

One of the newly repaired screens belonged to a window in Russell's room. Sara had hoped he would have returned before she got that far, for more reasons than one, actually, but since he hadn't, and she had no idea when he might get back, she decided to go ahead anyway. She *did* own the house, after all, and besides, she rationalized, with the weather turning warm for April, he'd probably be glad to be able to throw open the windows and get some fresh air. And if while she were working in his room she did happen to see something laying around—right in plain view, of course—that would tell her when he was planning to return or maybe even where he was staying, well, all the better. Maybe she would even give him a call and nonchalantly ask him to send her a check for the rent.

God, thought Sara distastefully as she changed from the navy blue linen suit that had been wasted on Stuart into her favorite gray sweats, she was beginning to think like a desperate woman. And with good reason.

She decided to tackle the living room windows first and spent the better part of an hour lining up the screens in the proper order. She had discovered the hard way that no two windows in the entire house were exactly the same size. That, combined with the fact that all the sashes and frames had settled over the years, meant that she had to insert the correct screen in exactly the right way and at precisely the right angle or no go. By the time she finished coaxing and shoving the screens into place on six living room windows and ten more in the adjacent sun

room, Sara was sweating and muttering words she hadn't realized she knew.

She was sick of sweating, sick of hitting her thumb with a
hammer, sick of spending her evenings touching up the chips
on woodwork that had more coats of paint than a chorus line
of Vegas show girls. The only thing she wanted to do more than
she wanted to curl up on the sofa with a book was collect the
rent from Russell LeFleur. *And* find another man interested in
renting a room in a town that had no industry and no tourist
attractions and was inconveniently located to almost everywhere.

Lugging the screens for the guest rooms, she headed for the
front door. Since the rooms' original doors had been sealed up
during the remodeling, the only way to enter either of them was
to go outside and walk around to the side entrance. Sara had
felt safer that way. Once inside the small hallway, there was a
solid, six-panel door on either side. Russell's room was on the
left.

Sara fished the key from her sweatpants pocket and inserted
it into the lock before it occurred to her that she probably ought
to at least give a perfunctory knock. She hadn't noticed his car
parked in its usual spot on the street, but then, she'd been preoccupied. If he had returned, it wouldn't do to just go barging
in on him.

She knocked.

No answer.

Of course not, she thought, turning the key in the lock, why
should life get any easier? She pushed the door and was surprised when it stopped short at the end of a four-inch chain
mounted just above eye level. Her irritation with Russell for
installing a chain lock without at least mentioning it to her first
was quickly replaced with puzzlement over how he'd managed
to fasten the darn thing from the outside.

Maybe it was one of those you could slide into place from out
here and then needed a key to release, she thought. Which
meant she wasn't going to be able to get in after all. "Great,"
she muttered, slipping her hand through the narrow opening to
explore the mechanism with her fingers.

The surprise she'd felt at discovering the lock in the first place was nothing to what gripped her as it suddenly gave way, sending her tumbling into the room.

She whacked her head on the edge of the door and would have landed face down on the floor if not for the intervention of a pair of strong arms.

The window shades were tightly drawn, and in the split second before a light was switched on in the dark room, a half dozen thoughts exploded inside Sara's already aching head. The first was that Russell was here after all . . . and that he'd caught her blithely letting herself into his room—after knocking, it was true—but he was probably annoyed just the same, and so was she at the way he'd whipped that damn door open. Only after all that did it occur to her that the arms that had rescued her were not only alarmingly strong, but long and hard-muscled and, warned some inner alarm system, most definitely *not* Russell's.

The light confirmed that fact, illuminating the sharp, very masculine lines of a face she'd never seen before. Amusement quickly replaced surprise in the eyes of the man gazing down at her from an intimidating height advantage.

"Friend or foe? The former, I hope."

His words, uttered in a slow, deep drawl, slid over Sara just as someone turned out the lights again, this time on the inside of her head.

Chapter Two

When Sara's eyes opened, she found herself confronting the same stranger. She registered shaggy brown hair, startling green eyes, and fear. Not his, her own. It had something to do with the chains imprisoning her. Oh, God, a shaggy-haired stranger and chains. It was a scene straight out of one of those true-life crime stories she'd seen on TV.

It took only a fraction of a second—not even long enough to squirm or work up a good scream—for Sara's grasp on reality to solidify sufficiently for her to understand that those weren't chains wrapped around her, but rather the man's arms. And they weren't binding her so much as holding her aloft as easily as though she were a lightweight doll, which she most definitely was not.

Now she squirmed.

"Let me go," she demanded. Had that raspy, tremulous whisper really come from her? She cleared her throat and tried again, afraid that only her ears could detect the minuscule increase in resolve. "Let me go."

"I'd love to," said the stranger. "But, honey, I'm afraid that at the moment, it's a real horse race as to who's got more ahold of whom."

The "whom" caught her off guard, coming as it had at the end of all that honey and horse race nonsense, and delivered in a smooth, unhurried accent that was so subtle Sara could only identify it as not coming from New England. She expected sloppy grammar. Of course she also expected that any second he might pull a knife, tie her up with the cord from the blinds and...

What did he mean, who's got more ahold of whom?

She suddenly lowered her gaze from his face to the spot where her arms were wrapped tightly around his throat. With a rush of embarrassment she realized that she was clinging to him so tightly he should be the one who was rasping. Instantly pulling her arms away, she folded them across her chest where they would be certain not to touch any part of him, not even accidentally. There was no telling what might incite a man of his sort.

"There. Now will you please let me go?"

"You sure you got your legs back?"

"I'm quite sure I never lost them."

"If you say so, honey. I only asked because it didn't feel that way when I was sweeping your butt off the floor a minute ago."

He grinned, and Sara registered straight white teeth and a full, sloping mustache the same deep chestnut brown as his hair. Only not as shaggy. Unlike Russell LeFleur's, this mustache did not hide the fact that its owner also possessed a mouth. A wide soft-looking mouth that settled easily into a smile, as if it spent most of its time that way. Something about that smile made Sara start to smile back automatically, before she remembered what was going on there. He was an intruder, for heaven's sake. A burglar, or worse. She stared at him with all the grim determination she could muster.

"Put me down." Suddenly recalling an expert on one of the talk shows saying that forging a human link with the attacker was sometimes the key to getting out of such a situation alive, she added more civilly, "I mean, please put me down, Mr...."

"Flynn."

"Mr. Flynn."

"Just Flynn."

"Yes, well, whatever. Please put me—"

Before she had finished, he dropped the arm supporting her legs so that they hit the floor with a thud, causing her to scramble for balance.

"There, there," he said, one arm still curled protectively around her back. "You can lean on me, honey."

"I most certainly will not." Sara's spine stiffened at the implication that she needed to lean on anyone for support. "I wouldn't have stumbled in the first place if you hadn't put me down that way."

"Put me down, that's what you said. You weren't all that specific about how I should go about it."

"Well, I certainly didn't mean for you to drop me when I wasn't ready."

"I didn't drop you," he pointed out. "I could have. I didn't."

"Yes, well..." Sara knew she wasn't the sort of woman who could be described as delicate, and truthfully, she was a little amazed that he hadn't dropped her, or at the very least, wheezed the entire time he was holding her. The fact that he hadn't was, she decided, a warning as to the man's strength. She quickly checked him out again, registering a lean, rangy body beneath the black jeans and well-worn brown leather jacket. He didn't look like her idea of a weight lifter. Still, it was probably best to proceed tactfully.

"I'm sorry," she said stiffly. "I didn't mean to criticize."

His smile slanted to life, and Sara realized that at least half the power of its impact was a result of the way his eyes glittered at the same time. Not the sort of mad glitter that would have sent her running for her life, just a sudden intensity, mixed with a heavy dose of amusement, all lurking behind lids that must be very heavy, indeed, based on her observation that he never quite opened them all the way.

"And I didn't mean to put you down without warning," he told her. "You want to give the whole thing another try?"

"No." Sara lurched backward as he stepped forward as if to take hold of her again. More than anything she wished he wasn't standing between her and the door. "God, no."

"There's no need to get all tense on me," he said, that smooth deep voice taking on a new, cajoling inflection.

"I am *not* tense. Although I have every right to be after being assailed in my own home."

"Assailed?" He hooked one eyebrow, and for half a second Sara felt a superior glow.

"Yes, Mr. Flynn, assailed. In case you don't understand the meaning of—"

"Oh, I understand what it means, all right. Assail," he said, as precisely as if he'd been assigned the word in a spelling bee. "To assault, attack, raid or storm." With each word he came a step closer. Sara, with her back to the wall, braced herself for the worst. "What I don't understand is whether saving you from falling on your behind falls under the heading of attacking, raiding or storming you?"

Heat rushed to the surface of Sara's face. "There wouldn't have been any need to save me from anything if you hadn't been lurking behind the door, waiting to grab me and—"

"I wasn't waiting for you. Truth be told, honey, I was as surprised to see what I'd reeled in as you were."

"I seriously doubt that."

"Pleasantly surprised, I should add."

"Look, Mr. Flynn, I don't know what you're doing here or—"

"But I'll bet you've got your suspicions, don't you . . ."

"Sara," she supplied in response to his questioning pause. *Forge a human link,* she reminded herself silently and added, "Sara McAllister."

"So, Sara, why do you think I'm here?"

"I have no idea. And I don't really want to think about it. So if you'll just leave," she suggested, grabbing wildly at straws, "perhaps we can forget any of this ever happened."

He shook his head, the downward slant of his mustache framing his regretful frown. "I wish I could. But I never leave a job unfinished."

A job. Oh, God, thought Sara, what sort of job did he have planned? There wasn't much worth stealing in Russell's room. Had he been here long enough to discover that? Was he now looking for greener pastures? A way to soothe his disappointment? Squaring her shoulders, she forced a bright, no-nonsense expression and attempted to move around him.

"Well, Mr. Flynn, you just do whatever—"

His arm shot out, slamming onto the top of the dresser beside her and forming a solid barrier to her escape.

"What's this?"

He said it almost idly, but there was nothing idle about the fear that shot through Sara as he slowly lifted the gun from the dresser and held it entirely too close to her face. Sweat beaded along her back, and her stomach muscles were churning so hard they hurt. She'd never before seen a gun up close. It looked sleek and efficient and she swore she could smell a lethal oily essence emanating from it. Using his thumb in a movement that struck her as terrifyingly well-practiced, Flynn spun the chamber and slid his finger almost caressingly against the trigger.

Sara squeezed her eyes shut.

"Please don't shoot me," she whispered.

"Okay," he whispered back.

She opened her eyes to find him smiling slightly, his expression caught between amused and bewildered, as if he hadn't fully made up his mind what to do with her. Hope washed over her in spite of the gun that was now tipped to rest lightly, almost absently, on his chest. She stood absolutely still. She'd seen *Die Hard*—both one and *Two*—and she knew that with one flick of that powerful wrist he could have that gun pointed her way and fired.

"I'll do whatever you want," she said softly. "Just . . . just don't shoot."

"I already told you I'm not going to shoot you."

Sara thought she detected a hint of impatience in his tone, as if he wanted desperately for her to believe him. As if it were even remotely possible that she would *ever* believe a word he said.

"What are you going to do?" she found the courage to ask.

"Talk."

"Talk?" she echoed, her voice raising in disbelief.

He shrugged. "You got a better idea?"

"No, no, of course not." *Human link, human link,* she repeated over and over in her head. He was playing right into her hands.

"Tell me about yourself, Sara," he said.

"Me? No, there's really nothing—" She broke off as he shifted his hold on the gun. She wet her lips. "What do you want to know?"

"The basics," he said with another shrug. "How old are you, what kind of work do you do, what do you know about Russell LeFleur?"

"You know Russell?" she said, her eyes widening. Somehow she'd figured this was just a random burglary, that of all the rented rooms in all the houses in all the world, he'd just happened to pick this one. "Are you a friend of... No, of course you're not. A friend wouldn't have broken in."

"Do you see anything broken?" he interrupted, his expression lazily indignant.

Sara glanced around quickly. "No."

"That's because I didn't break in. I'm not some street-corner thug looking for drug money."

That was a relief to Sara.

"How did you get in?" she asked.

"I picked the lock."

"Well, I'm sure a friend of Russell's wouldn't have picked the lock, either, or stand there waving a gun around."

"I'm not waving it around. In fact I think I've been pretty damn careful to see that no one gets hurt... accidentally."

"Yes, you have," she hastened to reassure him. "Very careful."

"Does the gun make you nervous, Sara?" he asked, his curious green gaze meeting hers over the tip of the barrel.

"No, not really. You said you wouldn't shoot me and I believe you." *Human link, human link.*

He smiled. "Good. I want you to trust me."

"Oh, I do, I do." *Like I'd trust Ma Barker and her gang,* she thought behind her brittle smile.

"So tell me about Russell."

"He lives here."

"I already know that, Sara. That's why I'm here. Tell me something I don't already know."

"I don't know that much to tell. He buys and sells rare coins..."

He made a noise deep in his chest. "Is that what he told you?"

"Yes. Isn't it true?"

"Half true. LeFleur sells coins."

"Is that why you're here?" she said, putting pieces together. "Are you looking for coins?"

"Why?" he countered, his sleepy gaze sharpening. "Do you know where there are some?"

Sara shook her head. "No. We, that is, Russell and I, hardly even talk. In fact, he's usually off somewhere and I never even come in his room. I'm only here now to put the screens in his windows."

"You're his landlady?" he asked, his look of vague surprise telling Sara that that had not been his first impression.

Coloring slightly, she nodded.

"Poor Sara. Has anyone ever told you that you have bad timing?"

"No one's ever had to. It's usually painfully obvious. Look, I may not know anything about Russell's coins, but I have a little money of my own." She swallowed hard, hoping that when he found out how little it actually was he wouldn't rethink his promise not to shoot. "I'll give you all of it if you'll just—" Again he gave that slow, heavy lidded shake of his head, almost as if she'd disappointed him. Swell, thought Sara, she couldn't even live up to the expectations of a common criminal.

"It's not money I want from you, Sara," he said softly.

"What do you—" She halted on a sudden, sharp intake of breath as he shifted his weight, leaning closer so that the heat of his body danced against hers. Sara trembled.

"You said anything," he reminded her gently.

"Oh, no..."

Hadn't she known? Hadn't she known all along it would come to this? So much for the human link theory, she was about to become a human sacrifice.

"Anything," he said again, his voice sounding as if his mouth were very close to her ear.

Sara had her eyes shut in dreadful anticipation. Was that the gun trailing along her throat, sliding lower, pressing against her breastbone?

"And what I'd really like," he continued, in that same slow, husky tone, "is something to eat."

She opened her eyes. He wasn't touching her, not with the gun, not with his hand, not at all. She had to get a grip on her imagination.

"Did you say eat?" she asked him.

"That's right. Nothing fancy. A sandwich maybe. Or an omelet." He tilted his head to one side. "You look like you fix a mean omelet."

Sara sucked in her stomach, wondering what he meant by that crack, then chided herself. Lord, she should be thanking her lucky stars that he wanted a sandwich and not her shivering body. Not that that should come as a big surprise. In her opinion, most men would make the same choice. But damn it, he wasn't most men. He was a lowlife, a criminal, a thug . . . in spite of what he wanted to think. Evidently, even bad guys had standards.

"That's all you want?" she asked. "An omelet?"

"For now," he countered, the gleam returning to his eye. "And only if it's not too much trouble."

"It's not," she assured him. It wasn't. It wasn't nearly as much trouble as, say, getting shot and killed. Heck, she'd fix him a four-star turkey dinner if it would buy time.

"We'll have to go to my place," she told him, indicating the door with her thumb.

He stepped aside. "Lead the way."

"Do you really think you need to bring that?" she asked, nodding at the gun in his hand.

For a second he appeared to weigh the request, then he nodded. "Yeah, I do, better to be safe than sorry."

"But we have to go outdoors to get into my side of the house. What if one of my neighbors sees you holding a gun on me?"

"No problem, I won't hold it on you." He slipped the barrel into the front of his jeans. "But this makes me sort of nervous," he said, raising his eyes from the front of his pants to meet hers. "So no sudden moves, okay?"

"None, I swear."

"Okay then, let's do it."

They stepped over the screens she'd left scattered in the hall and circled around to the front door of the house, Sara silently berating herself the entire way. Why had she warned him that the gun would attract attention? For once in her life she *wanted* to attract attention. She wanted somebody—*anybody*—to happen by and wonder what on earth Sara McAllister was doing leading a tall, tough-looking stranger into her home. She wanted them to wonder enough to look into it.

But even as she prayed desperately for that to happen, she knew it wouldn't. Even if someone did happen by on this quiet afternoon, they would simply think that poor Sara had finally found someone to rent that empty room she'd had advertised for weeks. And then they would probably shake their head and say, wouldn't Violet McAllister just turn in her grave to see what her daughter had been reduced to?

Stifling a groan of dismay, Sara climbed the porch steps, feeling Flynn a step behind her all the way. She was reaching for the doorknob when, like an answer to her prayers, a flash of red suddenly caught her eye and she nearly fell off the top step in her fervor to wave to the driver of the town's only shiny new BMW as it drove past.

"Hello, hello, Corrine," she shouted, signaling frantically to Stuart Bowers's blond, skinny wife, a woman whom—when pressed—Sara usually accorded a greeting that could freeze flames, and who usually returned the favor.

Not surprisingly, Corrine didn't even downshift as she sped past.

"Friend of yours?" inquired Flynn when her car had disappeared from view.

"Not so you'd notice," muttered Sara, turning back.

She slanted him a cautious glance as she moved past him, fearful of his reaction to her little outburst. After all, he had warned her not to make any sudden moves. He didn't look irritated, however. In fact, he didn't even seem to be aware that she had made a move. Hope flickered inside Sara as she entered the house. Maybe he wasn't as shrewd as he looked, and just maybe she could manage to rescue herself from this nightmare. As she led the way to the kitchen, a plan began to take shape in her head.

She would play along with him, fixing him whatever he wanted to eat, being the perfect hostage hostess, doing anything he wanted. *Anything.* The memory of how his deep voice had recently caressed that word made her gulp hard and shut off any more detailed thought in that direction. She would play along, but she would also be biding her time, just watching and waiting for a chance to make a run for it.

Well, maybe not a run, she thought. She wasn't all that fast, or brave. A disturbing picture of her sprawled facedown in the tulip bed, a bullet in her back, was enough to dissuade her from anything too dramatic. She would make a run for the phone, that was it. If she could manage to punch out 911, the authorities would be able to trace the call even if she couldn't fill them in on the details.

"Nice place," Flynn said, following her into the large kitchen.

"Thanks," replied Sara.

It was a nice room, big and airy and charming with its original oak fixtures and contemporary splashes of blue and white. At first glance that's all anyone saw. The leak beneath the kitchen sink and the wallpaper that had been scrubbed colorless in strategic spots and the draft that sifted through the old window cases from fall till spring were less apparent and considerably less charming. She and the house had something in common, thought Sara, hidden potential.

"Let's see," she said, peering into the refrigerator, "you're in luck. I have everything I need to make an omelet."

He was in luck? Who was she kidding? *He* wasn't the one cooking at gunpoint. He acted agreeable enough, but she didn't want to speculate about what his reaction might have been if she hadn't had the right ingredients.

"Great," he replied, glancing first out the wide windows beside the kitchen table and then coming to stand beside her to gaze out at the backyard through the window above the sink. Checking out escape routes, thought Sara. "You're sure this isn't too much trouble?"

She glanced at him, using the back of her hand clutching a package of mushrooms to brush loose tendrils of hair from her forehead. "Truthfully, Mr. Flynn, whether or not it's more trouble than riding a bike barefoot through a blizzard doesn't really matter as long as you're holding that gun, does it?"

He grinned. "Please, just plain Flynn will do fine."

Sara gritted her teeth. "Fine. Flynn."

"You're good at that," he observed a moment later as he watched her chop mushrooms.

"It doesn't require a terrific amount of talent."

"I'll bet it does. I'll bet it takes a lot of talent to do it that fast and make it look so easy. Where did you learn to handle a knife like that?"

"Well, I did take a c-c—" Sara stuttered as his words sunk in. A knife. She was holding a knife. "Cooking class. At the high school. Last year."

"Well, there you go," he said softly.

Sara finished chopping the mushrooms and turned toward him, bringing the knife up as she turned so that it stretched between their chests, very much the way he had held the gun there a little earlier.

"So, Flynn," she said and stopped.

He rested his hip against the sink and glanced idly from the knife to her. "Mmm?"

Get the hell out of here, she wanted to scream. Better yet, she wanted to make him stand there and sweat the way she had while she called the police to come and haul him off to jail where he belonged. She had the knife; she could do it. All she had to do was hold her hand steady and look like she would really use it and then . . .

And then he would probably wrestle her to the ground and turn it on her. A shudder racked her body as she thought of the fine-tuned pain a man with no morals could wreak with a knife. Better a bullet in the back, she decided.

"I just wanted to know if you wanted onions in your omelet, too?" she asked, lowering the knife to the counter. Lord, she really was a coward.

"Sure," he replied. "If it's not—"

"Too much trouble," Sara muttered along with him. "Right."

While she took out her anger at herself on a small, innocent onion, she melted margarine in the skillet. Next she reached into the cupboard beneath the counter for the blender. Straightening with it in her hands, she backed into Flynn.

"Sorry," he said, then resumed the soft, tuneless whistling that seemed to be a major character flaw and which was already driving Sara crazy.

She could feel him watching her as she dumped the ingredients into the blender, and she purposely used a lot of elbow action as she started it up, managing to bump, but not dislodge, him from his spot at her side.

"Do you have to stand so close?" she finally snapped.

He shrugged. "I like watching you."

"Yes, I can tell. But couldn't you watch from over there?" she asked, nodding at the table across the room. She recognized her tone as the one she reserved for her most annoying students.

"Why? Do I bother you when I stand too close, Sara?" he asked in a tone so deceptively innocent Sara saw red.

"No," she replied sweetly, thinking she was going to choke on this damn human link she was forging if this didn't end soon. "Not at all, *Flynn*. It's just that I've had this rash, you see, and I wasn't quite sure if it was poison ivy. Or maybe poison sumac," she added, thinking that sounded even more serious. "I wouldn't want you to get close enough to catch it."

"That's real considerate of you," he said, "but I never catch the stuff. I am an ace at recognizing it, though. Why don't you let me take a look at that rash of yours? Where did you say it is?"

"My...arms," she countered, immediately thrusting them behind her. "But there's really no need for you to go to any trouble."

"Sure there is. It's the least I can do when you think of all the trouble you're going to for me, and how concerned you were about me catching it in the first place. Come on, Sara," he said taking hold of her arms and trying to pull them forward.

"No, really, I..."

Her resistance only succeeded in bringing him closer, until they were standing so close, face to face, that the gun, still tucked into the front of his jeans, was pressing into her belly. Sara instantly surrendered. *Coward, coward, coward,* she berated herself. Taking one of her hands in each of his, he stepped back so that her arms were extended between them.

"Let's see now," he murmured, turning them over, then back. "Where did you say this rash was?"

"Up higher," Sara blurted. "I really don't think you can see it while I'm wearing this sweatshirt."

"Then I guess the next question is, what are you wearing underneath the sweatshirt?"

Chapter Three

"Underneath?" she echoed hollowly as he easily overrode her efforts to pull free. It was the first time he had touched her since he'd caught her when she fainted, and Sara was suddenly very aware of the temperature and texture of his skin. Warm and rough and hard. Like suntanned leather over steel. She looked down and was mesmerized by the contrast between the smooth, pale skin of her hand and the darker, hair-dusted unfamiliarity of his.

"Right," he said softly. "Underneath."

As if to illustrate where exactly underneath was, he lifted one hand to the crew neckline of her sweatshirt and slid a finger exploringly beneath the ribbed band.

Sara jerked to full awareness. "Nothing," she said. "That is, just my..."

"I see," Flynn replied after letting her struggle though a long pause. He didn't smile, exactly, but the way his eyes grew more hooded made Sara think that whatever he thought he saw, he was enjoying the view. "Then I guess we'll just have to push these sleeves a little higher," he decided.

"No, really," protested Sara even as he worked the cuffs up over her elbows, bunching the bulky fabric as high as it could be bunched. He studied her bare arms with a frown. "I still don't see anything."

Sara gave a quick look and shrugged. "What do you know? It must have gone as fast as it came."

"I've never known poison ivy to act that way," he remarked, letting her slide free in such a way that his fingertips touched every inch of her arms in the process.

"Really? Well, it comes and goes on me all the time. So I guess I'll just get back to work."

Sara thought she heard him laugh as she turned away to busy herself with the blender. It was a gritty, low-pitched sound, and she could almost feel it raking up and down her spine. But she didn't turn to see if she were right. If it was a sound of irritation rather than a chuckle, she'd rather not know about it.

She must be crazy to play games with a man like him. Never mind a common burglar or coin thief, for all she knew he could be an escaped mental patient. That thought was sobering enough to keep her attention focused on what she was doing until she placed the omelet, accompanied by the freshly squeezed lemonade he had requested after spotting the bowl of lemons on the table in front of him.

"You're not eating?" he asked at the sight of a single plate.

No, thought Sara, *I almost never feel like eating when I'm being held captive in my home at gunpoint.*

She simply shook her head.

"At least keep me company," he said, catching her by the wrist as she turned to go.

"I thought I'd just clean up."

"No way. You cooked, I'll do the dishes."

Just her luck, she thought, slipping into a chair. She had to run into the world's only liberated lowlife. She had hoped that while he was busy eating she might find an excuse to slip into the other room and grab the phone. Instead she found herself sitting across the table from him, the gun for a centerpiece, telling him more about herself than she wanted to.

It wasn't that she wanted to tell him anything, actually. He just had this way of making her forget the obvious constraints of their situation and ramble on. He had a way of making her feel comfortable, which was absurd considering that she had never been more uncomfortable in her whole life. Or more terrified, she reminded herself.

By the time he'd finished the omelet and the toasted English muffins and half the frozen cheesecake he'd let her defrost as long as it wasn't too much trouble, he knew that she was thirty-two and single with no prospects and that she taught several music classes at the local community college as well as giving private piano lessons on the baby grand in the music room.

"Will you play something for me?" he asked when he'd finished eating, which, she observed, he did as slowly as he seemed to do everything else.

"Play? No." The refusal, like the anxious shaking of her head and the invisible hands slowly twisting everything inside her into a giant knot, was automatic, and very familiar. "I couldn't. Really."

"Why?"

Why. Sara drew a shaky breath. How could she hope to explain to him feelings and fears that ran so deep?

"Because I have trouble playing in public. I always have."

He glanced around with a smile. "Where's the public?"

"I mean in front of other people. Strangers. Like you. I've tried. I can't. You see," she continued under his steady, contemplative gaze, "I once planned to be a concert pianist. That was my hope, anyway, and my parents' dream," she added, her voice hitting a somber note. "But on the night of the biggest recital of my life, with college scouts sitting out there in the audience at the high school auditorium, dangling scholarships in front of me, I froze."

"You mean you couldn't play?"

She shook her head. "It was as if I wasn't even sitting there at the keyboard. I was outside myself, staring at me, at how I looked out there all alone and what I was wearing, and suddenly I was overwhelmed by a sense that it was all wrong, everything, *me,* I was all wrong, and I just..." She folded her arms, pulling into herself at the recollections that sliced with a hot blade of humiliation even after all this time. "I wasn't able to play. And so I let them all down, my parents and my teachers, everybody."

"Yourself included," he said quietly.

Sara shrugged. "Anyway, I tried a few more times after that night and it happened all over again, and I swore that was it. No more playing in front of other people."

"Must make it sort of tough to teach others."

"That's different. One on one, I'm fine. But a performance—even a very informal one—just ties me up in knots."

"That's what we are here, Sara, one on one." He stood, picking the gun up from the table where it had been laying all this time, and used it to gesture toward the doorway. "Let's give it one more try, for me."

When he put it that way, thought Sara, walking ahead of him to the music room on squishy-feeling knees, how could she refuse? It was a small relief to collapse on the piano bench, but before she'd even caught her breath, her nervous gaze honed in on the parade of all those black and white keys, usually her most constant friends, now suddenly the enemies.

It was a magnificent piano, handmade of gleaming mahogany, a piano bought with high hopes for a daughter who was going to go places and do things. Only Sara had ended up not going anywhere or doing anything. Her whole life was confined to Sutton Cove and teaching kids, most of whom didn't want to be there. Each day was exactly like the one before and the one to follow. Until today, that is. Suddenly her palms began to sweat. She wiped them on her pants legs and glanced up to find Flynn observing the gesture with interest.

"Don't worry," he said, leaning on the piano, something she never permitted anyone to do. "I'll understand if you mess up."

"I never mess up," she snapped. "Not ever."

"Except that one time, back in high school, right?"

"I did not mess up that night," she insisted. "I had a panic attack or something. There's a big difference."

"Sure there is," he said in that utterly unruffled way of his. "I just wanted you to know I'd understand. If you did mess up, I mean."

Instantly, Sara's fingers descended onto the keys to sound the opening notes of a classical sonata she had been working on recently, a piece she found especially difficult and certainly not the one she would have chosen consciously. It hadn't happened consciously, however, it had just happened.

One second she was glaring at him, wishing she could wipe that sleepy smirk off his face, the next she was lost in the music, rising, falling, her soul dancing and crashing, the way it always happened when she played this way, an all-out, uninhibited way that she never, ever, played unless she was alone. Somehow, it was as if she *were* alone. For a few seconds after she finished, she sat with her head bowed, fingers still poised on the keys, as she dealt with the realization that she had played with such abandon in front of Flynn.

Finally the sound of his slow, emphatic clapping broke the silence.

"That was really something," he said.

Sara took a deep breath and looked up. "Thank you."

"You know, you've got a lot of fire in you for a woman who walks around like she's got a flagpole strapped to her back."

"Thank you again, Mr. Flynn. What an incredibly charming thing to say."

"Flynn."

"I know," she shouted as loudly as it's possible to shout through gritted teeth.

He smiled. "Where's the bathroom?"

"It's..." Sara dropped her hand to her side just as she was about to gesture toward the small bath off the kitchen. "Upstairs. It's upstairs, all the way to the end of the hall."

"Do you mind if..."

"No. No, of course not. Make yourself at home."

Mind? she thought as he loped toward the stairs. She'd been waiting for an opportunity like this all afternoon. As soon as he was out of sight she bolted for the kitchen, grabbing the phone off the wall and punching 911.

"Hurry, hurry, hurry," she whispered, spastically glancing over her shoulder, half-expecting to see Flynn and the gun in the doorway any second.

As soon as the operator answered she spilled out her name and address and told them about Flynn and the gun.

"Can you stay on the line?" the professionally calm voice inquired.

"No, no, God, no," Sara whispered into the receiver. "Just hurry, please."

When she turned again he was there, watching her.

"Is there a problem?" he asked.

He was on to her, Sara just knew it.

"No," she said, sliding the receiver onto the hook. "No problem."

"You seemed pretty riled with whomever you were talking to. I thought maybe there was a problem of some sort."

"No."

"Good." He leaned his shoulder against the doorjamb. "So who was it?"

"What?"

"On the phone. Who was it?"

"It was..." Sara's mind spun frantically, her heart hammering inside her chest. "One of my students. Calling to cancel his lesson."

"I see." He frowned. "Strange, I didn't hear the phone ring."

"It rings very softly," Sara explained, just as the phone rang with its usual shrill wail, echoing through the silent house and making her jump in surprise. "That is, it usually rings softly. Not always. It's sort of temperamental."

Smiling stoically, she picked up the phone and said hello, then stood there in agony as the emergency operator tried to verify her call. With Flynn so close by, a silent, somber observer, it was difficult for Sara to breathe, much less think up safe answers to the dangerous questions the woman posed.

"No, I told you it's no problem to reschedule your lesson for Saturday," she said into the mouthpiece. "Now I really do have to go. I have someone here with me right now," she added, hoping the woman on the phone would pick up on the significance of that, and that Flynn wouldn't. Miraculously, he didn't seem to. He smiled almost commiseratively as she hung up.

"Another student?" he asked.

"Same one," replied Sara, managing a shrug. "Kids."

He straightened and took a step toward her, sending Sara instinctively scurrying backward. Flynn only smiled.

"I guess if I'm planning to do those dishes like I promised, I better get to them."

Sara nervously joined him in clearing the table, putting things away as he rinsed and loaded dishes into the dishwasher. It was ridiculous, she thought. They might have been two old friends or a married couple who did this every night of their lives, if not for the fact that the entire time they were working side by side, Sara had one anxious eye on the gun tucked into his jeans and was listening for the sound of police sirens in the distance.

The house was quiet, except for Flynn's soft, aimless whistling, and it was finally pierced not by sirens, but by the sound of the doorbell.

Sara's gaze automatically jerked toward Flynn.

"That was quick," he remarked, looking not at all surprised. Or alarmed.

"You knew?" Sara asked on a soft breath of disbelief.

"That you called the police?" He nodded. "I knew. You're not exactly a world-class poker face, Sara."

"And you just stayed here and did dishes? You didn't run? Try to get away?"

He looked at her with faint amusement. "I don't believe in running away."

Sara paled, wondering if that meant he planned to go quietly or fight it out. "Please, I don't want any trouble."

"Me, either," he agreed readily. He nodded toward the front door as the doorbell sounded again. "We probably shouldn't let them get too antsy out there. Go open the door, Sara."

Moving stiffly, she walked ahead of him to the front door. Would there be state police as well as local waiting out there? she wondered. Waiting with guns drawn the way they always were in the reenactments she saw on television. She pictured a row of police cars lining the curb out front, red lights flashing, and a half dozen uniformed officers crouched in readiness, their guns cocked. And she pictured neighbors in every window, wondering what in the world was going on at the McAllister house.

She paused with her hand on the doorknob and felt her fear galvanize into a solid sheet of panic. What if they shot first and asked questions later? she worried suddenly. She might get hurt. Or Flynn might. She didn't know why that should matter one iota to her, but it did. She glanced anxiously over her shoulder to see him placing his gun on the hallway table.

"No sense inviting trouble," he said, flashing her that sardonic smile.

Inexplicably feeling less hostage and more Bonnie to his Clyde, Sara pulled open the door and peered around it to shout, "Don't shoot. He isn't armed."

"Ms. McAllister, right?" inquired the young officer standing on the porch.

Sara knew the man by sight, but not name. She looked past him to where his patrol car was parked. All by itself. Flashing lights off.

"That's right, I'm Sara McAllister," she replied, opening the door a little farther.

"I'm Sergeant Novack. Did you call for assistance?"

"Yes, I did." She gestured toward Flynn, now standing just a few steps away. "I want you to arrest this man."

The officer shifted his attention to Flynn, and Sara turned to see him step forward, an official-looking card in his outstretched hand.

"John Flynn," he said. "Bounty hunter. I have a bench warrant for the arrest of a man who lives in this house. He jumped bail in Massachusetts."

Sergeant Novack took a step into the house. "No kidding? A bail jumper right here in Sutton Cove, huh? Who is this guy?"

"He's going by Russell LeFleur," Flynn said as Sara listened in stunned silence. "But his real name is Benny Fortrell."

"What's he up on?"

"Grand theft. Benny specializes in rare coins. Eighteen months ago he snatched a set that was about to go on the auction block at a pricey Boston gallery. The centerpiece of the collection was a gold doubloon dating back to the colonial period, worth about a quarter of a million."

The policeman whistled through his teeth. "Nice pocket change. These coins never surfaced?"

"A few did. Not the Garrett gold doubloon. The job had Fortrell's marks all over it. His lawyer stalled and dragged his feet as long as he could, then a week before the trial was set to begin, Fortrell bolted."

"What's the jurisdiction?" asked Novack.

Flynn unfolded a typed sheet of paper he pulled from his shirt pocket and handed it to him. "Boston. First district."

The officer nodded and handed the paper back. "This guy dangerous?"

"Any man's dangerous when he's cornered."

"That's a fact," Novack agreed.

Sara dropped her arms to her sides. In the past minute or so, she'd crossed and uncrossed them a half dozen times. This was not going at all the way she'd anticipated. Never mind that a single policeman and not the SWAT team she'd expected had responded to her call for help. Now the one man who *did* show up was standing there chatting with Flynn as if they were passing time at a Fraternal Order of Police barbecue.

She didn't care *who* Flynn claimed to be or how many official-looking papers he flashed. He had broken into her house, assaulted her and held her at gunpoint, and she wanted something done about it.

"Excuse me," she said, capturing the attention of both men. "I hate to interrupt your little discussion, Sergeant Novack, but are you or are you not going to arrest this man?"

The policemen shot Flynn an awkward glance. "For what?" he asked Sara.

"For breaking and entering, for starters," she snapped. "I don't care what Russell or Benny or whatever his real name is accused of doing. That doesn't excuse this man for breaking into his room. He picked the lock, he told me so himself."

The policeman shifted his feet, his expression uneasy. "I'm afraid it does, ma'am. Excuse him, I mean. You see, ma'am, as long as he has a bench warrant for the arrest of this character, he's allowed to do just about anything he sees fit in order to hunt him down and haul him back to Boston to stand trial. Including using whatever means necessary to enter his place of residence.''

"Says who?" she demanded.

"The Supreme Court," Flynn said, his dry tone reflecting his amusement.

"Fine," she said after fuming for a moment. "But I haven't done anything and you don't have any warrant for my arrest, so I'll bet that piece of paper doesn't give you the right to enter my place of residence.''

"Of course not," agreed Flynn. "I didn't need a warrant once you invited me, Sara.''

From the corner of her eye Sara saw Novack squelch a knowing smile, and her anger soared. "I only invited you in because you were holding a gun on me at the time. The gun..." She pointed triumphantly at the gun on the table behind Flynn. "There it is right there. That's proof that he forced me to let him in here.''

"I'm assuming you have a permit for that gun," Novack said to him.

"Actually I don't," admitted Flynn.

Sara smirked.

"I do have a permit for this one, though," he added, eradicating her smile as he peeled open his leather jacket to reveal a gun nestled in a holster beneath his left arm. "I found that gun on the table here in the house and I hung onto it just to be on the safe side in case Benny returned while I was here.''

"So it belongs here in the house." Sergeant Novack turned to Sara. "Do you have a permit for the gun, Ms. McAllister?''

"I'm pretty sure she doesn't," Flynn explained before Sara could recover from having the focus suddenly shifted to her. "But I'll vouch for her.''

"*You'll* vouch for *me?*" shouted Sara. "Of all the ridiculous, asinine ... I don't care where he found the gun, he held it on me. He forced me to cook for him and—''

Flynn shook his head. "Sara, I can understand how you might feel a little foolish about this misunderstanding, but if you think back, I'm sure you'll recall that you *offered* to make the omelet for me. And the lemonade and the cheesecake. I kept asking if it was too much trouble and you kept saying no.''

Sara met his smile with an icy glare.

He glanced at Novack. "She even played the piano for me," he told the other man with a conspiratorial wink. "The lady's a hell of a musician."

Novack flipped shut the notepad in his hand. "All right, folks, there doesn't seem to be much more I can do—"

"Much more?" Sara interjected. "You haven't done anything."

"What would you like me to do, ma'am?"

"I already told you, arrest him."

"As far as I can tell, he hasn't done anything worth arresting him for. Unless somebody made accepting a home-cooked meal and a little entertainment a crime when I wasn't looking."

Sara felt a slow burn spread through her as the two men exchanged grins. "Fine. Laugh. But you haven't heard the end of this. I want him out of my house."

"Now that I can help you with," said Novack, glancing from her to Flynn.

"I'm going," Flynn said amiably, pausing on the way out to confront Sara's angry gaze. "But I'm not going far. I came here for Benny Fortrell, and I'm not leaving without him."

Chapter Four

Flynn shifted in the car's bucket seat and cursed for at least the hundredth time since he'd settled into it last night. His back ached and there was a kink in his neck and a killer cramp trying to take hold in his right leg. Sports cars were definitely not designed for sleeping.

The gleaming black Corvette, with its soft-as-butter leather upholstery and almost frighteningly powerful response to the slightest pressure on the accelerator, was his most prized possession. Hell, it was his *only* possession worth more than a day's pay, which only increased the significance of the importance he accorded it. The very fact that he was moved enough by the sight of it on the showroom floor to want to possess something so valuable, something it would hurt him to lose, was out of character.

Flynn loved everything about the car, its long, low-slung frame and its six-speed power train and its dual heated mirrors. And still, at that moment, he would gladly swap the 386 horses under its hood for the wide back seat of a good old-fashioned American sedan. Even one of those stodgy midsize jobs like the wimpy pale blue number parked in Sara Mc-Allister's drive would be an improvement over the close quarters he'd endured last night. The lady had made it pretty clear she didn't want him in her house, but could she be persuaded to let him sleep in her car? Flynn wondered.

Probably not. All in all, Sara didn't strike him as the compromising sort. If he knew anything about women, and he did, the only way she'd agree to him sleeping in her car was if he held a gun on her. And what, he thought with a sudden grin, were the odds of that approach working two days in a row?

His grin faded as he tried to work out the kink in his neck, but he couldn't completely shake his amusement as he recalled how thoroughly Sara had misread the situation yesterday. He probably ought to feel sorry about his key role in her misunderstanding. He didn't, however. If she'd just once asked for an explanation, instead of jumping to the conclusion that she had the situation—and him—all figured out, he would have told her the truth. But she hadn't asked, and he hadn't felt obligated to volunteer information. Flynn seldom felt obligated to do anything. So instead of having to reveal his whole hand right at the start, he'd had a chance to observe Sara McAllister up close, and in the process had enjoyed a pretty good omelet.

Thinking about the omelet caused his stomach to growl, a reminder that it was time for breakfast. He glanced wistfully at the house, imagining the smell of freshly brewed coffee and bacon sizzling in a pan. Dream on, he told himself. No matter how politely or contritely he approached the woman this morning, there wasn't a chance of an encore. Which struck him as pretty unfair. You'd think that providing breakfast would be the least she could do since she was the reason he'd spent the night twisted up behind this steering wheel in the first place.

After being ushered from her house by Sergeant Novack, he'd considered trying to find a motel nearby, but his instincts warned him to stick around, and he lived by his instincts. It wasn't only Benny Fortrell he'd hung around to watch for, though. He'd been a whole lot less concerned with Benny trying to sneak in than with the lady of the house trying to slip out.

He knew more about Benny's habits than he cared to. That happened when you took your work as seriously as Flynn did. It was Sara McAllister who puzzled him, and had ever since the paper trail on Benny had led him here to Sutton Cove. She was a wild card, and wild cards always put him on edge. The prim and easily intimidated Miss McAllister might simply be Benny's landlady, and then again she might be something more.

That was the main reason he'd prolonged the opportunity to talk with her and observe her yesterday. He needed to know the exact nature of her relationship with Fortrell. If she had slipped out last night, either to warn Benny or meet with him, he would have had his answer. She hadn't made a move, however. As he sat and watched, the lights in her house had gone off one after another, like dominoes falling in slow motion. First the outdoor lights, then the first floor, and finally the second, ending with the corner room at the front. Her bedroom, Flynn concluded.

Something told him that if he sat there and watched the house every night for a month, every night the lights would go out in that same order. That was in large part why he was leaning toward the hypothesis that she was strictly Benny's landlady. Plain and simple, he didn't think Sara McAllister was the type to get personally involved with a character like Fortrell.

From out of nowhere came the question of what sort of man she *would* get involved with. Definitely not his sort, Flynn thought with a sardonic smile. And not just because of the dirty trick he'd played on her, either. There was something about the way her lip had curled and she'd pressed a hand to her throat when he'd identified himself as a bounty hunter that told Flynn the revelation hadn't made quite the same favorable impression on her that it might have if he'd turned out to be a corporate lawyer. Or a podiatrist.

Not that it mattered. He didn't think Sara was his type, either. Although from a purely physical standpoint, it was tough to say for sure. Swaddled in those old, too-big gray sweats, she looked more like a shorter version of the guys he played basketball with at the *Y* than someone he'd want to face over a candlelit table. Still, even if she was hiding a centerfold-of-the-century body under there, it wouldn't change the natural order of things as he saw it.

When it came to women, Flynn didn't so much have one type he preferred as he had a type that he avoided. Blondes, brunettes, redheads; skinny or blessedly endowed, in his admittedly adventuresome past, he'd found something to like about them all. Usually the same thing, actually. He was much more specific about the sort of women he *avoided*. The sort with pianos and houseplants and sensible cars parked in their driveways. The sort who installed the window screens as soon as the temperature reached a certain degree in the spring and removed them just as methodically in the fall. The sort who lived life according to a Plan, and who had a space all reserved in that Plan for a Significant Other. Flynn had accepted long ago that he wasn't significant enough to be anyone's other.

He already knew enough about Sara to know that she was definitely a woman with a Plan. Hell, he'd bet she was so good at planning she made regular deposits to her nice healthy retirement account at the bank and kept one of those rope fire-escape ladders under her bed just to be on the safe side. A waste, thought Flynn, since he knew for a fact that there was no safe side anywhere.

Satisfied that Sara wasn't going to lead him to Benny, he stretched as best he could in the small car and did what he did every morning, decided what he was going to do for the next twenty-four hours. That was as far ahead as he ever planned, and in Flynn's opinion it was a very manageable and prudent way to live. It was also probably why he was the best at what he did. He was a master at breaking life down into chunks small enough to handle. Doing so helped a man to focus, and focus was very important to a hunter.

When he was working he was like a bloodhound who'd picked up the scent. You could barbecue a steak six feet off the trail and he wouldn't be distracted. *Focus.* That's what it took to find a man who didn't want to be found and to convince him, one way or another, that it was in his best interest to do the right thing. Focus also helped you to get through the long days of sitting and waiting, which were more often than not a part of the hunt.

Flynn had a feeling that today was going to be one of those days. He didn't mind sitting around. The fact is that the long lazy stretches of waiting broken by sudden, sometimes dangerous bouts of activity suited his temperament fine. He just didn't like sitting around in the same clothes he'd had on for three days.

Deciding to do something about that, he started the car and pulled away from Sara's house. He had to drive ten miles before he found a motel, a squat building off the old interstate. It looked grim and uninviting, which didn't matter since all he wanted was a place to grab a quick shower and put on some fresh clothes. As he headed for the office to check in, he automatically noted the license plates on the few cars parked out front. All local.

An hour later, feeling clean and revived after a long hot shower, he drove back to Sara's place and parked where he had a clear view of both the front and side entrances. He was good at this. He'd perfected the ability to hone in on the danger spots without losing sight of the entire scene. *Focus.*

He'd stopped at a drive-through for coffee and a bag of doughnuts on his way. He removed the lid from the paper cup and reached for a honey-glazed doughnut, then opened the newspaper he'd picked up at the motel and thumbed past the news and sports to reach the financial pages. He quickly scanned yesterday's closing quotes even as he kept watch on the street around him. Several times he noted that the curtains on Sara's living room windows stirred, and when she emerged to check her mailbox a while later, she glared at him from the porch. As if, he thought with amusement, a contemptuous look would be enough to either scare or embarrass him into backing off. He could spare Sara the effort by telling her that there were only two things that could make him back off when he was after something he wanted, and he didn't think she possessed either a pit bull terrier or the resolve to fire a gun at him. He wanted Benny Fortrell.

The instant a car pulled to the curb across the street, he pushed the remaining doughnuts and the newspaper aside and gave the situation his full attention. The car was a boxy foreign number; the driver was young and lanky, with fine blond

hair and a pale, bespectacled intensity Flynn associated with
people too smart for their own good. Definitely not Benny
Fortrell in disguise. Sara's boyfriend, perhaps? he wondered
with an unexpected quickening of interest. Was this skinny,
anemic-looking kid the type she went for?

If so, the woman had no idea how to dress to please a man.
She met the guy on the front porch wearing jeans of the baggy,
decidedly undesigner variety and a loose-fitting shirt exactly
like the one he was wearing except that his was black and hers
was white. As he watched with undisguised interest, Sara and
the man shook hands. That ruled out the boyfriend theory, and
for some reason that tickled him. As did the fact that Sara
didn't invite the guy inside, but instead led him down the porch
steps and around to the side of the house.

Flynn's curiosity peaked as they disappeared through the side
entrance. It was possible the guy had been sent by Benny to
deliver a message or retrieve something for him, but Flynn's
sixth sense for trouble usually alerted him to things like that.
His sixth sense was resting still as swamp water right now. It
couldn't hurt to know what was going on, though.

Whistling the undisciplined tune that was as much a part of
him as his appendix scar, he climbed from the car and ambled
around to the side door. As soon as he pulled it open and saw
Sara and her guest standing inside the room opposite Benny's
he knew the score, that the room opposite Benny's was vacant
and that Sara was doing her damnedest to get this guy to rent
it. And he knew what to do about it.

Knocking loudly on the solid wooden door she had left ajar,
he called out, "Exterminator."

They both turned at the sound of his voice, Sara's look of
confusion turning to something considerably sharper when she
saw that it was him standing there.

"What do you want?" she demanded.

"I want to help you get the bugs out, ma'am." He gave her
an exaggerated wink. "Just a little trade humor. Did you call
for an exterminator?"

She glared at him and Flynn noted, not for the first time, that
even with her teeth gritted, she was a damn good-looking
woman.

"No," she said, "I didn't."

"No kidding?" he countered, managing to look dumb-founded. "Well, someone sure did." He pulled a notepad from his jacket pocket. "This is 105 Weymouth, isn't it?" he asked, showing her the address he'd written down on his way there yesterday.

"You know it is."

"Then I've got the right place. I understand you're having a problem with carpet beetles?"

"No." Her eyebrows arched just a fraction. "Although I have seen slugs lurking around here lately."

Flynn whistled through his teeth. "Those suckers sure can be hard to get rid of."

"I'm sure I'll figure out a way."

"I'm sure you will. Or maybe they'll just go away on their own. Eventually."

"Crawl off into the sunset, you mean?"

"Exactly. Now about your carpet beetle infestation...."

"I am *not* infested with carpet beetles."

"Of course *you're* not, ma'am," he said, lowering his tone about the same degree hers had risen, "but can the carpet we're standing on make the same claim?"

The potential tenant, who had been standing by with an expression of mild confusion, looked taken aback. He glanced down at the carpet as if he wished he could float above it to the door.

"Listen," he said, "I think maybe I ought to look around a little before I jump into—"

"No," Sara said, grasping his arm, the sudden action seeming to alarm him almost as much as the bad news about the carpet did. "Don't let anything this man says scare you away."

"No," agreed Flynn, flashing the other man an amiable smile. "Don't let a few little carpet beetles scare you off. I've got some stuff in the back of the truck that'll zap those little charmers into extinction." He glanced around the room with narrowed eyes. "Of course, I wouldn't recommend you bring anything edible into this room for, oh, why don't we say five or six weeks to be on the safe side?" He eyed the younger man. "Do you have children, son?"

He shook his head.

"Then let's make it an even two months. No sense taking chances with those mutant genes."

The guy might as well have floated, he cleared out of there so fast. The terse thank-you he tossed Sara as he streaked by faded into a silence so tight it reverberated.

"I don't believe it," Sara said, shattering it at last.

"Me, either," agreed Flynn. "What kind of guy turns tail at the prospect of a few lousy beetles?"

"I meant *you*. I don't believe you... what you did. Do you know what your twisted sense of humor just cost me?"

He glanced around assessingly. "A buck fifty a month?"

"Two," she snapped. "Two hundred dollars a month."

"That's highway robbery, Sara. I'll give you one twenty-five."

"What did you say?"

"One hundred and twenty-five dollars a month. That's what I'm willing to pay you to rent this place."

She laughed in his face. "As if I would ever, in this or any other lifetime, let you stay under the same roof as me."

"It doesn't appear you have any other options," he pointed out, resting one shoulder against the solid wood molding surrounding the door. "Since I seem to be the only applicant who doesn't mind bunking down with bugs."

"Why would you? I'm sure it would be a step-up socially."

"So it's a deal?"

"Not on your life, not in your wildest dreams, not as long as I can still draw a breath."

"Is that a no?"

"You're damn right it is," she shot back, swinging the door open wide so she could move past him. She stopped just as she edged by and met his gaze. "You know, Flynn, this house has been in the McAllister family for years. I'd stoop to doing almost anything to hang on to it. *Almost* anything. I'm telling you this so you'll understand exactly how final my no is. You see, no matter how badly I need the rent from this room, if it comes down to you or nothing... I'd rather burn the place down."

"You know something, Sara?" he said, pleased to see his hunch was right, that there was a lot more to her than the meekness and docility of yesterday.

Suspicion mingled with the irritation in her dark blue eyes. "What?"

"You're a whole lot more fun when I'm not holding a gun on you."

Her smile stunned him. "Thanks. You have no idea what that means to me, coming from a glorified dogcatcher."

Glorified dogcatcher? As soon as he'd recovered, Flynn laughed out loud. He almost called after her as she stalked off; he had something else he wanted to ask her. But the way the long white shirt clung to her bottom as she strode away mesmerized him until she was out of sight. Just as well. His sixth sense extended to women as well as trouble, and something told him this wasn't the moment to ask Sara about sleeping in her car.

Not that the morning was a total washout, he thought as he headed outside. At least he didn't have to wonder anymore about what was under all those baggy clothes. Sara McAllister wasn't built like anyone he'd ever played basketball with.

"How am I going to get rid of him?" Sara wailed into the telephone receiver to Nancy. Sara had phoned her last night to tell her about John Flynn and the despicable way he'd bluffed his way into her home and a free meal. Nancy had advised that as long as the police had been notified, the best thing to do was to lock the doors and hope he'd be gone by morning.

He wasn't. Even now he was still sitting out there in his macho machine, pretending to doze when she knew darn right well he didn't miss a trick. The last time she'd peeked around the curtain to check on him, he'd irritated her even more by waving. That had irritated her past the point of rational thought, and so she had phoned Nancy at work looking for someone to share her outrage.

"I've been thinking..." Nancy said now, sounding more pensive than outraged. That wasn't necessarily a good sign, Sara knew from experience. But she was desperate. "And,"

Nancy continued, "I don't think you should do anything hasty."

"Hasty?" Sara retorted. "Nance, the man has been parked outside my house now for over twenty hours. Heaven only knows what the neighbors are thinking—*and* saying."

"Who cares?"

"I do. I don't like being gossiped about . . . especially when I haven't done anything to deserve it."

"So do something to deserve it."

"Nancy."

"Teasing, I was only teasing. But honestly, Sara, you admitted that this guy is great-looking—"

"Not great, all right. I said he was all right."

"Yes, but when I questioned you about the specifics, they added up to great. Tall, strong, devastating smile, perfect teeth, bedroom eyes . . ."

"I never used the expression bedroom eyes."

"You didn't have to. I could tell from your tone of voice when you went on about the exact shade of green they are and precisely how they crinkle at the edges, that we were definitely talking about a classic case of bedroom eyes."

"Humph."

"Which brings me back to my original point, perhaps you shouldn't be so hasty about getting rid of this Flynn guy. Would it hurt to invite him in for a cup of coffee? Get to know him a little? After all, he is working for the government."

"In a pig's eye, he is," countered Sara, twisting her neck to watch as he got out of his car and stretched. "He's working for himself, period. He makes his living off other people's misery and misfortune. People like Russell."

"May I remind you that Russell is a wanted criminal? And that Russell isn't even his real name?"

"I only have Flynn's word for that."

"His and the arrest warrant he showed that policeman last night."

"Mmm," Sara replied. "There was that, I suppose."

"Right. No matter how badly Flynn behaved yesterday, let's not lose sight of who the real bad guy is here."

"Oh, believe me, I'm not," declared Sara, keeping Flynn in sight as he did what looked like a hundred leaning push-ups off the hood of his car.

"Good. Maybe the poor man would even like a chance to apologize. Which you could provide him with over a cup of coffee."

"Never. Not a crumb, not a drop, not another morsel will that man ever get from me. I mean it, Nance, I wouldn't spit on John Flynn if he was dying of thirst."

"I'm relieved to hear that," her friend replied, her dry tone coming through the phone line loud and clear. "Thankfully, there's a lot of ground to explore between spitting on the man and getting to know him. So go explore."

"*Getting to know him?* I recognize that tone, Nance. Don't you ever think of anything else?"

"No...except maybe once in a while Mrs. Linberger's perm, which has already been setting five minutes too long. I gotta run, Sara. Don't do anything I wouldn't do."

"As if I could even think of something that would fall into that category."

"True. Keep me posted."

Big help she'd been, thought Sara as she hung up the phone. She was looking for a way to zap the man off the face of the earth and Nancy wanted her to invite him in for coffee. It was pretty bad, she thought dejectedly, when your best friend considered you such a lost cause she tried to pair you up with a bounty hunter, of all things.

Bounty hunter. There was something definitely unsavory about someone who spent his days hunting other human beings. For profit. Did he go home at night—on those nights when he went home, that is—and shout, "Hi, honey, I'm home. Bagged a big one today"?

Sara's forehead puckered. That raised an interesting and hitherto unconsidered matter... Was there a *honey* of some sort there to greet Flynn when he returned home? A wife, girlfriend, lover? Not that she cared. It would just be interesting to know. It wouldn't come as a surprise if there were a woman in his life. In spite of all his irritating traits, Flynn was undeniably an attractive man. In fact, she had downplayed his attributes to Nancy, knowing how such details could addle her friend's brain and cloud her judgment.

Nancy had a definite weakness where handsome men were concerned. But not Sara. Maybe because Nancy, who'd married Drew, associated gorgeous, sexy men with happy endings. Sara's frame of reference was decidedly different. Stuart had been handsome. Still was, actually, in spite of her hopes that marriage to Corrine would have caused him to go soft or gray or bald.

He had certainly been far too handsome for Sara. That had been obvious to everyone in Sutton Cove. There had been raised eyebrows when he'd first dated her and outright astonishment when he proposed. "What a lucky young lady you are," people would exclaim when they examined the engagement ring that had adorned her left hand so briefly that summer five years ago. She'd known that behind her back they were more blunt, wondering what a prize like Stuart saw in plain, plump Sara McAllister.

Sara had wondered, too, even as she walked through the world in a state of dazed bliss at the sudden and miraculous turn her life had taken. She knew she was lucky to have Stuart, and if she hadn't known, her mother's constant reminders would have convinced her quickly enough. And so she did everything she could to please him and show him how thankful she was that he had chosen her to love, paying no attention at all to all the thoughtless little things he said and did. When you were an ugly duckling picked by a prince, you didn't go around grumbling that his last name wasn't Charming.

Then Stuart was promoted to vice president at the bank around the same time her father died, leaving behind not the comfortable McAllister fortune everyone assumed, but rather a staggering pile of debt, gambling and other. And Stuart, in his new position, was privy to all the details. Not long afterward, everyone in town got the answer as to what he had seen in her. Barely a week before they were to be married, Stuart sat her down on the front porch and taught her a cold hard lesson in love; no inheritance, no wedding. He hadn't even bothered to lie about it. But then, he'd never been overly concerned about Sara's feelings, not in what he said or did, not even while they were having sex, so why should he have started then?

Now what was Flynn up to? Sara wondered, sliding from one window to the next to keep tabs on him as he walked a short way down the street, turned and ambled back. Probably just stretching his legs. It must be tough to sit cooped up in that little car all night and day. Especially for a man Flynn's size, and who looked like he was used to getting a lot of exercise. He didn't stay in that kind of shape by sitting and eating doughnuts. She was pretty sure that his work had its more physically challenging side. As well as a dangerous one.

It would be interesting, she had to admit, to hear firsthand about some of his experiences. Maybe it was because her own life was so predictable and unadventuresome that she was so fascinated by those who lived more recklessly. She read mysteries and thrillers by the score, and the closer to the edge of her seat a movie kept her, the better she liked it. She had a feeling Flynn was exactly the sort of brash, daring character who so enthralled her between the pages or on screen. Maybe, she thought, craning her neck to watch him pet the dog next door, that accounted for how enthralled she seemed to be with him in the flesh.

That telling choice of words, coupled with the fact that he picked that precise moment to glance toward the window and flash her a grin, sent Sara scurrying backward. This was ridiculous. It was a public street; if he wanted to sit out there, let him. She certainly had better things to do with her time than watch him. She reached the kitchen before she was able to discipline her thoughts enough to recall even one of those better things she had to do. The linen closet. She'd been meaning to reorganize it for months. Doing a three hundred and sixty degree turn, she started for the stairs just as the doorbell sounded.

Flynn.

She had no doubt it was him, probably hoping she had cooled down enough to reconsider his offer to rent the room. Well, she had cooled down, but the answer was still the same, and she had no qualms about telling him so.

Yanking open the front door, she said, "Look— Oh, Stuart, it's you."

"Were you expecting someone else?"

"Yes, I mean no, not exactly." She looked past him to where Flynn was now behind the wheel of his sports car, pretending to nap. Sara's sudden scowl reflected the fact that she knew better.

"Have I come at a bad time?" Stuart asked.

She swung her gaze to him and, seeing the wary look on his face, forced a reassuring smile. "No, this is fine. Would you like to come in?" she asked, aware for the first time of the old clothes she was wearing and that her hair was slipping loose from the barrette at the back of her neck. Great.

Although she truly had no lingering feelings for Stuart—except perhaps gratitude that they hadn't married—she always made an effort to look as good as she could whenever he was around. Mostly in the hope that he wouldn't feel the same way. Ordinarily, that would have been her first thought when she saw him standing on her doorstep. But not today. Flynn seemed to have taken up residence at the front of her brain and wouldn't be dislodged. Even now, leading Stuart into the living room, it was hard to work up more than a faint wish that there was some casual way she could excuse herself for a moment and return wearing a suit and heels.

"Would you like a cup of coffee?" she asked him.

"No, thanks. I really can't stay. I was on my way back from a meeting in Providence and I thought I'd stop by to discuss something that's been on my mind for a while now." He looked crisp in a European cut navy suit and white shirt. His blond hair was combed in a wave above his forehead, and he gave her that slight, earnest smile that used to make her knees weak. "I thought it best if we spoke about this privately. Away from the bank."

"It sounds serious," said Sara, trying to maintain eye contact with Stuart when a motion outside caught her attention and she noticed Flynn standing beside his car. Now what?

"It is serious, Sara. In fact, I think if this works out the way I'm hoping it will, it will change the course of both of our lives forever."

Darn it. Flynn had moved out of her line of vision. Maybe if she slid just a bit to the . . .

"Sara?"

"Yes? Oh, Stuart, I'm sorry."

"Is something wrong?"

"No, no, nothing. What were you saying? Something about changing the course of our lives?" Heavens, what *was* he saying about changing the course of their lives? Was it possible that after all this time, he... No, it wasn't possible.

"As an officer of the bank, I am, I'm sure you realize, privy to your complete financial picture. And I think you'd have to agree that it isn't what we would refer to as shipshape."

"No, I guess it's closer to shipwreck, isn't it, Stuart?"

That earned her his small compassionate smile. "Through no fault of your own, Sara. Your father's gambling debts set you on this path to financial ruin, and your mother's stubborn refusal to sell this house, even at the height of the real estate boom, only pushed matters further along. But there is a way out, if, and I say this as your friend as well as a member of the professional banking community, if— Sara, is there something out there?"

"Out where?"

"There." He gestured impatiently toward the front window. "Your eyes keep sliding in that direction."

"Do they? I'm sorry, it's probably just a bad habit. Go on, Stuart, about the way out."

"Yes, there *is* a way out, if you don't continue making the same mistake your mother did. The solution is for you to sell this house, Sara, and the time to do it is now. I know that won't be easy for you, so as your friend, I'm prepared to make you an offer generous enough to, shall we say, grease the gears a bit?"

He fired a full-blown, hundred-watt Bowers smile her way, the one that had once made her quiver inside. She wasn't quivering now. Instead, she fiddled with a button on her wrinkled shirt and met his gaze with a look of disbelief.

"I beg your pardon?"

"I said that I'm willing to make you an offer on the house. A generous offer."

"Stuart, I can't believe that you would come here to make an offer at all. You know how I feel about selling this house. You know the lengths I've gone to avoid selling and that I intend to hang on here as long as I can hoping that someway, somehow—''

"Hoping for a miracle, you mean?" Stuart interrupted in a caustic tone she'd heard him resort to on only a few occasions. "Face it, Sara, that's not going to happen. You're a woman alone, with minimal income and no assets to fall back on."

"Are you referring to financial assets or otherwise?"

"What the hell does that mean?"

"Well, since you thought it necessary to point out that I am a woman alone, I wondered what sort of assets I'm lacking that you considered most germane to my situation."

"Look, you might want to turn this into a debate of ancient history so that your feelings can get hurt all over again, but I don't. I came here to try to help you. You have absolutely no need for a place this size, and I do." He took a deep breath, puffing his chest up as his smile reemerged. "Corrine is expecting a baby in the fall."

"Congratulations."

"Thank you, Sara. Of course, the place we're in now won't do at all. We'll need more bedrooms, for starters, and a bigger yard, room for a swing set, and Corrine is already talking about putting a pool over there where that weeping willow is now."

"Corrine is talking about putting a pool in *my* yard? Cutting down *my* willow tree?"

He had the decency to look a little abashed. "Well, it's all speculation, of course. But—and I don't say this to be cruel—matters have reached the point where it's only a matter of time. You'll either sell this place or lose it." He patted her shoulder briefly, professionally. "Why not make it easy on everyone? If you sell now, Corrine and I will have the house of our dreams and you can find a place that's more . . . manageable."

"For a woman alone."

"Exactly." He stood and extracted a folded piece of paper from the inside pocket of his suitcoat. "Don't look at this now . . . You're too upset and I want to give you time to grow accustomed to the idea. This is my sales offer, and I'm confident you'll find it more than generous, considering how the price will plummet if foreclosure proceedings are started. Call me.''

Sara, ever mindful of her manners, trailed behind him as he found his way to the front door of the house of his dreams. All the way she bit her tongue to keep from blurting out, ''What about *my* dreams?'' What good would it do, since Stuart obviously couldn't care less and she was no longer even sure what those dreams really were.

Stuart opened the door and had already stepped onto the porch, turning to say goodbye, when Sara became aware that Flynn was already there, standing right beside him.

Just what she needed, round three.

She braced herself as Flynn smiled broadly at her without even glancing at Stuart.

''Hello, Sara,'' he said, extending his hand to her.

She took it automatically and as his fingers closed around hers, he gave a gentle, relentless pull.

It all happened so quickly, so smoothly, as if she were swept into a man's arms every day. His other hand curled around her waist, helping to pull her against him. And then she was staring up into his knowing green eyes, and his mouth, warm and soft and so very good at this, found hers.

Chapter Five

Sara knew she ought to protest, scream, do something.

Instead she stood there and let Flynn kiss her until he was finished. Which took a while. Flynn kissed the way he did everything else, with slow, lazy deliberation and not much concern with whether anyone else liked it or not. Which wasn't really an issue because, to her shame, Sara liked being kissed by him very much.

She liked the sure, practiced attention of his mouth and the abrasive tickle of his mustache and the solid power of his embrace. She liked all of it, so much so that for a second after he stopped kissing her she simply stood there, staring into his bemused eyes, completely oblivious to the fact that they weren't alone.

Not to mention the fact that he had no right or reason to kiss her in the first place.

The sound of Stuart clearing his throat brought all the awkward particulars of the situation back to her.

Pulling away from Flynn, she opened her mouth to demand an explanation but was thwarted when he spoke first.

"Are you ready to go?" he asked, his gaze holding hers in a way that signaled there was a message beneath the confusing question.

"Go?" Sara echoed tentatively.

"Right. Para sailing. Today's the day." He frowned at her. "You haven't forgotten that you promised me a lesson, have you?"

"Para sailing?" exclaimed Stuart, with a loud chuckle. "Sara? She wouldn't know a sail from a bedspread. The woman's a dud at anything the least bit physical."

Suddenly Sara wasn't sure which of the two men she'd most enjoying strangling.

While she struggled for words, Flynn for the first time turned to look at Stuart. He did so slowly, reluctantly, as if annoyed that anything should distract him from Sara, however briefly. At least that's the way it seemed to Sara and, irrational though it might be, at that second she felt closer to Flynn than she did to this man to whom she'd once been engaged.

"Is that what she told you?" he asked Stuart, a note of amusement in his voice.

"She didn't have to tell me," Stuart retorted. "I think I know Sara well enough to know she doesn't do things like that. Para sailing," he scoffed, shaking his head, "that's a good one."

Flynn gave a negligent shrug. "You obviously don't know the lady as well as you thought."

"Oh, I think I know her well enough. I'm Stuart Bowers," he said, thrusting his hand forward. "An old friend of Sara's," he added as if that ought to settle this matter of who knew whom and how well, as if Flynn and everyone else in the world ought to know that he, Stuart Bowers, was the man who'd dumped Sara practically on the church steps.

Flynn's expression of utter indifference delighted Sara.

He casually extended his hand to shake Stuart's. "John Flynn," he said. "A very new friend of Sara's."

As he said it, he let his gaze slide back to caress Sara, the small smile playing about his lips hinting at things beyond friendship and para sailing. Sara couldn't imagine what on earth had prompted him to behave this way, or why, but she knew the proper thing to do was put a stop to it immediately.

Unfortunately, at that moment, propriety wasn't in the driver's seat. She was enjoying the effect the charade was having on Stuart entirely too much to call a halt.

"Actually," she said to Flynn, hoping the nervous catch in her voice wasn't as obvious to their ears as her own, "I was just about to freshen up and change when Stuart dropped by. I'll only be a few minutes."

"I'll wait," he said, managing to give the two words enough virile intensity to send a shiver dancing along her spine.

"Well, good." She glanced at Stuart. "If you'll excuse us, Stuart . . ."

He suddenly looked less decisive about leaving. "Of course," he murmured. "And you'll think about what I said, Sara?"

"Oh, yes, I'll think about it."

"And you'll get back to me?"

"Yes, but . . ."

"Better yet, why don't I call you?"

"If you like," she said, edging inside the front door.

"In fact," Stuart continued as Flynn took a step inside to join her, positioning himself to break their eye contact, "I'll call you first thing tomorrow."

"Okay."

Flynn reached past her for the door and began to close it. "Goodbye, Stuart."

For a moment after the door swung shut there was silence on the other side. Sara couldn't suppress a feeling of satisfaction as she pictured Stuart's astonishment at being so summarily dismissed. Handsome and successful, Stuart was an important man in Sutton Cove and most people treated him as such. John Flynn wasn't like most people, however. Truthfully he wasn't like anyone she had ever known before; that was becoming clearer to Sara all the time.

Finally they heard Stuart's footsteps cross the porch and then the sound of his car starting. Sara breathed a sigh of relief before turning to confront Flynn.

"He's gone," she said.

"Sounds like it."

"I... You... We gave him the wrong impression, you know."

"Yeah." A wicked grin lifted the edges of his mustache. "Felt good, didn't it?"

Instinctively Sara opened her mouth to say that of course it hadn't felt good, that deceiving another person should never feel good, when she was brought up short by the truth. It *had* felt good to see Stuart the one floundering and taken aback for a change. It had felt wonderful, in fact. And it still did. Right about then she felt ten feet tall and buoyant enough to para sail without a sail.

"Didn't it feel good, Sara?" he prodded, crowding even closer to her in the small hallway.

"Yes," she admitted, unable to control the broad smile that claimed her mouth. "God, yes, it felt good. Did you see the look on his face?" She laughed out loud. "For years I've dreamed of being one up on Stuart, of turning the tables, and I finally did it! Not alone, of course," she added quickly. "I never could have pulled that off without you being there.... I never even would have thought of it."

"Glad I could help."

She caught her bottom lip with her teeth, suddenly thoughtful. "Why did you? I mean, what made you act that way in the first place? You don't even know Stuart."

"No, but I've known enough men like him in my lifetime. Guys who are all buttoned down and squared away, sure of what they want and how to go about getting it from whoever has it."

His description fit Stuart to a *T,* which only increased Sara's curiosity. "But how did you know he was like that?"

Flynn shrugged. "I saw him walk in here."

"You *saw* him? One look and you had him all figured out?"

"Basically. But I did also happen to overhear a little of your conversation."

"How little?"

"Enough to know the guy needed an attitude adjustment."

"You were eavesdropping," she accused.

"Impolite of me, I know," he admitted without looking the least bit contrite. "Unfortunately it's an occupational necessity. For all I knew you might have been discussing Benny."

"We weren't."

"I know that now." He narrowed his eyes to gaze speculatively at her. "So what's the ancient history between you and Bowers?"

"It's none of your business, that's what it is."

"Okay then, tell me about your problems with the house."

"I will not," she said, annoyed that he was the one being rude and she was the one blushing. "That's also none of your business."

"True, but I might be able to help anyway. The way I helped you handle Bowers."

"In the first place, I wouldn't have *handled* Stuart that way at all if not for you, so I wouldn't have needed your help. And in the second, I'm not sure what a *help* it will prove to be in the long run. I'm sure that once Stuart has time to think about it, we'll only have succeeded in annoying him."

"I'd settle for that," Flynn countered agreeably.

"You can afford to. He's not vice president of the bank holding the note on your house."

"The fact remains that we did more than annoy him. We *intrigued* him, Sara. Gave him something to think about."

"Oh please. By lying to him? As soon as he recovers he'll realize that's all it was."

"Not entirely," he said. "We didn't lie . . . too much. We simply created an illusion that he can either accept or reject. I'm betting he buys it wholesale . . . and it drives him crazy."

"You're wrong. Stuart isn't at all interested in what I do or whom I see."

"He's a hell of a lot more interested now than he was an hour ago, count on it."

Sara shook her head. "Stuart is married," she explained. "To that blonde in the red BMW whom I waved to yesterday."

"The one who treated you like you were invisible?"

"Yes," Sara replied tightly, "that one."

Flynn registered his opinion of Corrine with a soft whistle. "I didn't think Bowers had it in him."

"And she's pregnant."

"I heard. None of that changes things, though. We still threw Bowers a curve he won't be able to resist thinking about.

It's the nature of the beast, Sara. Men like Bowers always want what they think they can't have."

He had grossly misread the situation, thought Sara. But she wasn't about to humiliate herself by confessing that Stuart hadn't wanted her when she was available and that the only thing he wanted now was the roof over her head. Especially not when Flynn was looking at her in that heavy-lidded, assessing way again, as if questions that would turn her cheeks scarlet were running through his mind.

"You seem to know an awful lot about Stuart's type," she observed, growing increasingly uneasy under his gaze.

"I told you, I've dealt with men like him before."

"And just maybe you are a little like him." Some unfamiliar craving for danger must have delivered the words to her tongue. Seeing the flicker of surprise they brought Flynn made part of her wish she could take them back and part of her brace for his response.

He shook his head slowly. "You're wrong, Sara. Very wrong."

"Are you telling me you never want what you can't have?"

His mouth twitched at the corners. Heavens, where was she getting this stuff? It was as if Nancy had taken control of her senses.

"Never," he replied, something in his gaze making Sara's heart begin to hammer.

Some men didn't have to speak to make their thoughts heard. Flynn was one of them. Sara withstood the potent silence for as long as she could before surrendering with an awkward shrug. "Well, at any rate, it was an interesting experience. And I'm at a loss as to whether I should be thanking you or—"

"For what?" he interjected.

"For what happened with Stuart, for what you said and…" She fidgeted with the collar of her shirt. "And did."

"Did?"

"You know, kissing me."

"Ah," he said, nodding. "Of course. No thanks are necessary, Sara, but I think maybe an explanation is."

"You already explained."

"Obviously not specifically enough," he replied, his tone dry. "This is what I was referring to a minute ago, when I said that not all of what happened was a lie. It's true that what I said about para sailing and all that was for Stuart's benefit, but you should know that I had a very different reason for kissing you."

Overriding all her well-honed instincts for avoiding confrontation and embarrassment, Sara asked, "What reason?"

"Same reason I do everything." His deep laconic tone and slow movement toward her had a hypnotic effect. "Because I wanted to."

This kiss came as less of a surprise and more of a body blow. Maybe it was because they were alone or because on some subliminal level Sara had invited this and now welcomed it. Maybe it hadn't been all that subliminal. Maybe she wanted to kiss him with the same hunger he obviously wanted to kiss her. It was a scary thought.

With one hand cupping the back of her head and the other moving slowly along her spine, Flynn's mouth took possession of hers much the way it had on the porch a while ago. He kept the contact light and easy, tilting his head for better position and inspiring gentle flutters of pleasure inside Sara. For a while.

Sara wasn't wholly aware that the kiss was changing until she was already caught up in the rougher, more dangerous skirmish it had become. Flynn's tongue parted her lips and swept inside her mouth, teasing, searching, provoking a burst of sensual excitement. As she lifted her hands to his shoulders for support, Sara groped to bring forth the protest she knew she should be making right about now.

When was the last time she had been kissed this way? Never, she realized through the sensual haze he'd brought upon her. Never exactly like this. Never with this magical blend of power and care. For even as his mouth rocked hard against hers and his embrace tightened as if he'd like nothing better than to pull her into him, his fingers wound gently through her hair, the touch light and exquisite, making her feel both stalked and cherished. And crazy. Crazy for allowing him to do this, crazy for liking it. Crazy for wanting more…and more. No, there had been no other kiss like this. Not ever. Not even close.

Her hands shifted slightly on his shoulders, coming into contact with the warm smooth skin at the side of his throat, and even that innocuous contact made her senses race faster. A muffled moaning sound drifted past the frayed edges of her consciousness, and Sara realized dimly, and with only the weakest twinge of conscience, that she had made the sound. Flynn kissed her cheek and closed eyelids, then ran his open mouth down her neck, the combination of hot, soft mouth and rough whiskers incredibly arousing. His hands slid down to frame her rib cage and for just a second, at her very core, there was a flicker of something as hard as granite. Not conscience...this was something tougher and more implacable, and as Flynn slipped his hands beneath her shirt and touched her skin just above the waistband of her jeans, it dragged Sara back to reality.

She wasn't some love-struck teenager, or one of those svelte models captured in the throes of supposed passion for designer advertisements, not by a long shot. She was just acting like one.

"Please," she said, polite as always. She slid her hands to the front of Flynn's broad shoulders to try to lever him away, only to discover that all those lean hard muscles weren't for show. Intensely aware of the size and heat of him, she whispered, "Please, we have to stop."

"Any particular reason?" he asked, his gravelly voice caressing her throat. His head was still bent, his mouth still trying to bring her under his spell and doing a good job of it until his fingers began to dance higher on her midsection, exploring places that were much too vulnerable for Sara. Soft places she was always vowing to exercise into tighter, tauter, more touchable shape.

"I mean it, Flynn, really. We don't even know each other."

He laughed softly against her skin. "That's not a prerequisite."

"It is for me," she countered, conviction giving added firmness to her words. Arching away from his mouth, she added, "Stop."

He stopped.

"Okay," he said, the husky edge in his voice revealing that he'd been as inflamed by the kiss as she had. Sara avoided looking for further proof, afraid she'd find it. "I don't share your compunctions, but if you want to get to know me first, that's fine with me. Since there's not much to know, it shouldn't take more than an hour and then . . ."

He trailed off and reached for her, his eyes dark, his kiss an eloquent expression of what he wanted to happen in an hour. As soon as his hands found their way under her shirt, Sara squirmed free.

"All right," he said with a sigh. "Exactly what do you want to know about me?"

Sara rolled her eyes. "It doesn't work that way, Flynn, like you're filling out a job application."

"I agree. You shouldn't try to fit feelings into little boxes and blanks. You should just go with them."

"That's easy to say."

"It's just as easy to do. Come here and I'll show you, Sara."

She shook her head, nervously trying to smooth her hair into place. "I'm sorry if I let things get a little out of hand and . . ."

She faltered as he quirked an eyebrow.

"And perhaps I led you to believe that I . . . that we . . ." She paused to breathe, prompting his amused smile to deepen. "Let's just say I'm sorry if I sent the wrong signals. I may have let you steamroll me into going along with that bit with Stuart, but that was very unlike me. I assure you that I *won't* be pressured into going along with this."

"You're serious about this. I can't do more than kiss you until we get to know each other better?"

"That's right," she said, then caught herself. "No. I'm not even sure about the kisses."

He reached for her. "Shall I run it past you one more time so you can make up your mind?"

"That's not necessary."

"All right then, how do you suggest we get to know each other?"

Sara's mind shut down. She should be getting rid of him, not proposing ways for them to be together.

"We could talk, I suppose," she said at last. "Exchange ideas, discuss mutual interests."

Flynn grimaced and Sara felt it in her tummy. There was *nothing* unappealing about the man . . . except perhaps the gun she knew was nestled inside his jacket.

"Exchange ideas and mutual interests," he repeated. "That sounds like a lot of work, Sara. More like a world summit than what I have in mind. Whatever happened to dating?"

"That would be fine, too, I suppose."

"Good. Have dinner with me tonight."

"All right," she agreed, anticipation already stirring within.

"Then afterward maybe we can move in together."

"Forget it, Flynn, I should have known better than to—"

"It was a joke, Sara. I was just hoping that since we're getting to know each other so well, you might reconsider your reluctance to rent me that room."

"It wasn't reluctance. It was a flat-out no."

"But that was before Stuart showed up. We're allies now, Sara."

"I'm not sure I'd choose the word allies, exactly. But I guess I have revised my opinion of you a bit."

"Then it's settled."

"I didn't say that."

"Then let me sweeten the pot," he countered, "so that we can both walk away from this winners. I need to be here, Sara, you know that. And from the sounds of it, you need cash in order to hang onto this place."

"True, but I'm afraid the two hundred dollars rent won't do it."

"How about five grand?"

She laughed, then frowned. "Let me get this straight. You want to pay me five thousand dollars to rent that room?"

"Not only for the room. For your cooperation . . . and your assistance, if it comes right down to it. I want Benny Fortrell. If you do what you can to see that I get him, I'm willing to split the recovery fee with you."

Sara wavered. Benny—Russell—was her boarder. On the other hand, he was also wanted by the law.

"Trust me, Sara, the guy is slime," Flynn said, tipping the scales in his favor.

"So we'd sort of be partners, is that it?"

His eyes widened briefly, then he gave a nod. "Sort of. Not permanently, of course."

"Of course not. I knew that. But for this case?"

"For this case, sure, why not?"

Sara stuck out her hand. "It's a deal."

After she gave him the key to the room and he'd left, Sara gave in to the excitement bubbling inside by dancing around the living room. Of course as Flynn said, it wasn't permanent. And it wasn't official and it *definitely* wasn't something she would ever tell anyone about, but for a while she, plain ordinary old Sara McAllister, was going to be a bounty hunter.

Chapter Six

"You're going to what?"

Sara shrugged, relishing the unprecedented look of astonishment on Nancy's face. "I'm going to help Flynn catch Benny Fortrell."

"Who is really Russell LeFleur?"

"Actually it's the other way around. Russell is really Benny."

"Whatever," said Nancy with an impatient wave of her hand. "A rose by any other name and all that... The fact is this guy is a wanted criminal."

"Right."

"Whom we already know owns at least *one* gun, the one Flynn found laying around in his room?"

"Uh-huh."

"Which would lead one to believe that he's capable of using it if provoked?"

"I suppose."

"And in spite of all this, you've agreed to team up with the guy who's trying to catch him?"

"Right."

"Have you lost your mind?" Nancy demanded.

"There's no need to shout," countered Sara, holding aloft two blouses on hangers as she tried to decide which one to wear for her dinner date with Flynn. *Date.* Just the word started anticipation humming within.

"There's every need to shout," Nancy shot back. "How else am I going to get through to you? Will you stop that?" She snatched the hangers from Sara's hands.

They were standing in Sara's kitchen, where Nancy had found her when she dropped by on her way home from the shop. Naturally, Sara hadn't been able to resist confiding in her. That's what best friends were for.

"I can't stop," she told Nancy as she reclaimed the hangers. "I have less than an hour before Flynn comes to pick me up and I still haven't decided what to wear."

"The blue one," Nancy replied automatically as she glanced at the two blouses Sara had just finished ironing.

Sara used her foot to swing open the door of the small bathroom off the kitchen and held the blue blouse up to her as she studied the effect in the mirror hung there. "You really think so?"

"If you have to choose between those two, I do. Don't you own anything softer, knit maybe... slinky? You know, something your mother wouldn't have wanted you to be caught dead in?"

"No."

Nancy sighed a familiar sigh. "In that case, wear the blue, but tuck it in at least."

Sara wrinkled her nose. "I hate tucking things in. It makes me look—"

"I know," interjected her friend, "fat. That's all up here," she insisted, tapping the side of Sara's head. "How many times do I have to tell you you're not fat, hell, Sara, you're not even pleasingly plump anymore. You're gorgeous... or at least you would be if you bought some clothes that fit and let me do something with your hair and—"

"Don't start."

"All right, I won't...not on that subject anyway. But, Sara, I'm not sure it's a good idea for you to get involved with John Flynn."

"I don't believe it. Can I get this on tape? For years you've been nagging me to get involved with anything single and equipped with a *Y* chromosome. Now, when I do finally decide to accept a dinner invitation from an attractive man, you're the one who's not sure."

"It's not the dinner invitation that has me worried. And it's not even Flynn the man I have doubts about; it's Flynn the bounty hunter. Besides, there's a big difference between getting involved, which I may have encouraged you to do from time to time—"

"*May* have?"

"All right, I encouraged you. I never said anything about going into business with a man you don't even know, for heaven's sake."

"I'm not going into business with him," Sara explained. "I'm just helping out a little on this one case. You have to admit it makes perfect sense since Benny lives in my house."

"It doesn't make any sense, and I don't like it. This could be dangerous, Sara."

"Life's dangerous."

"Oh, Lord, you're even beginning to talk like a bounty hunter."

Sara shot her a dubious look. "How many bounty hunters do you know?"

"Not counting you and Steve McQueen in *Wanted, Dead Or Alive*?"

"Not counting me and Steve."

Nancy shrugged. "None actually."

"I rest my case. Which earrings do you think I ought to wear with this outfit?" she asked, holding up the blouse along with the khaki skirt she'd already decided on. "Gold hoops maybe?"

"Fine. Sara, this isn't at all like you."

"Then you should be glad. You're always nagging me to be less cautious and more adventuresome, less like me, more like you.... I'm finally taking your advice."

"Maybe that's why I feel so responsible. I never expected you to take me so literally. I just don't want anything to happen to you," Nancy said, her tone becoming unusually subdued, her eyes clouded with concern as she stared into the mirror where Sara was once again primping.

Sara turned to face her with a smile. "Thanks, but nothing's going to happen to me. I haven't turned *that* adventuresome overnight. I don't plan on taking any chances, believe me."

"Exactly what do you plan to do?" Nancy demanded, exasperation creeping into her voice.

"Take things as they come," Sara countered, the airy wave of her hand reflecting her uncharacteristic mood. "Even that's a big step for me, you have to admit. When's the last time I went out with a man whose grandparents didn't know mine?"

Nancy barely smiled. "That's part of what has me worried, Sara. When I said I didn't want anything to happen to you, I didn't mean only this bounty hunter foolishness...which I still say is just plain too dangerous to fool around with. I mean, what's this Flynn character after? And how come, when you usually have no trouble avoiding and discouraging whatever male attention comes your way, he's suddenly got you acting like a sixteen-year-old on her way to the prom?"

Good question. One that Sara had been asking herself all afternoon without coming up with even a vaguely coherent answer. Her experience with Stuart had left her a little gun-shy where men were concerned. All right, make that a lot gun-shy. But somehow, things were different with Flynn. Not that she trusted him, not by a long shot. She didn't even want to think about the unfamiliar and unsettling feelings Flynn inspired, much less discuss them . . . not even with Nancy.

Why on earth was she going out with him, a man she hardly knew, a man who had only yesterday held on a gun on her—albeit an unloaded one—a man whose attitude and behavior and work were all totally inappropriate? A man who scared the hell out of her?

Sara was suddenly stricken by the thought that perhaps it was *because* he'd held a gun on her that she found him so alluring. Oh, not the gun itself, she wasn't into that sort of thing, but the fact that he was so good at handling one, and that he'd obviously had occasion to use one in the past, and that his life was so different from her own. Maybe the attraction was that Flynn was so dangerously different from any man she'd ever known, much less spent an evening with. Was it possible that she, sane, sensible Sara McAllister, had a secret weakness for dangerous men?

No, it absolutely could not be that, she told herself hastily. Then what? Sara breathed a small sigh of relief as her mind at last latched onto an acceptable motivation for the way she was acting.

"I already told you what Flynn is after—Benny Fortrell," she said to Nancy. "And as for me, I'm interested in the money, of course. The five thousand dollars he's promised me if I help him catch Benny."

A frown wrinkled Nancy's brow. "I still say that sounds suspiciously generous on his part."

"Not when you consider that Flynn stands to make the same amount, *if* he brings Benny in. And as he explained to me, the sooner that happens, the lower his total outlay for expenses. Something about reaching the point of diminishing returns."

"All right, so you rent the room to Flynn and he pays you the five thousand dollars. Where does this romantic dinner for two fit into the scheme?"

"Only in your overactive imagination. No one said anything about romance, just dinner. I expect that we'll spend most of the evening discussing the case," Sara managed to say with a straight face. "And what he expects of me... In the line of assistance, I mean."

"You're sure that's it?"

"Of course. Nancy, you know how badly I can use this money. I told you about Stuart's offer."

"Yes." Nancy's frown sharpened into a look of distaste. "What a total sleaze he turned out to be. I've got to hand it to Flynn, the way he handled Stuart is at least one point in his favor."

The memory of how Flynn had handled *her* in the process of handling Stuart brought Sara a rush of warmth. For some reason, she hadn't given Nancy *all* the details of their encounter that afternoon, and now she hurriedly steered the subject onto less charged territory.

"Stuart's visit made me face up to how little time I have left," she said. "Right about now I'd have dinner with the devil himself if it meant paying the mortgage."

She could have added that, in a way, that's exactly what she felt like she was doing, getting ready to have dinner with her own personal devil, one who gave new meaning to the notion of temptation.

Instead, she glanced at the clock. "Oh, no, I'm never going to be ready in time if I don't get moving."

"Hint taken. I'm out of here," Nancy replied, reaching for her purse. "Is it all right if I grab that volume of the encyclopedia for Katie?"

"Of course," Sara told her, hurrying toward the stairs.

Nancy's youngest was doing a report on Thomas Jefferson, and since Sara's house was on the way home and the library wasn't, she had stopped by with the intent of collecting the required encyclopedia and the latest update on Sara's suddenly fascinating life at the same time.

"Help yourself to whatever you need," Sara called to Nancy.

"Thanks," she replied, turning toward the den. "And Sara . . ."

Sara paused and glanced at her over the banister.

"Be careful," urged Nancy.

"Relax, Nancy, this is me, remember? I'm always careful."

Another rock-solid truth that was suddenly less solid and less true, thought Sara as she tossed the blouse and skirt on the bed and started to strip off the sweats she'd put on after her shower.

At one time, being careful and playing it safe had been her way of life, her creed. She shook her head as she pulled a slip from her drawer. What did she mean by *at one time,* as if it were ancient history? As recently as this morning that had still been true. And only one thing had happened since then to change the way she thought. Flynn had happened.

He'd kissed her, twice, and suddenly the words *careful* and *safe* were no longer uppermost on her list of priorities. Because no matter how she'd avoided dwelling on the specific possibilities of the night ahead, in her heart she knew that there was nothing safe about spending an evening with Flynn. And nothing the least bit careful about the way she was looking forward to it.

The doorbell rang before Nancy had located the book she was looking for. She'd be lying if she said she was sorry. In fact, she'd purposely taken her sweet time perusing the encyclopedia shelves in the hope that John Flynn would show up a little early. Maybe seeing him for herself would quell some of her uneasiness about the whole situation. Sure, to hear Sara tell it he was a cross between Clint Eastwood and Mel Gibson, but Sara wasn't always the most reliable judge of men. One look would tell Nancy all she needed to know about Mr. John Flynn.

"I'll get it," she shouted up the stairs to Sara, receiving a frantic yelp in reply. Obviously Sara wasn't ready yet. Good. That would give them time for a little get-acquainted chat. Cradling the heavy volume in one arm, she pulled open the front door, took one look at the man standing there and felt her smile freeze in place.

"Oh no," she muttered.

John Flynn—Nancy was absolutely sure that's who it was based on Sara's description—lifted his eyebrows, eyebrows that were dark and expressive and every bit as uncompromisingly masculine as everything else about him.

"I beg your pardon," he said.

"Mmm?" murmured Nancy, her mind frantically cataloging details, most of which Sara had downplayed considerably.

"You said *oh, no.*"

"I did? Right. I meant, oh, no, it's not the paperboy after all. That darn kid is always late." Nancy stuck out her free hand. "Hi, I'm Sara's friend Nancy. You must be John Flynn."

"Just Flynn will do fine," he said, shaking her hand, the wariness lingering in his eyes even as he flashed her a carelessly lethal smile.

"Sara will be down in a minute. Why don't you come on in?"

He followed her into the living room.

"Have a seat," she urged.

"No, thanks, I've done too much sitting already today."

"Can I get you something to drink?"

"Thanks, I'm fine," he said.

Fine didn't come close, thought Nancy, watching as he ambled across the room, stopping by the piano in the adjacent sun room to glance at the McAllister family photos displayed there. John Flynn was gorgeous and sexy and absolutely no match for Sara.

He was wearing a cream colored V-neck cotton sweater over a black T-shirt and khaki slacks. And no socks under his shoes. It didn't matter. Most men wouldn't look half as well-dressed in a tux, she thought ruefully. Flynn's appeal had little to do with clothes and everything to do with style.

While he might not have Stuart Bowers's classic, perfectly symmetrical features, he had something more potent, something that was hard to define but that, if it could be bottled and sold, would guarantee that the male of the species would win the battle of the sexes once and for all. It was a blend of raw sex appeal and charisma . . . unstudied, effortless and with the potential to devastate the unprepared and inexperienced. Like Sara, for instance.

Nancy joined him by the piano, intent on performing whatever damage control she could manage before Sara appeared.

"So, Flynn," she said, trying not to sound like an overbearing parent. "What are your plans for Sara?"

He slowly lifted his gaze from the framed photograph he was holding and met hers. "Is that your subtle way of asking if my intentions toward her are honorable?" he inquired, laughter lurking in his deep voice.

"Actually, I was wondering where you plan to take her to dinner. But as long as you brought it up . . . are they? Honorable, that is?"

His green eyes narrowed as he glanced at the stairs, then back to Nancy. "Did Sara put you up to this?"

"God, no," Nancy retorted. "She'd be mortified if she thought I was interfering."

"Then why are you?" It was said lightly, but Nancy heard in his tone the rock solid resistance of a man who doesn't like to be asked questions.

"Because Sara is my friend," she said, opting for honesty since something warned her that a man like Flynn would see through anything else. "My *best* friend. And I don't want to see her get hurt."

His mustache slanted above a wry smile. "I invited her to dinner, Nancy. That's usually pretty safe terrain."

"Yes, well, safety is all relative, you see." She spoke quickly, with a nervous glance toward the stairs. "The fact is that Sara is, well, she's sort of... She hasn't... Oh, the hell with it. Let's stop beating around the bush, Flynn, it's obvious you've been around—and in all the ways that count, unless I miss my guess. You breeze into town looking for Russell or Benny or whatever the heck his name is, and instead you find Sara. Something tells me that she's not your usual type of woman, and yet you ask her out anyway, and I guess I'm just curious as to why."

"Maybe I didn't have anything better to do."

"That's what I figured, but you see, Sara does. What I mean is, she deserves better. Sara's not the kind of woman who can be steamrolled into having a good time with you for a few days and then just blow it off afterward."

"Don't you think I know that?" snapped Flynn, his eyes flashing. "I know all about what kind of woman Sara is, damn it."

Nancy stood silently, taken aback by his sudden vehemence.

He seemed a bit surprised by it himself as his mouth quirked into a self-effacing smile. "Sorry, it's been a long day."

"Right. Maybe I shouldn't—"

"No," he interrupted. "You were right to say what you said. Sara is your friend, and I am a stranger passing through."

Nancy shrugged. "It's just that we've been friends since we were kids and it's sort of become a habit to look out for each other, especially since Sara's folks died."

Flynn nodded, then held out the picture he'd been studying when she approached. "Is this them with Sara in this picture?"

"Yes," Nancy replied, thinking how Sara would cringe if she knew he were looking at this particular picture. Sara banished most photos of herself, keeping this one around only because it was her favorite of her parents. She sometimes joked about having it copied with herself cropped out of it.

Nancy watched as Flynn gazed intently at the image of a younger, considerably heavier Sara.

"How old was she when this was taken?" he asked.

"Almost eighteen. It was taken the night of the senior recital, before..."

Flynn nodded as Nancy caught herself and left the comment unfinished. "She told me about it."

"She *told* you?" As far as Nancy knew, Sara never, ever discussed that night with anyone.

He looked up, nodding again as he placed the picture on the piano. "Yeah, she did. You don't have to worry, Nancy. I'll have dinner with Sara tonight and that will be the end of it."

Looking into his eyes, Nancy was suddenly, inexplicably sorry she had interfered. "Look, Flynn, I wasn't trying to stop you from seeing her again—"

"You didn't," he cut in. "I knew the minute I asked Sara out that it was a mistake. And I never make the same mistake twice."

Oh, yeah, jeered the cynic within Flynn after Nancy had said goodbye and left. How about kissing Sara? That had been a mistake, and he'd gone ahead and done that twice. In fact that's what had landed him where he was, standing in Sara's living room having just finished trying to reassure her best friend that he wasn't going to hurt her. Which, until just a few minutes ago, had been at least a fifty-fifty possibility.

He'd enjoyed kissing Sara—and everything else before she'd called a halt to it. At the time, all he could think of was kissing and touching her some more. And so, with that in mind, he had proposed this preposterous date *and* offered to split his fee with her. He shook his head, pacing across the living room. Amazing the trouble a man could get himself into when he let his hormones do his thinking.

He sure hadn't needed a reminder that Sara was not his kind of woman. He'd known it all along. The soft, tempting feel of her beneath those baggy clothes had simply caused him to close his mind to the truth for a while. Seeing that picture of Sara with her folks had put things into perspective for him even before her friend's none too subtle questioning of his motives.

Sara had been at least ten years younger in the picture, and at least thirty pounds heavier. Beneath the softly rounded cheeks and body, however, there had been hints of the beautiful woman she was today. Hints, he thought ruefully, which were much too subtle for most guys at seventeen or eighteen years of age—himself included—to have appreciated. Sara hadn't mentioned her weight when she told him about the recital but, thinking about it now, he imagined that must have been a difficult time for her, and he had the sudden, crazy wish that he had known her back then.

He shook off the thought with a small, disparaging chuckle. He would have been nineteen then, halfway between being booted out by an uncle and aunt who hadn't wanted to take him in in the first place and a four-year hitch in the army. And so overloaded with his own problems he wouldn't have been able to help Sara or anyone else with theirs. Enlisting had been the culmination of the lowest period of his life, so it was a relief for Flynn when the sound of Sara's footsteps on the stairs spared him for having to think about it any further.

"Hi," she said, stopping on the bottom step. "Sorry I kept you waiting."

"It was worth it."

The response was automatic and the second it left his lips Flynn cursed himself silently. He was determined to get through this evening without giving Sara the erroneous idea that he was interested in her as anything other than a means to an end. Benny. It shouldn't be too hard. For a fleeting moment as she descended the stairs, her long, silk-stocking-clad legs sliding enticingly into view, he'd panicked. Would he be able to stick to his noble intentions if she were wearing something that showed off the womanly body he now knew she kept hidden beneath all those gathers and layers? He needn't have worried. The skirt and blouse she was wearing looked like something left over from the time the picture on the piano had been taken, and the kindest description of the tan pumps on her feet was "sensible."

She shrugged awkwardly at his offhand compliment. As if, Flynn thought grimly, she weren't accustomed to fielding praise from men. And suddenly, in defiance of his good intentions, not to mention common sense, he smiled and reached for her hand and said, "You have beautiful hair, Sara. Do you ever wear it down?"

He intentionally held her gaze prisoner with the sheer intensity of his, bathing her with attention as her cheeks turned pink and she shifted uneasily. She liked it, though. He could tell by the way her eyes grew bright with pleasure, and whether it was wise or not, he was glad he'd said it.

"Thank you," she said finally. With the hand he wasn't holding she smoothed the golden brown hair that was gathered into some sort of knot at the back of her neck. That knot made Flynn think of the women in *Little House on the Prairie*. And it made him wonder how many hairpins he'd have to remove before it tumbled loose in his hands.

"It's sort of a pain putting it up all the time," she said, her tone clipped. Nervous. "Actually, I've been thinking lately about cutting it."

Flynn shook his head. "No, don't do that. Not until I've seen it down." He stroked his thumb across her palm and watched the sensation it caused widen her eyes almost imperceptibly. "Promise me, Sara."

She nodded, just as he'd known she would. The gaze, the lowered voice, the thumb action. Except for that one time he'd unknowingly tried it on a call girl in a bar and almost lost his thumb, it always worked. So why had he used it on Sara? *What the hell are you doing?* he asked himself as he abruptly released her hand.

"All set?" he asked Sara.

"Just let me grab my jacket," she said, moving around him to pull open the closet door. "It's warm now, but it might turn cold later."

"Right," Flynn muttered with disdain that was totally self-directed. "Better to be safe than sorry."

Outside he helped Sara into the car then dropped into the driver's seat beside her and reached into the back for the large Burger King bag he'd left there.

"I hope you're hungry," he said. "I got Whoppers, Chicken Tenders, a couple of large fries, onion rings."

She stared at him over the Whopper he held out. "You're joking, right?"

He shook his head, managing to look sheepish. "No joke. You don't like burgers?"

"I like them fine. It's just that when you invited me to dinner, I didn't expect Burger King."

"Another man might interpret that as snobbishness, Sara."

"There's nothing—"

"But not me," he continued, overriding her indignant retort. "I could have tried to impress you by ordering Chinese, but that can be tricky to eat in a car this small." He handed her the Whopper. "I know this isn't fancy..."

"It's not even hot, Flynn."

"It was when I got here, but forget that. I'm hoping that quantity will transcend temperature...and atmosphere, which," he conceded with a quick glance around, "is also lacking here. However, the car does have the one overriding advantage I looked for when deciding where we should eat tonight."

"Bucket seats?" muttered Sara.

"No, a view of the door to Benny's place."

"Benny," she gasped. "Oh, my goodness, I forgot all about him."

"Luckily I didn't," countered Flynn, offering her a container of fries. "Or else we both might have been out five thousand dollars."

"You're right, what if he had come back while we were off having dinner?"

"I thought you'd see it my way, partner. And to seal our arrangement..." He again reached into the space behind the seats.

"Champagne?" exclaimed Sara as he held the bottle aloft.

"Vintage French." He frowned at her. "Let me guess—you don't drink."

"I don't. Ordinarily. But..."

"But then, what's ordinary about tonight?" he finished softly when she trailed off. "Come on, Sara, indulge me."

"Well, maybe a little bit."

"Good. Now open your window for me, Sara."

With a small, uncertain laugh, she did as he instructed and Flynn sent the cork firing through the open window onto her neighbor's lawn.

"Bull's-eye," he said. "I never miss."

Sara rolled her eyes, grinning wholeheartedly now. "I guess if your target is big enough, you never will."

"Details, details," he scoffed. "Glasses are in the glove compartment."

She carefully removed the glasses and peeled away the linen napkins he'd used to wrap them, then held them as Flynn poured. While they ate, she answered his questions about the town and a few about Benny. In total disregard for their surroundings and the term "fast food," the dinner proceeded unhurriedly, taking nearly as long as it would have in a five-star restaurant. Afterward, Flynn gathered the paper wrappings into the empty bag and tossed it in the back before filling their glasses for the third time.

"Crystal champagne flutes in the glove compartment," Sara drawled, holding the glass up to the streetlight that had flickered on a while earlier as darkness settled over the quiet neighborhood. "Now why doesn't that surprise me?"

"I'll bite. Why doesn't that surprise you?"

She studied him over the top of her glass, her blue eyes as solemn as the eyes of a woman on her third glass of champagne can be. "Because," she said at last, "you're not a man who does things halfway. You don't let a little thing like eavesdropping stop you from finding out what you want to know and you don't take time off for dinner when you're on a stakeout and you don't drink champagne from a paper cup."

"Is that good or bad, I wonder?"

"Oh, it's good, very good. Being so absolutely sure of what you want and having the guts to go after it, how can that be anything but good?" She sipped her champagne and shrugged. "Sometimes I'm not even sure what I want, never mind how to get it."

"I thought you wanted to save your house?"

"So did I." She sighed, then seemed to collect herself. "I mean I did...I do. But that's really something I have to do, that I'm supposed to do. Do you know what I mean?"

She twisted toward him and the emotion brimming in her wide-eyed gaze caught Flynn off guard, like a gulp of hundred and fifty proof rum he once had years ago. The impact burned along the same path the rum had, landing hard in the pit of his stomach.

"I think so," he said. "Sometimes there's a big difference between what you should do and what you want to do."

Like right now, he thought.

"Exactly," she said, resting her cheek against the high leather seat back. "I *should* do whatever I can to save the McAllister house."

"Okay. Now what do you *want* to do?"

Back off, warned a voice inside him. *You don't want to know.*

But the trouble was he did. He really did. At that moment, he wanted very much to know what it was that Sara McAllister dreamed about.

He watched closely as the expression on her face softened and grew distant, and her small smile drew his attention to her mouth, bringing to him memories of the way her lips felt and tasted. Then he saw her catch herself and pull back from whatever thoughts she'd succumbed to. She squared her shoulders and crossed her legs primly at the ankle.

"I don't know," she said with a stiff laugh.

Liar, he thought, irrationally disappointed.

"I used to know," she went on, almost wistfully, "but it's not so easy anymore." She smiled at him. "Believe it or not, I was once a lot like you...a pretty gutsy, go-for-it type of person."

"I believe it," he told her. "It takes a pretty gutsy person not to crack when they think someone's holding a gun on them."

"I didn't just think it," she pointed out.

Flynn shrugged. "I suppose it was a matter of perspective."

"Perspective being which end of the barrel you were standing at."

"I'll go with that definition. A lot of women would have cried."

"I'm not the type."

"The type who cries?" he asked, intrigued.

"The type who can get her own way by sobbing helplessly. That only works if you are petite and adorable. Anyway," she said, after another sip of champagne, and while Flynn was still wrestling with how absolutely skewed her self-image was, "the last time I did anything truly gutsy, I was eight years old."

Flynn fought the urge to grab her and teach her his definition of adorable. "What gutsy thing did you do?"

She pointed to the flashing red lights mounted on top of a radio transmitter in the distance. "I once chased a fire engine all the way out to that transmitter. I was on my bicycle."

Surprised, Flynn looked from her to the tower and back. "That's got to be five miles."

"Five and six tenths. Each way."

He laughed at her precision, and the pride in her voice as she recalled the feat. "That's a lot of pedaling for a little girl."

"Yes, it was, but it was worth every blister... and the lecture I got when my folks found out I'd been there."

"You weren't allowed to go that far?" he inquired, having no real idea of what eight-year-olds who grew up in normal families were permitted to do.

"Absolutely not. And I never did... till that day. Fire engines were my weakness," she confessed, laughing. "I could never resist the call of the sirens and the flashing lights. Whenever one passed my house, I would take off after it, but usually I gave up after a few blocks. When I set out that day, I never expected to chase it so far. Once I started, though," she said, that dreamy look returning to her face, "I couldn't stop until I reached the end. Until I saw whatever there was to see. Suddenly whatever was pushing me on was stronger than my fear of getting in trouble or getting hurt or even getting lost. That day, there was no turning back."

Flynn stared at her, her golden hair and creamy skin almost iridescent in the shadowy interior of the car. He wished she'd just go right on talking so that maybe that look would never leave her face, and he wished that he could touch her...just one more time.

He almost did touch her when she absently ran her tongue across her lips; he almost reached out and pulled her into his arms and picked up where she'd stopped him hours earlier. Then she saved both of them by flashing him a self-conscious smile.

"That was a long time ago," she said.

"You're still the same person," he reminded her. "That gutsy eight-year-old Sara who knew what she wanted and went for it is still inside you somewhere."

"I don't think so."

"Then what happened to her?"

Sara shrugged and avoided his gaze. "Lots of things. Mostly she just grew up, I guess."

No, Flynn wanted to shout, almost as much as he wanted to grab her and shake her. Or did he really want to grab her and make love to her? This was crazy. The whole night was crazy and this conversation was crazy and craziest of all was the stupid, sad way he felt inside thinking about what had happened to that little girl who'd pedaled her bike for all she was worth and didn't give a damn about the consequences.

He stared out the driver's side window. Social conventions weren't his forte, and he found himself wondering how much longer they had to sit there before this date could come to an end.

The rustling sound of Sara shifting in the seat beside him drew his attention. He turned to see her stretch her long legs out in front of her until they bumped into the metal wall beneath the dashboard.

"You must be getting cramped, cooped up in here," he observed.

"No... Well, maybe a little. And it *is* getting late."

"Not that late," he heard himself say.

"Still, you're probably even more cramped than I am. You've been sitting all day and your legs are longer than mine. We could go inside."

"No." Hearing the severity in his tone, he added, "I ought to keep an eye on the door in case Benny shows up."

"Are you going to sit out here all night?"

He shook his head. "That's why I wanted the room, so I could get some sleep. But for the time being, I feel more in control out here."

More in control than he would, say, sitting in her cozy living room, he thought sardonically. The question was, more in control of what? Not knowing made him uneasy, and he shifted restlessly as the silence stretched.

"Look..."

"Why..."

They both stopped and forced smiles.

"You first," he said.

"I was just going to say that I probably ought to go on inside. I mean, it might attract Benny's attention if he pulled up and saw us sitting out here together."

"That's true," he agreed, although he knew he was parked where they wouldn't draw Benny's attention. That kind of mistake he never made. "I hadn't thought of that."

As she reached for her door handle, he got out and circled around to help her. They walked in silence along the brick path and up the porch steps.

Sara turned as they reached the front door, her smile awkward. Shy almost, thought Flynn, steeling himself from the sappy effect that smile was having on his insides. She was too damn old to be shy. And he was too old to let it get to him.

She fumbled in her purse for her key and hesitated again before finally unlocking the door, then again once he'd pushed it open. She stood with her shoulder wedged between the screen door and the house, holding it open only about a foot.

"Thanks for dinner," she said with that same smile.

"It was nothing." He let himself smile back. "Literally."

"No, it was great. Really. I had fun."

"Me, too," he said, sorry it was true. Sorrier still that he'd admitted it to her. "We'll have to do it again next time you've got a runner staying here."

"Runner?"

"Shoptalk for a bail jumper."

"Oh."

Silence.

"You can't cook in your room, you know," she announced suddenly.

"I gathered that. There being no kitchen and all."

"I thought maybe you carried around a hot plate."

Flynn shook his head. "Champagne glasses are the extent of my domesticity. No cooking," he added, making an X on his chest. "Cross my heart."

Sara groaned. "Please, I wasn't trying to be the grumpy landlady. I was going to say that, if you want, you can come on over and eat with me. I mean since you really should stick around and we are in this together and all."

Aw, come on, Sara, he thought, *make this easy on me.... Be the mean landlady.*

"We'll see," he said. "I usually like to make my own schedule."

"That's no problem. Living alone, I'm flexible about mealtimes."

"We'll see," he said again, and then because she made no move to go in, and because standing so close to her in the moonlight made him feel like if he didn't touch her, he would die, Flynn did the only thing he could do... he took the matter out of her hands.

Pulling open the screen door that was all that separated them, he tipped his head in the direction of the hall beyond. "You can go on inside, Sara," he said, more gruffly than he intended. "Because I've already decided I'm not going to kiss you good-night."

Chapter Seven

He'd decided, Sara muttered under her breath as she rolled her blouse into a ball and fired it at the hamper in the bathroom. Her panty hose and underwear followed in like fashion. *He'd decided not to kiss her good-night.*

As if it were entirely *his* decision to make. What if *she* had already decided she wasn't going to kiss him good-night? She'd bet that would have taken Mr. John so-sure-of-himself-it-made-her-sick Flynn down a few notches.

Oh, how she wished he *had* tried to kiss her so that she could have had the pleasure of stopping him in his tracks. Failing that, she wished she'd at least had the presence of mind to tell him that's what would have happened if he'd tried, instead of responding to his announcement with a wishy-washy good-night. But more than anything, she thought as she rinsed the cleansing cream from her face and confronted her dejected, unadorned reflection in the bathroom mirror, she wished it were true.

It wasn't. The pitiful, embarrassing truth was that she'd wanted Flynn to kiss her again. She'd been imagining it all afternoon and had fully expected the kiss to happen and had been shamelessly stalling there by the front door, confident that any second he would . . .

Sara cringed and shook her head, trying to stop herself from reliving—for what felt like the hundredth time—the moment when Flynn had bluntly informed her that he was not interested in kissing her good-night. No, she corrected herself in an attempt to salvage what dignity she could, he never said he wasn't *interested,* simply that he'd *decided* not to. It didn't help.

She turned off the bedroom light before pulling down the covers. Then she walked over and yanked the window shades down, something she never did, usually preferring to lie there and see the stars and moon peeking through the branches of the tree outside her window. It was as though she felt she needed extra protection tonight. That was a good one, she thought. Extra protection from a man who wanted no part of her.

Feeling another wave of residual humiliation building, she crumpled onto the mattress and pulled the blanket up to her chin, thinking she would prefer to pull it right over her head and hide under there forever. Certainly she never wanted to face Flynn again. *Ever.* Why had she let him talk her into renting him that room in the first place? For the money, she reminded herself, drawing at least a little consolation from having such a practical and noble motive.

Whatever she was doing, she was doing to save her family home, she reminded herself, and not simply because she was a weak, lonely woman who'd been taken in by a good-looking charmer. To keep Stuart and Corrine from getting their hands on this place and chopping down her willow tree, she would do almost anything. And nearly had.

She gulped in the darkness and assured herself that tonight's little fiasco would simply serve as a reminder of the kind of man not to get involved with. A reminder she'd evidently needed, in spite of the fact that she'd thought herself to be completely immune to his breed.

Her father had been a handsome, wickedly charming man. And though she'd loved him dearly and always would, she was still struggling with the burden of the gambling debts he'd left behind, debts that he'd secretly accumulated while showing the rest of the world—including his own family—only the amiable, happy-go-lucky side of himself. A side all too similar to John Flynn's laid-back style.

Her second lesson on the species had come from Stuart, of course, whose charm and appeal were of a very different sort than Flynn's, but who nonetheless possessed both in spades. And Stuart and Flynn did have at least one thing in common as far as Sara was concerned: they were both mercenaries at heart, willing to do or say whatever necessary to get what they wanted. Clearly, neither one wanted her.

Make that two things they had in common.

Sleep wouldn't come. Maybe, thought Sara, it was because with the shades so tightly drawn, the room was too dark. If she knew for certain that Flynn wasn't sitting out there keeping watch, she'd crawl out of bed and raise them again. The absolute blackness around her, combined with her restlessness, made every little creak and rattle she heard seem portentous. And there were a lot of creaks and rattles in a house this old.

The night was warm, and she'd left the windows open a little, and now even the sounds filtering in from outdoors seemed magnified, the distant barking of a dog, the scrape of overhanging branches against the roof as they danced in the breeze blowing off the nearby ocean, the occasional sound of tires on pavement as a car drove past. Funny, she never realized there was so much traffic at this time on a weeknight.

Sara found herself absently counting the cars that passed, measuring the time that elapsed between them. It was better than thinking about her date with Flynn, she rationalized. On another night, one when she wasn't purposely trying to distract herself, she might not have been so immediately attuned to the sound of Benny's car pulling to the curb in the same place he always parked. But she was aware of it now.

Had Flynn also heard it? If he were still sitting out there in his car, he would have seen Benny pull up. But if he weren't, thought Sara, he might not realize that Benny was here until he heard him entering his room. Would that be too late for Flynn to get the jump on him? She wasn't sure, but instinct and a lifetime of watching detective movies told her that it was far better to be forewarned.

Holding her breath, Sara listened ... for a voice, the sound of a car door, anything that would tell her Flynn was on top of the situation.

Nothing. The house seemed to be holding its breath, as well, leaving the night deathly quiet around her. Now that she thought about it, she'd yet to hear the sound of Benny getting out of his car or walking along the driveway. Curiosity gnawed at her until there was only one thing to do.

Sliding from her bed to prevent any suspiciously moving shadows from appearing on the shade, she crept to the window and moved the shade just enough to see the street below. The streetlights were positioned so that she could easily see that Flynn's car was empty, and that Benny's wasn't. As she watched, the man she'd first known as Russell LeFleur stepped from his car and went around to open the trunk.

With the raised trunk lid between them, Sara couldn't see a thing. What was he doing back there? she wondered as one moment stretched into another. Visions of suitcases full of money and stolen coins and guns filled her head. It was the thought of the guns that did it. As much as she personally despised Flynn at this particular moment, she would still rather see him apprehend Benny with a minimum of fuss—and live to hand over her share of the reward—than be hurt, or worse, in a hurried surprise attack. The best way to insure that things went smoothly was to warn him that Benny was here. And the only one around to sound the warning was Sara.

But how? He didn't have a phone in his room and she could hardly go sashaying out the front door in her nightgown without arousing Benny's suspicions. For all she knew, he was already suspicious. Maybe Benny was on to them and had been staking out Flynn the whole time Flynn had been staking out the house. Waiting for his guard to drop. Maybe behind that trunk lid he was right this second snapping a silencer onto a .45 Magnum.

A part of Sara rolled her eyes at her own overly dramatic conjecturing. Another, currently much stronger part felt an urgent need to act. If only she had left intact the original door between the house and the rental wing, she thought, fumbling in the darkness for her robe. Her hand landed on something soft and robelike, which turned out to be a pair of sweatpants. Close enough, she thought, hurriedly stepping into them and yanking them up over her nightgown. Not exactly the sort of slinky apparel the heroine of a James Bond movie would wear to slip off into the night and warn 007, but it would have to do.

As it turned out, *slipped off into the night* didn't quite describe her exit through the kitchen window. *Fell out,* came closer. *Plopped to the ground* also had a ring of authenticity. The one bright spot was that she managed to plop beside the trash can and not on top of it. And she did it all without making a sound, thanks to her bare feet; *007, here I come,* she thought as she kept close to the house and edged her way toward the side door and Flynn.

With each step she prayed that she didn't collide with Benny as he rounded the corner of the house, and that Flynn wasn't sleeping so soundly she couldn't wake him with a quiet knock, and most importantly, that she wouldn't suddenly come to her senses and realize what a stupid, foolhardy thing she was doing. What had she promised Nancy about not taking any risks? Whatever it was, she'd meant it at the time. But that time seemed very far away as she used her key to open the outer door and—ignoring her natural instinct to reach for the light switch—stepped into the darkened hallway.

Before the door had even closed behind her she felt someone brush against her in the darkness and she screamed.

"What the hell . . . ?"

It was Flynn's voice. She'd recognize that irritable tone anywhere. And it was Flynn's hand covering her mouth and Flynn's arms that closed around her, feeling every bit as strong and overpowering as they had the first time they'd encountered each other in much this same way. Only this time, Sara wasn't about to pass out.

"What are you doing here?" he demanded as she tried to wrench away from him. She managed to free herself except for her wrist, which was ensnared by something hard and suspiciously metallic. She reached for the hallway light and switched it on.

"Handcuffs?" she gasped. "You handcuffed me?"

She had only a fleeting glimpse of Flynn's murderous expression before he flipped out the light again, returning them to darkness. "Why don't you just open the door and yell to Benny that we're here waiting for him?"

"You mean you already knew he was here?"

"Did you think I was waiting here in the dark to cuff myself to you?"

She wasn't just handcuffed, she was handcuffed to *him*. That explained why she kept being yanked against him.

"Why don't you look before you slap those things on a person?" she grumbled.

"Why don't you stay out of places where you don't belong?"

"Don't belong? May I remind you that this is *my* house?"

"Yeah, but Benny's *my* runner."

"*Our* runner," she snapped.

"Oh, for Pete's sake."

"We had a deal."

"I thought you were smart enough to know that your part of the deal was to stay out of my way."

"Stay out of your way? Of all the— Ouch!"

He jerked on her wrist a second time and Sara heard the scrape of metal against metal. "Hold still, will you? I can't fit the key in with you moving around."

"I'm moving because you're twisting my wrist."

"Consider yourself lucky. I'd much rather be wringing your neck."

"That's the thanks I get for trying to help. For trying to live up to my end of our bargain."

"Give me a break. The only bargain we had is that I would have said anything I had to in order to get into this room."

"And *done* anything you had to?" she shot back, cursing herself for feeling hurt by his admission. Hadn't she already figured that out on her own?

He gripped her wrist tighter, forcing her to hold still. "What the hell is that supposed to mean?"

"It means—"

"Shh." Again his hand covered her mouth in the darkness. "He's coming."

His voice was so low, Sara might have thought she'd imagined he'd spoken if not for the small ripple of sensation she felt as his warm breath touched her ear. Then she, too, heard Benny's footsteps approaching. She felt the tension emanating from Flynn's body and sensed that he was poised and ready to act, and suddenly she wasn't as afraid as she knew she ought to be.

Benny's footsteps came closer. He was at the door... unlocking it... pushing it open...

"Ahh..."

The small, high-pitched yelp was ripped from Sara against her will as the metal strip at the bottom of the door sliced across her bare toes. She squelched it, but not quickly enough.

The moon cast enough light for her to see Benny's quizzical frown as he peered into the small hallway.

"Miss McAllister? Is that... Oh, no," he suddenly exclaimed, giving the door a shove and fleeing as Flynn did his best to maneuver around the door and out of the hallway with Sara still attached to his wrist.

"Move, will you?" he yelled, pulling her along the driveway.

"I'm trying! My foot... Oh, ow..."

Her toes where bleeding and already throbbing painfully, and the way he was dragging her sideways put her off stride. Add to that the fact that she wasn't all that fleet of foot to begin with and it didn't make for much of a chase.

The sound of an engine starting reached them a half second before they saw Benny's car streak off down the street.

"I don't believe it," Flynn said, coming to a halt so suddenly she collided with his back. He repeated the thought, this time with a colorful addition to express just how much he didn't believe it. "I had him. Right here. I had him."

"Almost," Sara concurred in what she thought to be a very sympathetic manner.

Flynn turned on her, as much as it's possible to turn on someone who's handcuffed to you. "And whose fault is that?"

"Whose handcuffs are they?"

"Who came barreling in where she didn't belong?"

"Who forgot to tell his partner her part in the plan?"

"What plan? There is no plan. There's just me. I know what has to be done and I do it. No plan and no partner. Got it?"

I've got it, said a little voice inside Sara. Ordinarily, she would have said it out loud and then slunk into the house as soon as he freed her and drowned her embarrassment in super chunky peanut butter eaten straight from the jar.

She wasn't sure why she wasn't saying that now, or where she was getting the temerity to look him straight in the eye and say, "Not so fast, Flynn. We had a deal. You got the room and I got in on this case."

"Oh, please," he said with a disparaging grimace. He stuck his hand in his pants pocket. "Where the hell is the key so I can get out of here?"

"Do I have time to bandage my toes?"

"Your toes?" He paused with the key in hand and glanced at her feet and at the blood trickling onto the driveway. "What the hell happened to you?"

"My foot got caught under the door when he pushed it open. Why do you think I yelled the way I did?"

He shrugged. "I thought you were scared."

"I was. But not scared enough to yell."

"That cut looks nasty," he said, his tone suddenly more gruff than angry. "Better get something on it right away."

"That's why I asked if I had time to bandage it."

He unlocked the handcuffs and shook them off, then slipped them into his pocket. "You've got the rest of your life, as far as I'm concerned."

"I meant do I have time before we leave? We are going after him, aren't we?"

He looked at her and laughed. "I'm going after him, that's for sure. You're staying here to look after your toes and your piano and whatever else it is you did before I came barging into your life. And don't worry about your money," he said over his shoulder as he started up the drive toward the house, "I'll send you a check."

Maybe it was that offhand remark about the check, or the fact that he thought he could so easily dismiss her and walk away the same way he had offhandedly decided not to kiss her good-night. Or maybe it wasn't Flynn at all. Maybe it was simply a real bad case of spring fever, thought Sara.

Had it been spring when she chased that fire truck for miles? Funny, she couldn't remember. She could only remember the feel of the wind in her hair and the way her heart had been pounding and the feeling of anticipation that had risen inside her like a volcano ready to erupt. The same feeling that was rising in her now.

She ran into the house as quickly as she was able to run and collected a tube of first-aid cream and a box of Band-Aids from the medicine cabinet, then grabbed her purse, an old sweater and a pair of sneakers from the hall closet. Stuffing everything into a tote bag that was also hanging there, she slammed the door behind her and managed to make it out to the sidewalk as Flynn came hurrying down the driveway, shrugging into his leather jacket.

He paused and glanced at her quizzically. The amusement lurking in his gaze wiped out any second thoughts Sara might have been starting to have.

"Going somewhere?" he inquired.

"Yes. I'm going with you," she announced.

"The hell you are, woman."

He started across the street and Sara kept pace.

He stopped. "Quit acting crazy, Sara. Go on back inside where you belong."

"Where I belong?" she countered, her spine stiffening.

"That's right. Nothing personal, Sara, so don't go climbing up on some feminist soapbox. The fact is, you don't belong with me."

"I do until this case is over."

He laughed and took another step. Sara did the same, and his smile fell away.

"Why are you doing this?"

"I want my share of the money."

"I told you that I'd mail you a check as soon as this is over."

"That's not good enough."

"What's the matter, Sara, don't you trust me?"

Sara smiled. "Let's just say I trust you more when I can see you. Besides, how do I know that if you go after Benny alone, you won't just mess things up again?"

"*Me* mess things up?"

"You should have made sure it was him before you went throwing those handcuffs around."

"Since when are you an authority on the finer points of apprehending a runner?"

"I don't have to be an authority to know that much. It's just common sense."

"Right. So's this." He shifted the duffel bag he was carrying to his shoulder and turned away. "So long, Sara."

"Ignoring me won't work, Flynn," she said as she followed along. "I'm going with you."

"You're welcome to try," he retorted, covering the rest of the distance to the car in three long strides.

He was fast, but Sara was determined. And a little bit desperate. She knew that if she stopped and thought about it, she would do the sensible thing and go home. Where she belonged. So she purposely didn't let herself think about what she was doing or why on earth she was doing it; instead she concentrated on the strange, wonderful excitement that was stirring down deep inside, its simple, insistent rhythm driving her forward. *Now or never, now or never, now or...*

She slipped into the car seat at the same time he did, both their doors slamming in unison.

"Get out of the car, Sara," Flynn ordered, no trace of amusement left in his expression or his tone.

"No. We had a deal."

"Deal be damned," he exploded. "I don't have time to sit here playing games with you."

"Then drive."

"You want to make me push you out?" he demanded, reaching across her to shove open the passenger door. "Is that it?"

Sara held onto the seat with both hands and met his gaze. "You're welcome to try."

For a minute, as he loomed over her side of the car, Sara thought he was going to do it, push her out and leave her there.

Then he reared back and raked all ten fingers through his hair in exasperation.

"Why are you doing this?" he asked again.

"Because we had—"

"Yeah, a deal, right." He reached into his pocket and pulled out his wallet. "Look, I'll give the money now, at least as much as I can, and I give you my word I'll—"

"It's not just the money."

"Then what is it?"

"I don't know. I guess now that I know what's happening, I just want to be part of it. I want to know how it ends."

"Fine. I'll write you a letter with all the details."

She shook her head. "I want to see it for myself. Just this once, I want to see for myself."

"Damn it, Sara, you're too old to go chasing after fire trucks."

Her eyes glittered stubbornly. "I don't need you to tell me how old I am. Or where I belong or what I ought to do."

He stared at her, then swore under his breath and reached across her again, this time to yank the door shut.

"You want to be part of this?" he demanded. "You want to live dangerously? You want to see for yourself all the wild, ugly things that are missing from your life? Well, you got it, sweetheart." He turned the key in the ignition, and the car's powerful engine sounded to Sara like a jet preparing for takeoff. "But, lady, you better fasten your seat belt."

They drove south on Interstate 95 for nearly two hours before either of them said a word. The clock on the dash blinked 1:33 a.m., her foot was killing her, and Flynn was scowling through the windshield as if he were on the road to hell and in a hurry to get there. Sara had thought it best to postpone any attempts at conversation until he at least loosened his grip on the steering wheel.

Unfortunately, it didn't look like that was going to happen anytime soon, so in an instinctive effort to smooth the waters between them, she cleared her throat and said, "May I ask where we're headed?"

"You can ask."

"I take it that means you're not going to answer?"

"Take it however you like."

"All right, how about if I try to guess where we're going? Will you at least tell me if I'm warm?"

At last he took his gaze off the road ahead long enough to flick her with a look cold enough to freeze her into silence for another sixty miles. "I already told you all I plan to . . . I don't play games."

Oh, no? thought Sara, turning away from him with a shrug. *How about that little game of pretend he'd played in Benny's room? And the game he'd played for Stuart's benefit? And the biggest, funniest game of all . . . asking her out?* He played games, all right, only usually he decided when and with whom and made all the rules. The fact that he hadn't this time was no doubt what had made him so irate. It would pass, she told herself. And if it didn't . . .

Sara burrowed deeper into the bucket seat, worrying hard about what she had gotten herself into. She was alone with a man who didn't want her around, headed she had no idea where, with no more than the clothes on her back, next to no money and a credit card that was perilously close to the limit. It was a lot to worry about and eventually all her anxiety receptors overloaded and she fell asleep.

She awoke with a start when she felt the car stop and the engine shut off. Rubbing her eyes, she gazed from the sprawling, brightly lit building in front of them to Flynn.

"Where are we?" she asked.

He glared at her. "Truck stop. If I'm going to keep going, I need coffee."

"Shall I come with you?" she asked as he swung the door open.

"Suit yourself."

Sara hesitated and he didn't wait for her.

A cup of hot coffee would taste good, she thought, watching him disappear into the truck stop. And she could use the ladies' room to freshen up and do a better job of bandaging her foot than she'd been able to in the small car. Buttoning her sweater to conceal the nightgown underneath, she hurried after him.

She'd just stepped through the front door and located the rest rooms when Flynn appeared.

"Good, you're here."

Sara raised her brows slightly. "I didn't think you cared."

"I don't. But I figured as long as we're here, we might as well eat breakfast. I don't plan on stopping again in a hurry."

"Breakfast? What time is it?"

"Four-thirty. Not that it matters. I told you, I make my own schedule."

"Breakfast sounds wonderful," she said, flashing a smile she hoped would irritate the hell out of him. "Just let me slip in here and freshen up and . . ."

"Later," he interrupted, taking her by the elbow and steering her toward the restaurant area. "After we get our order in."

"Flynn, wait. I can't go in there looking like this."

"It's a truck stop, Sara, not the Ritz."

"Just the same, my hair . . ." She made an anxious swipe at the tousled strands, freezing as he whipped around to regard her and her hair with a nasty smile.

"Take it from me, Sara, at the moment your hair is the least of your worries. Now let's go."

What had he meant by that? she wondered as she allowed him to maneuver her toward an empty booth. It was either that or cause a scene in front of the dozen or so truckers and other travelers scattered around the brightly lit restaurant. She didn't like scenes.

Had he meant that her hair didn't look as awful as the rest of her looked? Or that her appearance in general, as horrible as she knew it had to be, was the last thing she should be worried about considering everything else that was happening? Opening the plastic coated menu the waitress brought, Sara added the problem of what to most worry about to the growing list of things to just plain worry about.

The menu offered the standard roadside fare. Flynn ordered bacon and eggs, with side orders of hash browns and pancakes. Pancakes. Sara's mouth watered. How long had it been since she'd thrown caution to the wind and indulged her love for pancakes topped with melting butter and thick maple . . .

"What'll it be?" the waitress prompted.

"Oh, let's see." She glanced once more at the pancakes pictured on the menu and closed it. "I'll have two eggs, poached. No butter. And toast, dry. And orange juice, please. Small."

After the waitress left Sara excused herself and went to the ladies' room. It took a while to clean and re-bandage the cuts on her toes, which weren't as deep as she'd first feared, and to do what she could with her hair. She splashed water on her face, wishing she had blush and lipstick in her purse, and returned to the table just as the waitress was filling Flynn's coffee mug.

She wrinkled her nose as she took a sip of her lukewarm coffee.

"Cold?" Flynn inquired, watching her.

"A little." She frowned as he shoved his fresh mug toward her. "What are you doing?"

"Giving you mine instead. I'll drink it cold."

"I wasn't complaining."

"And I'm not complaining now. Just drink your coffee, okay? How's the foot?" he asked after they'd each taken a sip.

"Not as bad as I thought. Only one toe got the worst of it, and the bleeding has stopped."

"Good."

"Thank you for being so concerned."

He glanced up quickly, as if wondering whether she were being sincere or sarcastic.

"I mean it," Sara told him.

Flynn shrugged. "I just didn't want a lame partner whom I might end up having to carry."

"You mean it?" she countered, leaning forward, excitement sparking inside. "About me being your partner?"

"Do I have a choice?"

"You know you do. You said it yourself, you could just push me out of your car if you wanted to. You're strong enough. Or if that's too much trouble, you could have just taken off and left me while I was in the ladies' room."

Sara was glad that possibility was only occurring to her now and not when she was in the middle of applying the Band-Aid to her toe and would have had to come limping out to make sure he was still here.

"You're right," he said. "I could have."

"But . . ." she prompted.

"But we had a deal, in your eyes, anyway. And since I didn't do a good job of explaining up front just how limited a partnership this was meant to be, I'll stand by it."

"Does that mean you'll tell me where we're going?"

"Virginia."

"Virginia?" she echoed, startled, although she had no idea what she'd expected him to reply. "Why Virginia?"

"I've got a hunch that Benny's headed for Norfolk."

"What sort of hunch?"

"One of the coins Benny's trying to fence, the one I'm betting he needs to fence in order to put some real distance between him and the warrant hanging over his head, is too rare and too easily traced for most dealers to handle, even the disreputable ones. This calls for a dealer who specializes in risks."

"Would he need to go all the way to Virginia to find someone like that?"

"He might, to find one that he trusted. There's a guy like that down there whom Benny has done business with before. I have a feeling Benny's already been there trying to work out a deal with this guy, and that he's headed there a little more desperate and a lot more willing to barter now that he knows I'm closing in."

"If you know that's where he's headed, why not just alert the police to pick him up down there—better yet, have him stopped along the way?"

He looked at her with fresh disgust. "I didn't say I *knew* that's where he was headed. I said I have a hunch. Cops are singularly unimpressed by hunches, especially when they come from bounty hunters. Then there's the little matter of the money . . . *our* money."

"What about it?"

"I can hardly have the police round up Benny and transport him back to Boston, then show up to collect my fee. You want the pay, you have to play, Sara. That's just the way it is."

"I see." She frowned, another thought occurring to her. "But maybe Benny already sold the coin to this man. He could be headed anywhere."

"Maybe. That's why they call it hunting, Sara. But if it makes you feel better, that's not likely. If he had already dumped the coin, I doubt he'd have showed up at your place."

"How come?"

"There was nothing in that room worth coming back for."

"So why did you hang around?"

He shrugged, studying the salt and pepper shakers as he spoke. "You have to make choices in this business. Until tonight, there were any number of places I knew Benny *might* have turned up. I couldn't be at all of them at once, so I picked your place."

But why? Sara wanted to persist, longing to know whether meeting her had even a little to do with his decision to hang around, and at the same time not wanting to hear him say that it hadn't.

"It's like trying to do a jigsaw puzzle in the dark," she said. "How can you know what to do next?"

"Experience," he said with another shrug. "And a hunch."

"And that's enough to drive two thousand miles?"

"It is when it's all you've got."

"And that's all we've got," she agreed, feeling more a part of this adventure all the time. And liking the feeling.

"Not quite," Flynn returned, eyeing her assessingly, as if not sure whether or not he should say what he was about to. "We also have this." He pulled a scrap of bright pink paper from his jacket pocket and handed it to her. "I found it by the door when I went back to the room for my things. Benny must have dropped it in his hurry to get away."

"A receipt."

Flynn nodded, observing her as she studied it.

"From someplace in Norfolk," she noted, "which is why you decided which dealer he was going to see?"

"It makes as much sense as anything."

"It still seems to require a giant leap of faith on your part."

"I've got the faith that counts in this business—faith in myself to get the job done."

Sara eyed him challengingly. "How do you know that *I* didn't drop this receipt?"

"I don't know," he admitted, reaching for the neon colored scrap and pointing to the logo at the top. "I just had a gut-level feeling that you wouldn't be carrying around a receipt from a place called the Pink Pussycat."

"Oh," responded Sara, relieved that the waitress arrived right then with their food and spared her a prolonged roasting under the heated amusement he was directing her way.

The middle-aged brunette serving them deposited the plates on the table and hustled back to her conversation with the trio of truckers seated at the counter. Sara stared at her eggs for a few seconds, then sighed and used an extra paper napkin to blot some of the grease pooled on top of them.

"Those eggs aren't poached," Flynn pointed out as he drowned his pancakes in maple syrup. The sweet rich smell wafted Sara's way.

"No," she said. "Apparently not."

He speared a piece of bacon with his fork and delivered it to his mouth. "What are you going to do about it?"

"I beg your pardon?"

"I asked you what you're going to do about the eggs."

"Well . . ." She gave a soft, uneasy laugh. "What do you propose I do?"

"They're your eggs, Sara. The way I see it, you ordered poached eggs and didn't get them. If I asked for something and didn't get it, I'd let somebody know about it."

"You're right, of course. I just don't usually like to make a fuss, but . . . you *are* right. I'm going to call the waitress over here and tell her I got the wrong order."

She lifted her hand in a subtle wave, the sort she might use to summon the maître d' at a five-star restaurant.

The brunette ignored her.

Flynn chewed his pancakes, watching the unfolding drama as if it were a mildly interesting television show and he had nothing better to do.

Sara waved more briskly.

"Excuse me," she said, then realized she'd have to practically shout to be heard over the country music coming from the overhead speakers. "Excuse me . . ."

The waitress shifted, sending relief streaming through Sara who at this point would have preferred to just forget the whole thing and eat whatever was in front of her. Her relief faded as she realized the other woman wasn't responding to her call, as Sara had assumed. Instead she slid between two of the burly truckers and plopped down on the empty stool there. Plopped, thought Sara, with the panache of a woman who expected to be there for a while.

Flynn chuckled, wiped his mouth on his napkin and tossed it aside. "Give me your plate," he said.

"There's no need for you—"

"There is if we ever want to get out of here," he cut in. "Here, help yourself to some of my pancakes while I get this taken care of."

He walked up the waitress, tapped her on the shoulder and smiled as he explained the problem. And she smiled back, an enchanted sort of smile that Sara would bet that Flynn was accustomed to receiving from women. Did she smile at him that same way? Probably, she thought glumly. It was a hard thing to avoid. Where Flynn was concerned, all her reflexes seemed to be directly linked to her hormones.

He returned and sat down. "All set. Two poached eggs coming right up."

"Just like that," Sara remarked, not sure whether to be charmed or irked at how masterfully he'd stepped in and made things right.

"Just like that. Lesson number one, Sara, the first step in getting what you want is asking for it."

Chapter Eight

Their conversation in the restaurant did not set the tone for the trip. Back behind the wheel of the car, Flynn was once more silent, his expression grim and remote enough to discourage any questions or small talk. He was the epitome of a man with a job to do. Which made perfect sense, thought Sara, remembering why they were there.

Make that why *he* was there. As the sun rose over the interstate, it became increasingly difficult to pretend to herself that she was there because she truly thought that Flynn needed her help to secure the reward on Benny's head, or because she'd believed their deal to mean she was to have an active role in his capture, or for any reason other than that she just plain wanted to be there.

And just why was that? she asked herself as the early morning sun slanted through the windshield and illuminated the numerous lint balls clinging to the ancient sweater that covered a flowered cotton nightgown that was nearly as old. She slunk a little lower in her seat, as if that would prevent Flynn from getting a good look at what she was wearing. Why had she so desperately wanted to come with him?

Impulse? On the part of a woman who bought panty hose and underwear on a rotating schedule? Nah. She thought harder. Maybe it was simply as she'd suggested last night, a hunger for adventure, a yearning to see something beyond the narrow boundaries of Sutton Cove. A yearning, she reminded herself, which had been inside her forever, nurtured by her favorite books and movies and condemned by circumstances beyond her control to remain hidden and unfulfilled. Until last night . . . Until that yearning suddenly overpowered logic and common sense and everything else . . . until Flynn.

There was no avoiding it. Circumstances hadn't changed in the past forty-eight hours, unless you considered the slight change from bad to worse that had been defined by Stuart's visit. *She* was what had changed. And once again, the only logical explanation for that change was Flynn. Somehow, some way, he'd released something deep inside her that Sara hadn't even known was there, or had forgotten about, or had simply been afraid to deal with.

She had no choice but to deal with it now that she was on her way to Norfolk and heaven only knew what kind of danger. Her well-exercised pragmatism kicked in to tell her she had two choices: she could continue on, moving farther away from home and everything safe and familiar with each passing moment, trusting in fate and Flynn, or she could tell him to drop her off at the next town so she could catch a bus home.

He would do it in a second, Sara had no doubt. In fact she was sure he'd be happy to do it, ecstatic to do it, extremely vocally relieved to do it. And she would be . . .

A sudden, aching pressure began behind her eyes as she thought about the prospect of bailing out. She would be right back where she started. Back in Sutton Cove, back in her beloved but overwhelming house, back between a rock and a hard place. Installing screens. Waiting for Stuart to begin foreclosure proceedings. Alone. And lonely. Lonely in the way she'd learned it was possible to be even in a small, close-knit town full of friends and people you'd known forever.

In the end, that's what decided it. She might not be making the sensible choice by staying with Flynn. In fact, in the light of day she felt more than a little foolish about the way she'd acted last night. Not to mention feeling apprehensive, wondering what sort of working relationship would be possible with a man who suddenly seemed to think that talking and breathing were mutually exclusive activities. But inexplicably, in spite of the lack of conversation, one thing she didn't feel was lonely. And for now, that was good enough.

They stopped twice more after that, for coffee and to use the rest rooms. It was midday, Norfolk less than fifty miles away, and Sara had rehearsed what had to be said a dozen times, from a dozen different angles, when she finally decided she was ready.

"Flynn?" she said.

"Mmm."

"We have to talk."

Oh, no, we don't, sweetheart, thought Flynn. He knew exactly what he *had* to do. He had to find Benny. That was a point of honor, more so than ever after last night and Sara's ridiculous suggestion that somehow *he* was responsible for botching things up. And, since he'd made a deal with her—a deal she had grossly misinterpreted, but a deal just the same—he supposed he had to let her tag along. Which meant he had to be with her and he had to eat with her and he had to sit for hour after hour so close to her that every time she moved, her scent pulled his thoughts where he didn't want them to go. All that was what he *had* to do. He damned well didn't have to talk to her, though. And he wasn't about to.

"Talk about what?" he replied.

"My clothes."

He glanced at her briefly, unsmiling. "What do you want to say about them?"

"I don't want to *say* anything. You may not have noticed, but the fact is I left in such a hurry last night, I didn't take anything with me except what's on my back."

"So?"

"So," she snapped, "you can hardly expect me to go around wearing a nightgown tucked into a pair of old sweatpants."

Flynn noted with satisfaction the frustration in her voice. Why should he be the only one who was feeling frustrated? "Why not?"

"Why not?" The question took her by surprise. "Well, because it's not appropriate, for one thing."

"I never did put much stock in what's *appropriate*, Sara."

"Obviously. If you did, you wouldn't go around breaking into people's homes... and lying to them... and threatening them with guns—"

"I never threatened—"

"Even if only indirectly, by pointing it at them and letting them believe you might shoot. That's sort of like a sin of omission," she declared, obviously pleased she'd thought of it. "You omitted telling me what was really going on."

"Uh-uh. I distinctly remember telling you that I would not shoot you."

"Yes, but not in a sincere way that would make me believe you."

"I have no control over what you believe."

"Inappropriate," she said again, in that snippy, dismissive way she sometimes had, as if she were a judge passing sentence. "It seems to me that most of what you choose to do falls into that category. Like right now," she added with a regal nod toward the speedometer. "Breaking the speed limit."

"I'm not breaking it, I'm pushing it a little."

"You call eighty miles an hour a little?"

"Sara, everybody knows the speed limit on the freeway is just a suggestion."

"No, everyone does not know it. I, for instance, did not know it, and I don't believe it. And neither, I'll bet, does that state trooper behind us."

"Ah, damn." His gaze shot to the rearview mirror. Just what he needed, a speeding ticket. This would cost him time he didn't have. Maybe hours, if they required him to pay it before moving on. He was rummaging through his memory for information on Virginia's policy on traffic offenders when he realized there wasn't a trooper in sight anywhere behind him. He shot Sara a look of disgust. "Very funny."

"I'd say revealing is a better word. Obviously you're not as blasé about speeding as you pretend to be."

He was tired and hungry, and the black spots floating in front of his eyes after so many hours of staring at the road ahead didn't help his mood any.

"You know, Sara," he said in a slow, deliberate tone, "I can't help wondering—since I'm so damned *inappropriate*, and you're so damned holier-than-thou appropriate—why the hell are you so hot to spend time alone with me?"

Her jaw dropped to release a small, satisfying gasp. "I am no such thing."

"Oh, no?" he said, flashing her a nasty grin. "Then how come you're sitting there doing just that?"

"Because," she said, her discomfort almost palpable inside the small car as she obviously struggled for words. He had to hand it to her, though, when she finally found them, she fired them at him with grit and determination. "It's very simple, Flynn, I'm here because I want my money."

"Oh, right, the money." The highway stretched in a straight line for as far as he could see, making it safe for him to subject her to another direct grin.

"And I also want some new clothes," she added, just as he turned her way and his gaze collided with hers. He held it there for as long as he dared while doing eighty, and not nearly as long as he wanted to.

Damn, he thought, dragging his attention back to the road. This was exactly why he hadn't wanted to talk to her. Because he knew that if they talked, sooner or later he was going to give in and look at her. If he looked, he knew there was a better than fifty-fifty chance their eyes would meet, and he had finally figured out that that's where the greatest danger lay with Sara.

Sara's eyes. Big and blue as sky over water, and luminous, the windows, if not to her soul, at least to the woman inside her. A woman Flynn didn't want to make the mistake of getting to know any better. He knew it would be a mistake, and that was enough.

The woman inside Sara was full of dreams and opinions and spunk. She wasn't afraid to ask questions, because she wasn't afraid that the answers might be inappropriate. And she wasn't afraid of him. It was the woman inside Sara who had kept her cool even while believing he held a gun on her, and it was the woman inside who'd let him kiss her, and had kissed him back, hard, and it was the woman inside who'd just done what he himself had urged her to do at that first truck stop—*ask* for what she wanted.

"Well?" that woman prodded him now.

Flynn kept his eyes focused straight ahead as he said, "We'll see."

This was all wrong, thought Flynn as he pulled into downtown Norfolk later. The first thing he should be doing was checking out the coin dealer for information on Benny. Not hunting for a store that sold women's clothes.

He finally found one that looked promising, Swanson's Department Store. Backing into a vacant parking space, he scanned the front windows where a little bit of everything, from bathing suits to cookware, was on display. The question was, would they have anything Sara liked? He swore at himself. Who cared? Let her like what they had. After all, they weren't down here on a shopping spree.

"Make it fast," he warned her.

"I can't."

That brought his head around quick enough. "You *can't*? Can't what?"

"Go in there," she explained, waving her hand toward the store's entrance. "Not dressed like this."

His eyes narrowed suspiciously. "Let me get this straight. You want new clothes, but you can't go in there and buy them because you aren't wearing the right clothes?"

"Yes . . . No. That is, it's not as ridiculous as you make it sound."

"Oh, no? Well, then, why don't you try making it sound less ridiculous for me?"

"Think about it, Flynn," she said, a note of urgency in her voice.

He didn't want to think about it.

"Technically, I'm not even wearing clothes," she whispered, as if someone else were around to hear.

No, he definitely did not want to think about this.

"I mean look at me!" she went on.

He didn't want to look.

"This is a nightgown, for Pete's sake," she said, yanking open her sweater to reveal what was under it.

He for damn sure didn't want to see. He didn't want to see the rosebuds on that soft-looking fabric or how smooth and pale the skin of her throat was, and he definitely didn't want to see the alluring shadows he thought he saw through the fabric.

He raked his hair with one hand. "Will you stop that?"

Sara looked confused. "Stop what?"

"Trying to appeal to my..." Flynn swallowed and ran his hand over his stubbled jaw. "Sympathy."

"I wasn't," she retorted. But at least she buttoned a couple of the buttons on her sweater. "I was trying to appeal to your common sense. There's no way I can go walking into a store dressed this way."

"So what do you suggest we— Oh, no." He caught the entreaty in her eyes and shook his head.

"Please, Flynn. I'll make a list of what I need. It won't be much, I promise. All you have to do is walk in and buy what's on the list. I'll even give you my credit card."

He didn't want to do this. Not that he hadn't bought women's clothes before. He had. On numerous occasions. And he'd bet what he'd bought had been a lot more personal and tempting than anything that would be on Sara's list of essentials. He still didn't want to do it.

He turned to tell her to buy her own clothes or do without and fell smack into that wide blue land of no return that existed in her eyes.

"Make the damn list," he growled.

While she hurriedly scribbled on the back of an envelope he found for her in the glove compartment, Flynn stared out the window and wished he still smoked. This was definitely a Marlboro moment.

At last she handed him the envelope. Flynn ran his gaze down the list of items and sizes. She'd been pretty general in her requests, which was lucky for her, because he didn't have any

intention of walking his feet off looking for a T-shirt in a particular shade of pink.

She needed, he realized as he reached the final items on the
list, everything. His mouth went suddenly dry. And that really
ticked him off. He, who always knew exactly the right thing to
say to a woman and who had a lifetime batting average of
nearly a thousand in that department, was suddenly getting
cotton mouth over the thought of buying Sara's underwear.

"Is this a B?" he asked, managing to sound a whole lot more
disinterested than he felt as he indicated to her the final item on
the list. The word "bra" and the size, were written in smaller
print than the rest, as if not to call too much attention to them.

She blushed and nodded. "Yes. It is."

"Yeah, that's what I thought," he countered, lowering his
gaze to her sweater for just a fraction of a second, just long
enough to be inappropriate. "I'll be right back."

"Wait," she said, reaching out to touch his arm. The point
of contact might have been a magnet the way both their gazes
shot to that spot and froze. It was as if they were witnessing
something baffling in its complexity, instead of just a woman's hand resting on a man's arm. Something that happened
every day, thousands of times a day. Nothing to get hot at the
back of the neck about, Flynn chided himself. Nothing at all.

"I . . . I want to give you my credit card to pay for all that
stuff. The thing is," she continued, pulling away to fish the card
from her oversize purse, "I'm not sure exactly how close to the
limit I am on this card, and so, well, could you—"

"Forget it, Sara," he said, opening the car door.

"No, here, you have to take it." She had the card out and was
leaning across the seat to press it on him. "I don't expect you
to pay for my clothes."

And he didn't expect to want to. But at that moment, hearing the tremulous note of embarrassment in her soft voice made
him think of yesterday and the way she'd sounded when she was
facing that Bowers jerk. She'd sounded embarrassed then, too,
and trapped. For no reason he was comfortable thinking about,
Flynn was at that moment willing to spend whatever necessary
to spring the traps Sara was caught in.

"I said forget it. If it makes you feel better, I'll deduct whatever it costs from the reward money."

"But what if we don't find Benny? Then there won't be any reward money."

He glanced at her over his shoulder and smiled. "Trust me."

Yeah, right, thought Sara, watching as he walked away, mesmerized by the loose-limbed stride that carried him into the department store. Trust him . . . in his dreams. Trust was not exactly the prime emotion inspired by men like John Flynn.

Reckless curiosity was more like it, perhaps a dash of excitement, and— Oh, why try and fight it? Lust. It was a package deal. Something about the combination of leather and high-performance machinery and long, lean, muscled male body had a preordained effect on females in the vicinity.

Thinking about that made Sara feel a little better. As if none of the disturbing feelings setting up camp inside her were her fault. It was all biological. Historical even. This same pattern of stimulus-response could probably be traced back to a caveman wearing the remnants of last night's kill and swinging a state-of-the-art club.

Sara was almost smiling with relief when it occurred to her that she was sitting there, trying to bolster her self-image by comparing herself to a cave woman...and it was working. She had to get hold of herself.

Resting her head against the high seat back, she pressed her hands to her cheeks and felt the heat that had built up there. Not surprising. Making that list for Flynn had been very embarrassing. But not, she reminded herself, as embarrassing as it would have been to walk in there and face the salespeople dressed like a bag lady. Actually, worse than a bag lady, thought Sara with a sudden giggle. Most bag ladies probably had underwear.

Flynn returned a short while later carrying two large shopping bags—one more than Sara estimated he should have needed to hold the few things on her list. That raised the intriguing question of what extras he had been inspired to buy for her and prompted a fleeting parade of images of red lacy things, unlike anything she had ever in her life owned, to flash through Sara's mind.

He handed the bags into the car to her, then slid behind the wheel. Squeezing one bag into the space by her feet, Sara positioned the other on her lap and reached into it, foolishly expecting to feel lace, and prepared to be embarrassed and angry and thrilled, and not necessarily in that order.

Her stupid heart was racing and she couldn't even wipe the smile of anticipation from her face until her hand closed on something soft and thick and familiar.

"Sweats," she announced, pulling from the bag a Nike sweatshirt in a horrible mustard shade. The matching pants were packed right below it. Trying not to think about the disappointment that was lodged like a dagger in her throat, she said, "I didn't put sweats on the list."

"You didn't?" He looked surprised. Phony surprised, thought Sara, feeling both confused and annoyed.

"No. I didn't. I put down that I wanted two pairs of jeans, a couple of T-shirts and a sweater."

"Yeah, well, I thought jeans might be tricky. You know, getting the size right."

"I wrote down the size."

"The lady in there said they run small. I didn't figure you'd want 'em if they were tight, so I decided to play it safe."

"With sweats," she concluded, feeling like a wife who just got a washing machine for Christmas. Which was ridiculous, since she wasn't Flynn's wife by a long shot and she actually liked sweats. She wore them all the time back home. Maybe that was it. This wasn't home. She'd taken a big chance and made a huge fool out of herself to get here and the last thing she wanted was for it to be just like home. Or to look just like the Sara who belonged there.

She rummaged through the rest of the things in the bag, then in the other one. "It's all sweats."

"And underwear," Flynn added. "I stuck that on the bottom."

"Ah, yes." It was there on the bottom, all right. The reason Sara hadn't noticed it sooner was that, like the sweatshirts and pants, it was sturdy, one-hundred-percent cotton. Only it wasn't mustard colored or lime green. It was white, pure, boring, virginal white, and that was what sent Sara over the edge of her own inhibitions.

"Give me the receipt, Flynn," she ordered, holding out her hand expectantly.

"What for?

"The receipt for the clothes. What else?"

"I meant, what do you want the receipt for?"

"So I can exchange them," she snapped.

"Why would you want to do that?"

She held the mustard sweatshirt up to her chest and glared at him over it. "I don't know, Flynn. You tell me."

He shrugged. "This isn't exactly Bloomingdales, you know. I went with what they had."

"Where? In the Hefty Man department?"

He was beginning to look a little uneasy. "I know it's sort of big, but I wanted to be on the safe side."

"In case we needed to use it as a tent? Flynn, look at this thing."

"I did look at it. It looked about the same as the one you were wearing yesterday."

"Maybe," she agreed, coloring at the mention of the outfit Nancy was forever telling her was laughably oversize, "but that was yesterday. Now are you going to hand over the receipt or shall I just trash all this and start from scratch?"

He handed her the receipt and Sara swallowed her pride and returned the clothes to the store. Somehow she managed to hold her head up and stare down the snooty saleswoman who handled the return.

"You mean you're exchanging everything?" she asked.

Sara nodded. "Everything."

Every last bulky reminder of the way she must look in Flynn's eyes, thought Sara. With the credit slip for the purchases in hand, she faltered briefly. If she didn't want what Flynn had bought, what did she want? She wanted to make him see her in a different way, she realized suddenly. She wanted to see *herself* in a different way.

With that in mind, she cut a path through the designer sportswear department, falling back on the memory of hundreds of shopping excursions with Nancy and letting her subconscious be her guide. Over and over she stared at the racks and asked herself what good old Nancy would select. In the process, she unleashed a long-standing desire for black knit leggings that she had always dismissed as being too revealing, and hip-hugging ribbed knit tops in Popsicle shades—too young—and leather boots with heels...too flashy. She bought slinky trouser socks and a wide hot-pink belt that accented all the tops. It had been years since she'd tried on a belt and it came as a shock to discover that she took a medium. Not an extra large, not even a large, a medium.

Maybe the belt size gave her courage. Something did, because after changing in the ladies' room and applying makeup in shades that the lady at the cosmetic counter had promised would bring out the tigress in her, she stopped in front of the store's beauty salon and stared at the blowups of gorgeous models with shining, perfectly cut hair.

She hesitated briefly, feeling a twinge of disloyalty to Nancy. The feeling quickly fell away. She knew exactly what Nancy would say if she was here. She would say, "Go for it, Sara."

Catching her refection in the shiny metallic strip that bordered the shop window, Sara smiled in amazement at her new image from the neck down and said softly, "Go for it, Sara."

All in all, she kept Flynn waiting much longer than she'd intended to and, she was certain, much longer than he had expected, and she was sorry about that. She was not sorry however, about the result of taking that extra time. Not at all.

Leonard, the hairstylist who cut her hair into a style that brushed her shoulders and framed her face with short wispy pieces, kissed his fingers as he peered over her shoulder at her reflection in the mirror.

"It is magnificent," he exclaimed. "It is movement. It is you!"

And Sara, who never believed flattery when it was directed her way, almost agreed.

Then she went outside, to where an obviously impatient Flynn was leaning on the hood of the car, and his reaction told her all she needed to know about how she looked.

She hesitated a second as she stepped through the front door, slipping on the sunglasses she'd bought as she passed the accessories counter, and watched Flynn watching her. Then she moved toward him, and in spite of the dark glasses hiding his eyes, she saw the surprise that rocked him, and she knew, with a sweet rush of understanding, she *knew* that until that very second, he hadn't recognized her and he'd been staring at her the way he had because he was a man and that's what a man does when he sees a beautiful woman. *A beautiful woman.* The words twirled inside her head like one of those brightly colored banners used by gymnasts. *A beautiful woman.* She was a beautiful woman.

Her knees felt watery as she stopped in front of Flynn and said, "Hi."

"Hi," he replied. Then he pushed the sunglasses to the top of his head and took a long, slow look at her, down and up and down again. Finally he met her gaze; that smug little smile he was so expert at was on his lips.

"So," he said, "what took you so long?"

Sara felt the urge to swing her sleek black and tan leather purse at his head. Before she had the chance, his smile broadened into something warm and genuine.

"You look great, Sara. Really great. I had no idea..." He broke off, his mustache slanted above a rueful smile. "No, that's not true. The truth is I had a pretty good idea that this is exactly how you'd look if you ever got around to buying some clothes that fit you right. Which is probably why I didn't buy them for you in the first place."

"You mean you purposely bought me things that were a dozen sizes too big?"

He nodded, his smile stretching into a grin.

"But why?"

"Think about it, Sara."

Her brow furrowed.

Flynn shook his head and moved to open the passenger side door. "Think about it on the way to the Majestic Coin Shop."

"We're going there now?" she asked as she walked slowly around the car, cognizant with each careful step of the heels on the new boots, and climbed in.

"Right now. Unless you wanted to stop somewhere else on the way?" he added dryly. "Maybe for a facial? Or to have your nails done?"

"I don't think so," Sara retorted sweetly. "I maxed out on my credit card."

Flynn look at her from beneath raised brows. "I thought you were going to exchange the stuff I bought?"

"I did." Smiling, she patted the shopping bag at her feet. "It didn't quite balance out, though."

"No," he agreed, giving her another of those looks that made Sara feel as if she'd gone a week and a half without breathing. "I guess not. But if it's any consolation," he added as he started the engine, "it was worth every penny."

And then some, thought Sara, pleasure as warm and sweet as maple syrup spreading through her. When was the last time she had felt this wonderful? Never, she realized. Never once in her whole life had she felt this way. Beautiful and desirable... and powerful. She wasn't sure why one should be so entwined with the other, but it was.

She tossed her head just to feel her hair dance against her neck and imagined how much better it would feel if it were Flynn's hands moving it, rubbing the silky strands between his fingers and against her skin.

"Whatcha thinking?" he asked, eyeing her speculatively.

"About the Majestic Coin Shop," Sara lied. "I was wondering if whoever's there will tell us what we want to know."

"Oh, I don't think we'll have any problem," replied Flynn, a wicked smile taking shape as he ran his eyes over her legs. "Especially now that I've got the right bait."

"I'm the bait?" she asked, not sure she liked the sound of that.

He nodded. The gaze he ran over her was frankly approving. "Dressed like that, you are."

Sara thought that over for the rest of the short drive to the Majestic Coin Shop, which was located in a run-down waterfront area not far from the naval shipyard. It didn't take a genius to figure out the part the bait played in a situation like this. Besides, she read a lot of detective novels. She knew that the glamorous sidekick always managed to distract and confuse the quarry and before he knew it, he'd told them what they wanted to know. Of course, there was one little problem that Sara wondered if she should mention to Flynn, namely the fact that "distract and confuse" was not usually the effect she had on men. "Bore and anesthetize" was more like it.

No, no, no, Sara chided herself, absently reaching up to feel her hair. That was the old Sara. The new Sara was up to being the bait in any scheme Flynn could dream up, and she was ready to prove it.

He parked a short distance from the coin shop and came around to open her door.

"Ready to go fishing, Sara?"

"As ready as I'll ever be," she replied, taking the hand he offered to help her out and managing to control her wobbling as she got to her feet. "This is so exciting."

"What is?"

"This." She gestured around them at the waterfront bars and bait shops, the street crawling with characters and overhung with a heavy odor of fish and salt air. "The reason we're here . . . all of it."

Flynn looked dubious. "I guess," he said finally.

"You know," Sara confided as they approached the shop entrance. "I was afraid you were going to tell me to wait in the car."

"I'd planned to," he countered, reaching for the door. "Don't make me sorry I didn't."

The Majestic Coin Shop was small, about fourteen by sixteen feet in Sara's estimation. Trays of coins were piled in the glass display counters that ran along the side and rear of the store. The shades and bars covering the front windows and the flickering fluorescent tubes overhead didn't supply much in the way of light or ambience. It was hard to make out what might lie in the shop's shadowy corners and the slice of back room visible around the crookedly hung curtain divider. Something told Sara that was probably for the best.

Drawing confidence from Flynn's presence close by, she paused in the middle of the empty shop and did her best to look worldly. It must have worked, because the gum-chewing man lounging behind the rear counter got up, scratched his chest and looked interested. Then he peered past her to Flynn and his expression hardened to a wary mask.

"Do something for you?" he asked with open hostility.

His manner explained why customers weren't exactly lined up out front, thought Sara.

"Maybe," Flynn replied, ambling toward the counter. Sara kept pace. He surpassed the other man significantly in both height and muscle, a fact Sara could tell was not lost on the middle-aged shopkeeper. "I'm looking for a coin."

The man snorted. "That's a step in the right direction."

"This coin, to be specific," Flynn continued, pulling what looked like a magazine clipping from his pocket. Glancing over his shoulder, Sara realized that the coin in the inset photo must be the Garrett gold doubloon, the coin he'd told her was worth a quarter of a million dollars on the auction block in Boston. It was hard to imagine the man before them dealing with anything of such importance and value.

As if to confirm her bad impression, he pulled a toothpick from his shirt pocket and began picking his teeth. "Don't got nothing like that here."

"No, I didn't expect you'd have it here," Flynn said, sarcasm heavy in his voice. "Can you get it for me?"

The man looked long and hard at Flynn, his lip slowly curling in distaste. "Nope."

"You sure? Take another look." Flynn shoved the clipping closer to him. The man looked at it as if it were of no more significance to him than dryer lint.

"I got other gold pieces you can look at," he said finally, shrugging.

"I'm not interested in any others," Flynn retorted.

The man met his gaze. "Any special reason you're so interested in this here piece?"

"Let's just say I'm a . . . collector."

The man's smile was slow and nasty. "Yeah, and while we're at it, let's say I'm Peter Pan, and the broad here is Tinkerbell. Maybe her and me ought to—"

"Uh-uh," interjected Flynn, reaching across the counter in a movement so swift Sara didn't even see it happening, to take hold of the man by the shirtfront and jerk him onto his toes.

"Rule number one, speculation about the lady is not allowed."

"Sure thing, officer," the man shot back, his attempt at defiance losing some of its steam due to the fact that he was struggling to breath around Flynn's stranglehold on his shirt. "What is she? Your partner or your wife?"

"There you go speculating again," remarked Flynn. His relaxed manner, a direct counterpoint to the other man's, amazed Sara—and thrilled her. She felt like she'd stepped into one of her favorite novels and was standing alongside the fierce but ultracontrolled hero. Of course, she wouldn't want things here to escalate the way they so often did in books, to the point where the hero's savage side was unleashed.

She nervously scraped her fingertips against her palms. "Flynn, maybe..."

"Not now, Sara," he said without looking at her. "This gentlemen and I are working out a business deal."

"No way," the man spat. "I don't do no deals with cops."

"But he's not really—" began Sara.

"Not now, Sara," repeated Flynn, less cordially this time. "I think that perhaps what you meant to say was that you don't make deals with local cops. But you see, I'm not local." He released the man and smoothed his shirt into place for him before pulling an ID from his pocket and flashing it before him. "Boston PD."

It was not the ID he had shown the police officer that first night at her house, Sara was sure—as sure as she was that it wasn't a genuine Boston police ID. John Flynn was frighteningly good at subterfuge.

The shopkeeper looked from the ID to Flynn, the toothpick back in place. "You think it makes a rat's ass worth of difference to me what precinct you call home?"

"No, but I'm betting this makes a great big rat's ass of difference to you," Flynn countered as he fanned one-hundred-dollar bills on the counter. One hundred...three hundred...five hundred... Sara stopped counting.

The shopkeeper didn't. She watched the muscles at the side of his scrawny neck flex and bulge as he went about the process.

"That's a lot of green," he said at last. "But it ain't near where what that gold doubloon is worth, and you and I both know it."

"Just like you and I both know who's got it," Flynn shot back. "Are we going to let that little weasel Benny have all the fun?" He glanced around. "I took one look at this dump and knew you weren't the dealer, just a way station between Benny and whoever's really handling the transaction. I'm sure you're getting your cut, but I took one look at you and surmised that whatever it is, it's not enough. And that you're not the sort of guy who'd be opposed to picking up a little extra scratch...." He pushed the money closer to the man. "Just for giving me a name."

He licked his lips. "They find out I did this, they'll make me sorry."

"I'm not going to talk," Flynn assured him.

His eyes darted to Sara. "Yeah, but broads aren't always so—"

"She does what I say," said Flynn.

Sara swung around to look at him. "Flynn, I really..."

"Not now, Sara."

The shopkeeper stared at the money some more, then reached for it. Flynn brought a hand down hard on top of his.

"The name," Flynn prodded.

"I put Benny in touch with a fellow... I don't know for sure the deal will even go through. This fellow's been out of the country for a while. Just got back and he—"

"Can the travelogue. Tell me his name."

"Ivan. Ivan Mulhouse. Runs a fancy operation down—"

"Where?"

"I was getting to it. Sheesh, you cops are all the same. Antsy. Miami. He's got a fancy-shmancy setup down in Miami Beach. In the Seagate Building on Biscayne."

Flynn released his hand and smiled. "Thanks."

Sara decided to wait until they were in the car to discuss the flaw in the otherwise successful visit.

She stared at him and intoned, "She does what I say?"

"You do," Flynn countered, his tone matter-of-fact. He yawned and rolled his shoulders the way she often did if she'd been sitting a long time at the piano and her muscles were cramped. Then he shot her a look. "You'd better."

"I beg your pardon?"

"Begging's not necessary. Obedience is. At least, as long as you insist on tagging along. Otherwise . . ."

"All right. All right. I'll do as you suggest."

"You'll do as I say."

Sara conceded with a nod. "As you say. But you still didn't have to go saying so, especially not to a man like that."

"Sweetheart, obedience is one of two things a man like that understands in a woman. You would have liked it even less if I'd commented on the other."

"I'm sure." She folded her arms across her chest, but as awkward as it was for her to talk about such things, she couldn't resist. "Is that what you meant by my being bait?"

"Hell, no." He looked indignant. "Sara, do you honestly think I would ever . . ." He shook his head. "That was just a joke."

"But I thought that's why you brought me in there with you."

"I brought you with me because I figured it was safe enough and you'd get a big kick out of it. At the first hint of trouble you'd have been out of there."

"Oh," she said, feeling a little less intrepid than she had a second ago. "At least he told us who Benny's going to sell the coin to."

"Hopefully."

"You don't think he was telling the truth about Ivan Mulhouse?"

"What I think is that Miami is a hell of a way to go on a wild-goose chase. Especially when you've been driving as hard as I have."

"I can fix that," she announced. "Let me drive."

"Absolutely not."

"Come on, Flynn. I'm a good driver. I wanted to offer hours ago, but you didn't seem to be in a very receptive mood."

"I wasn't, and I'm not. Not when it comes to letting you drive my car."

"Listen, I understand how men can be about their cars," she said, not conscious that she had reached out to pat his arm until the contact sent a bolt of sensual awareness through her. She pulled away. "My father once owned a Buick that he called 'Baby' and refused to let my mother drive."

Flynn looked disgusted. "This is not a Buick. To me, it's almost not even a car...it's...family. Go ahead, laugh. That's the way it is. I don't have real family. I don't own a house or a lot of *appropriate* clothes and things. What I own is this." He tapped the steering wheel the way Roy Rogers used to scratch Trigger's nose, gently and with affection. "We've been through a lot together and I've never put so much as a scratch on the paint job."

"I didn't ask you to let me scratch it, just drive it."

"Why do I think they would be one and the same?"

"Because you're jumping to conclusions based on outdated stereotypes. It so happens I won the Defensive Driver Award in my driver's training class and I've never so much as been in an accident, not even a tiny one."

"Which means the odds are against you. Face it, Sara, with that clean a record you're an accident waiting to happen and you're not going to happen in my car."

"If anyone around here is an accident in waiting, it's you," she shot back. "You're about to fall asleep sitting there...admit it."

He shrugged. "So I'm a little tired."

"A little? Come on, switch places with me."

He stared at her, his expression grim, but at least he didn't say what he had when she first broached the subject... *absolutely not.* "You probably can't even drive a stick," he said at last.

"Ha! I cut my teeth on a stick shift, automotively speaking, that is."

Flynn looked at her again, shook his head and sighed. "I just know I'm going to regret this, but... Come on, I'll let you give it a try."

Not until she was strapped into the driver's seat did it occur to Sara how very different things looked from behind the wheel of a Corvette than they did from behind the wheel of her mother's old sedan, the first car she'd ever driven. Oh, well, she thought, cosmetics aside, how different could they really be? When you got right down there under the hood, a car was a car, just a bunch of nuts and hoses.

And horsepower, she thought as she shifted into first and touched her foot to the gas pedal. How could she have forgotten all those horses? She wasn't quite used to the feel of the new boots, and the Corvette shot forward, directly into the path of a pickup truck being driven by a man with extraordinarily quick reflexes. By some act of God, they didn't collide. She did, however, manage to stall the engine.

"Forget it," Flynn growled as she went to turn the key in the ignition. "I can't stomach any more of this."

"Will you calm down? I just need to get acclimated here."

"I thought you said you drove a stick?"

"I did. But that was a while ago... All right, so it was years ago. And it was on the wheel, not down on the floor like this one. Don't groan," she admonished. "I'm a fast learner."

Somehow she managed to get them on the highway with a minimum of bucking and grinding of gears. Flynn's jaw remained very, very tight the whole time, and when they were finally cruising along at a steady speed and his eyes drifted shut, Sara wasn't entirely sure whether he'd simply fallen asleep or passed out from the trauma of it all.

Chapter Nine

Sara drove for hours and Flynn slept. Following his directions, she left Virginia behind and entered North Carolina, heading southwest until she once again picked up Interstate 95. And Flynn slept. She drove past signs for places she recognized, like Raleigh, and for many others that she'd never heard of, places with names like Battleboro and Ringwood. She loved it. She loved the speed and unfamiliarity and not knowing what the landscape would look like around the next bend. And all the while she was loving it, Flynn slept.

He didn't even wake when she pulled into a rest area to stretch her legs and to leave a hurried, intentionally vague message on Nancy's answering machine explaining that she would be away for a few days and asking her to call several of Sara's students and cancel their lessons. Sara felt good after making the call, and oddly free, as if now she had truly left all the responsibilities and baggage of her real life behind...at least for a while.

Pulling onto the interstate, she had a little bit of trouble shifting into second and she considered the fact that Flynn even slept through the resulting gnashing of gears and teeth to be proof of just how beat he was. With that in mind, she decided to hold off stopping for dinner for as long as she could.

Being more speed conscious than he was, she didn't cover ground as quickly as Flynn had and by the time they neared Fayetteville, her stomach had been growling for nearly an hour. Visions of fast food hamburgers drifted across the endless ribbon of black pavement ahead. Only Sara didn't want anything else that came prepackaged. She wanted a real meal and she wanted to sit down at a table, preferably one covered with a tablecloth, to eat it. And she did not want to hear the rumble of sixteen wheelers in the background.

The problem was, she had a hunch that if she suggested that to Flynn, he'd veto the idea out of hand, insisting it would waste too much time. So she wouldn't ask him, Sara decided. If they were already stopped at some quaint little off-the-beaten-path restaurant when he woke up, he could hardly refuse to go in. He was bound to awake as ravenous as she was, and once they were already there, how much more time could it take to have a nice dinner? The bonus was that it would give them a chance to talk and unwind, and that prospect appealed to Sara on all sorts of levels.

Her mind made up, she began watching the roadside signs more carefully. At the next sign promising food, lodging and fuel, she would get off the highway. How hard could it be to find a restaurant? Not very, she should think. Back home, there were a half a dozen such places on the outskirts of Sutton Cove alone.

Once off the highway, she took a right and drove slowly past the lineup of burger joints and pizza places without seeing anything remotely like the charming café she was envisioning. No problem. If you wanted something off the beaten path, you had to expect to drive a little way *off* the beaten path. About ten miles farther along the road, she finally came across a sign advertising the Village Inn and pulled to the side to read it. There was a drawing of a very colonial-looking white clapboard inn, and beneath, written in gold scroll, Fine Dining and Rooms of Distinction.

Success, thought Sara. This was exactly what she had in mind. She knew in her heart the food at the Village Inn was going to be wonderful; she could already taste the biscuits and was debating whether or not to splurge on sour cream for her baked potato. And as for the rooms of distinction, well, maybe Flynn wouldn't feel like driving anymore tonight after enjoying a big meal. Stretching out on a real bed held great appeal, she thought as she rotated her shoulders as much as the shoulder harness permitted. And just maybe, after they sat and talked and perhaps shared a bottle of wine, just maybe . . .

Sara felt suddenly warm. She wouldn't think about that now. Narrowing her eyes, she strained to read the directions given in smaller print on the sign. There was no direct lighting there and it was getting darker all the time. Three miles down and turn left at the light. No problem.

She drove a short distance before thinking to check the odometer so she would know when she'd gone three miles. She peered over the top of the leather-wrapped steering wheel, then through it, before finally locating it right below the speedometer and next to a row of other gauges. She wondered if Flynn's car had a trip counter similar to her own. That would make it so much easier.

Leaning forward, she felt around the controls for a knob and was jerked to full attention by the blast of the horn from a car coming from the opposite direction. Sara sat upright and yanked the wheel to steer the car onto her own side of the road. And not any too soon, she realized as the other car sped past. She glanced anxiously at Flynn, who, mercifully, slept on.

Maybe she just ought to forget the trip counter. She would just remember that the odometer had read 28,565 when she started, so she should be turning somewhere around 28,568. Or had it been 28,563 when she started? Which would mean she should turn at 28,566, which was right about now. To complicate matters, a blinking yellow light came into view up ahead. Was that the light where she was supposed to turn? Sara wondered. Somehow, she'd expected it to be an ordinary stop light. Why weren't directions more specific? And when, she wondered, slowing to a halt at the light and looking around, had the road narrowed and the scenery turned so rustic?

The urge to do a U-turn and forget the whole thing rose inside her. Sara began to chew her lip uncertainly, then stopped herself. No, damn it. She would not turn around like some cowardly little mouse. *The way she ordinarily would,* squeaked a small inner voice. How often did an adventure like this come along? Never, that's how often. Just as she'd never before eaten at truck stops or driven a sports car or been to Miami. Heck, she'd never before been outside of New England. She was now, however, and she wasn't going to waste this opportunity by doing things halfway.

She was going to find the Village Inn.

She just might have, too, if not for the way the road she turned onto forked into another that was so narrow and curvy and dark. Very, very dark. No streetlights, no street signs, nothing but a twelve-foot-wide strip of pavement—at least Sara assumed it was pavement—edged by a ditch running along both sides. Of course, she didn't know about the ditches at first. If she had, she might not have driven down the road so far. Or so fast. But she didn't find out about the ditch until her right wheels went into it.

"What the hell...?" Flynn shouted and bolted upright in his seat.

He was, Sara noted, finally awake.

He looked around in confusion, rubbed his eyes with the backs of his hands and looked again. "Where the hell are we?" He looked directly at her. "Sara? Where are we?"

"Well . . . I'm not exactly sure."

"You're not sure?"

"Not *exactly* sure."

"Where's the highway?"

"Back there." She pointed over her shoulder, then adjusted her aim. "Or maybe there."

"I don't believe it." He said it again, adding the same *X*-rated qualifier he had the night Benny got away. "How did we get here?"

Sara did her best to explain.

"Dinner? You left the freeway and drove into this hellhole to have dinner at a place you never even heard of before?"

"Yelling isn't going to help matters, Flynn."

"Yes, it is," he shot back. "Because yelling is going to release some of the anger I'd otherwise have to release by breaking something." He shoved open his door as best he could,
considering the angle the car was at, and looked into the ditch.
"I don't believe it. We could have busted an axle. Blown a tire.
You probably killed my rims, at the very least." He groaned.

"Look, I'll pay for any damage that was done to the stupid
car."

He swung around to look at her. "You don't get it. You just
don't get it. Get out of the car, Sara."

Real panic beat inside her. "Be reasonable, Flynn. I know
you're upset, but you can't leave me out here alone and..."

"Nobody said anything about leaving you anywhere, although if I'd used my head and left you... Ah, forget it. I want
you out of the car so I can push it onto the road."

"Oh."

Sara hurried to unfasten her seat belt and get out, managing
to make it to the road before Flynn. He walked slowly around
the car, examining it from all angles and shaking his head a lot,
before reaching inside to fiddle with the stick shift. Yanking off
his jacket, he tossed it on the ground from where Sara immediately retrieved it. It was the least she could do. Circling to the
back of the car, Flynn bent down and planted his hands on the
trunk.

"Can I help?" she asked.

"Sure."

"Great," replied Sara, grateful for the chance to redeem
herself somewhat. "What should I do?"

"Same as always. Stay out of my way."

Pique blended with feelings of regret as she did as he instructed and stayed well out of the way until he had all four
wheels of the small car on the road. His face ruddy and beaded
with sweat, he once again examined the car, then grudgingly
pronounced no real damage done.

Sara sagged with relief.

"You okay?" Flynn asked, stepping closer, his eyes narrowed as he stared at her through the darkness all around them.
He still had that same disgruntled expression.

"I'm fine. Just a little shook up from the way the car jerked when we left the road."

"Look . . ." He heaved a sigh, glancing away from her, then back. "I'm sorry I yelled at you."

"I'm sorry I drove your car into the ditch. And I'm sorry I bugged you to let me drive in the first place," she went on, feeling the heavy sting of oncoming tears and hating it. "I'm sorry I ever had the bright idea to leave the highway and find a nice quiet romantic restaurant. I'm sorry I'm even here."

"That makes two of us." He immediately winced and added, "Ah, Sara, I didn't mean that." He raised his hand as if to touch her shoulder, but stopped short and let it drop to his side. "I get crazy about the car sometimes, because . . . Well, just because I do."

"You have a right to," she countered, keeping her head down as she pressed the back of her hand to her eyes to forestall the tears from actually making an appearance.

"Were you really trying to find someplace romantic?"

Sara registered the small change in his tone, the soft note of speculation buried in its rough depths, and shook her head. "No."

"Liar."

The word was more caress than accusation. His voice had dropped to become even softer, also grittier, and closer. He was moving closer, Sara realized with a jolt, so close that she was aware of him with each separate millimeter of her skin. His nearness made her tingle as if she were standing in a cloud of static electricity.

"You know," he said, lifting his hand and running his fingers lightly through her hair, fingering the newly short pieces around her face. The gentle contact felt exactly as Sara had imagined it would: exciting, provocative, arousing. "Leaving the highway the way you did could prove to be a very costly mistake."

Somehow Sara managed to draw enough breath to say, "Why's that?"

"For starters, you could have done real damage to the car. Do you have any idea what it costs to repair a Corvette these days?"

"No," she replied, mesmerized by the shape of his mustache framed mouth hovering so close in the darkness. The night around them was sweet and heavy and silent, broken only by the intermittent sound of crickets. "What does it cost?"

Flynn shrugged as if distracted and let his thumb coast along her cheek and down the side of her throat. "A lot."

"Oh." She tipped her head just a little to the side, wanting to permit, not hinder, the further exploration of his fingers. "But I didn't do any damage."

"True. But you did cost me time I can't afford to waste. Not to mention the fact that we could very well be lost out here." He curled his fingers around her shoulders, his chest barely brushing hers as he slowly leaned closer. "I'll lose even more time trying to find my way to the highway."

"What's your point, Flynn?" she whispered, although she knew very well what it was. The point was, there *was* no point. All this talk was just a verbal prop, camouflage for the work of his hands and eyes and mouth.

"Sara, it's payback time."

"Payback? I'm afraid you're out of luck. As I told you in Norfolk, I'm tapped out."

He laughed softly. "On the contrary...I don't think any man has even begun to tap what's inside you, Sara."

He wove his fingers together to brace the back of her head and stared at her as if seeing her for the first time.

"If I didn't know better," said Sara softly, "I'd think you were suggesting that you're the man to change that."

Judging by the slight widening of his eyes, her response had taken Flynn by surprise. He wasn't alone. It was the kind of thing she might ordinarily think, but would never say.

Flynn smiled a bit savagely. "You'd think right."

To her amazement, far from feeling alarmed, Sara felt exhilarated. For the first time ever she was flirting with a man without being tongue-tied and overwhelmed by doubts. She wasn't sure if it were the haircut or the new clothes or a combination of both, as well as the thrill of their shared adventure, but when Flynn looked at her in that heavy-lidded way that seemed to say that she was beautiful and he was interested, Sara *felt* beautiful.

"I'm going to set you free, Sara." The gravel-edged oath came as he lowered his head to hers. "Free from yourself."

"What about your decision?" she asked teasingly, slowing his descent by bracing her hands against his chest.

Flynn frowned without pulling away. "Decision?"

"Uh-huh. Your decision not to kiss me good-night, remember?"

"Ah. That decision. Not a factor. I have no intention of kissing you good-night."

Disappointment rippled through Sara. She was kicking herself for reminding him about it when he added, "At least not for a long, long time. You see, Sara, when a man kisses a woman good-night, it means the night is over." He gripped her firmly by the arms so that she couldn't have pulled away even if she wanted to. "This night is just beginning."

Sara was prepared for a kiss like the ones they'd shared before; she'd been dreaming about it at odd moments ever since. But this was nothing like those others. There was no slow buildup to passion this time. From the instant Flynn jerked her body against his and opened his mouth over hers, every touch of his hand, every fierce thrust of his tongue, was a raw proclamation of his desire.

They weren't teenagers and this wasn't a first date, and Flynn wasn't making any secret of what he had in mind. Part of Sara immediately responded by pumping forth a stream of ingrained doubts and insecurities, as well as platitudes that her mother had drilled into her at a formative age. Warnings about what nice girls did and didn't do, and what men were after, and what they usually did if you gave in and gave it to them too soon. Rules about what was and wasn't appropriate. That word again. The part of Sara closest to the surface was absolutely certain that making love while pressed against a man's car invariably qualified as inappropriate.

The trouble was that Flynn's caresses were reaching past that part of her, the part she relied on to deal with the outside world, and touching what lay buried beneath. For Sara, that was very private, uncharted territory.

His mouth found her ear, his breath bringing a warm, tingly rush of pleasure, the touch of his tongue sending sparks of excitement racing over her skin. He unfastened her belt and tossed it into the car behind her, then ran his palms over her hips and bottom and began to slowly slide her shirt higher.

Sara closed her eyes and tried to shut herself off to everything but the newly discovered pleasure of being touched by a man this way. His hands maneuvered her top up past her waist. The coolness of the night air on the bare skin of her midriff was a startling contrast with the heat and roughness of Flynn's touch. His fingers slid higher, touching, seeking, ultimately shoving her bra out of the way to free her breasts. He nestled them in the warmth of his cupped palms, his thumbs playing with the aroused peaks. Sara groaned and fought panic.

Just as she began to win the battle with herself, Flynn slid one hand lower. The elastic waistband of her knit slacks required no preliminary unsnapping and unzipping, and his touch spread like fire across the stomach muscles she flexed to make as firm as possible. The long, lean fingers that she had watched working the stick shift now worked on her with the same finesse, rubbing, pushing steadily lower....

Sara shivered. Oh, God, she'd thought she could handle this. She hadn't thought he would demand so much, so fast, and most shocking of all, she hadn't considered that she might want this every bit as furiously as he did. At least part of her wanted him—the part that wanted to keep her eyes and mind closed and ride the feelings he was creating in her. It would be so easy... as easy as riding the hard, muscled thigh he'd slid between hers, its rocking motion steady and erotic.

Instinctively, Sara gripped him with her thighs. Flynn made a sound of raw approval and pressed higher and suddenly, proving that nerves can deliver reality as efficiently as they do pleasure, Sara's inner censor kicked in and she went still... at least on the inside, where a lifetime of inhibitions were clamoring to be heard and heeded.

"No," Flynn growled. "No, damn it, don't stop me."

Sara was startled. She hadn't protested, had barely moved. How could Flynn be so attuned to the slightest change in her response? How could he anticipate what had hardly taken shape in her own mind?

"Please don't stop me, Sara," he pleaded, confirming that he'd done exactly that—read her mind. "At least, not for the same reason you did last time."

Sara regarded him warily as he slid his hands from inside her clothes and lifted his head to look down at her, his expression troubled. She heard an unexpected note of uncertainty in his husky voice as he continued, as though he were struggling for the right words.

"I know you have hang-ups of your own. Hell, who doesn't?" he muttered, holding on to her when she tried to move away. He lifted his hand to her face. "I saw that old picture of you on the piano, Sara. I think I know why you tense up and start to pull away every time I touch your body. But there's no need to. You are a very beautiful and desirable woman."

"I think full-figured would be a better term," Sara suggested, rolling her eyes and folding her arms tightly across her chest.

Flynn shook his head. "Is that supposed to be bad?"

"Have you read a fashion magazine lately?"

"No."

"That explains your misconception. Look, Flynn, I know I don't still look exactly the way I did in that old photo, but I sure don't look like the *me* of my fantasies . . . or anyone else's, for that matter."

"Goes to show what you know about my fantasies," he countered softly. "Fact is, you look exactly like the woman in the fantasies I've been having for the past couple of days."

"I do?" she said, disbelieving still, but willing to be convinced, so willing it hurt.

"Yeah, you do . . . not that I intend to stand here discussing them with you. I'm not much in the mood for discussing anything at the moment." He slid his hands down to her hips. "I know you have doubts, Sara. That's not entirely unreasonable, considering. If you want to have doubts about me, fine, or about whether you want this to happen, okay, but not about yourself," he insisted, tilting her forward just enough that she was pressed against the front of his jeans where even now his arousal was unmistakable. "Or that I find you incredibly sexy and desirable."

At another time, with another man, the deliberate contact would have been crude and unwelcome, but not with Flynn. Rather than feeling offended, Sara was thrilled that she had been able to excite him so thoroughly.

He slid his hands under her hair and massaged the back of her neck in a way that made Sara's legs weak.

"You turn me on," he said. "I don't want you to, but you do anyway, and that's very unlike me. I'd bet a whole lot that this is all very unlike you too, and that I'm the last man you'd choose to have make you feel the way you were feeling a few minutes ago."

"Maybe we don't always have a choice in these things."

Something dark flashed across his face. "Damn it, Sara, you always have a choice. Sometimes it's just easier to pretend you don't. Remember the first rule about getting what you want?"

"You mean what you said about having to ask for it?"

He nodded with a small, grim smile. "Well, sweetheart, you've been asking for it in one way or another ever since we climbed into that car together."

"Are you suggesting that I . . ."

"I'm just calling it like I see it. I have had some experience in this area."

"That doesn't come as a surprise to me."

"Thanks," he said, ignoring her attempt at sarcasm. "We're both grown-ups, Sara. We both know we started something when I kissed you the other day and you let me. If I'd just gone away like I planned to, maybe nothing ever would have come of it. But I didn't go away, and this thing with us has been in the air ever since."

"I don't know what you're talking about."

"Sure you do."

She met his gaze defiantly before flinching under his hard stare.

"All right," she conceded with an awkward toss of her head, "maybe I do know. But I feel . . . strange standing here talking about it this way."

"Don't worry. I told you I'm not interested in talking and I meant it. But for some unknown reason, I feel obligated to mention rule number two."

"Rule two?"

"Right, for getting what you want. Make sure that what you've got in your sights is the real thing." He grasped her chin to turn her gaze toward him, and held it there. "Take a good look, Sara. Are you sure I'm really what you want?"

A resounding *yes* echoed through her so forcefully Sara thought for a second she might have actually shouted it. Only Flynn's steady, expectant gaze assured her that she hadn't.

"Well, when you put it so bluntly, it's rather difficult to assess—"

"No," he interrupted. "It isn't difficult at all. It's simple, really, probably as simple and basic as it's ever going to be for you, Sara. No promises or starry-eyed dreams to muddy things. You see, with me, Sara, this is all you get."

"I see," she replied, her stiff tone concealing the wound his words had inflicted. "You're making it clear up front that while you're not opposed to a quick roll in the hay—or should I say on the car hood—in the long run, I am not the woman for you."

"You're a fine woman, Sara." There was a haunting note of regret in his voice. "What I'm trying to say is that I'm not the man for any woman. Not you, not anyone. That's just the way it is."

"But—"

He cut her off. "End of story, Sara." He trailed his fingers slowly along the side of her throat, rediscovering all the sensitive places he'd set fire to earlier. The embers still burned. "I can make you very happy tonight, Sara. I know I can, and I want to. I want to let me show you how beautiful you are…. How good it can be…" He held his hand still. "But this time, I want to make sure we both understand the terms of the deal up front."

"The terms being that we have a … fling, a purely physical relationship, an affair that lasts only as long as—"

"Sex," he cut in. "I'm talking about sex, Sara. Good sex." He smiled wryly. "Safe sex, I promise you. But that's the only promise I'm making."

Sara knew she should be shocked and offended by his blunt proposition. Instead, God help her, she was tempted. She was thirty-two years old, old enough to make up her own mind about what she could and couldn't do. And old enough to know that propositions like this didn't come along every day. Was it always better to be safe than sorry, as her mother had so often preached?

Sara wasn't so sure. Something deep inside her was urging her to take a chance . . . on fate, on herself, on Flynn. She harbored a gut-level feeling that even a few nights with Flynn would be worth the risk. And also a silly, romantic hope that maybe . . . maybe . . .

Maybe what? demanded her common sense. Maybe she, plain old Sara McAllister, could hold Flynn when what she was certain were dozens—perhaps scores—of more sophisticated, more glamorous, *skinnier* women hadn't managed to? Not likely.

The trouble with gut-level feelings, she realized as the silence grew long and she stood in the heat of Flynn's increasingly sardonic gaze, was that before they could be acted upon they had to run a powerful gauntlet of fears and doubts and good manners. What chance did something fresh from the heart have in such a contest?

None, really. As the seconds ticked away, Sara's urge to go with her feelings grew weak and battered. The death knell came when it occurred to her that if sex were all Flynn had to offer, he was probably frighteningly proficient at it. With high standards and expectations. Her stomach knotted. Sure, he'd promised her that it would be great for them; he was probably assuming that at her age she was reasonably experienced and able and willing to pull her own weight. Sara cringed inwardly at her own choice of words.

He assumed wrong, she thought, pondering what it would feel like to open herself so completely to Flynn in this regard, and fail. What would it be like to be confined in so small a space with him afterward? What if he turned out to be the type who had to prove himself the consummate lover with every woman he had and insisted on trying again even after she'd proven hopeless? Worse, what if he didn't *want* to try again?

"I think," she said at last, scraping her dry tongue over equally dry lips, "that perhaps we both should give this some more thought."

"Right," he said, his expression revealing that he was neither surprised nor pleased. He swung open the passenger door. "Get in the car, Sara."

Get in the car, Sara. Get out of the car, Sara. This trip was beginning to feel like the Twilight Zone with a doorman. A silent doorman, she thought, equally silent herself as Flynn slowly retraced their route to the main road she'd turned off earlier. After what had transpired, what was there left for them to say?

"Right."

"What?"

"I said you should have turned right there," Sara informed him. "I took a left there and so to get to the highway, you should have gone right instead of left."

"Right."

"That's right."

He glanced at her sharply. "Cut it out, Sara, I'm not in any mood for a comedy routine."

"I wasn't trying to be funny," she insisted, her voice rising in frustration. "You're going the wrong way."

"The wrong way to get back to the highway. But I'm not looking for the highway."

"What are you looking for?" she asked, her throat tight with anticipation as she surmised the answer and what it might mean.

"You wanted to eat at the Village Inn, didn't you? We're going to eat at the Village Inn. And don't ask me why," he snapped, his gaze fixed on the road ahead, "because I don't know."

Chapter Ten

The Village Inn turned out to be a thirty rather than a three-mile drive from where Sara had made her disastrous wrong turn. Realizing that, Sara concluded with some disgust that she must have misread the sign.

No matter. The drive allowed plenty of time for Flynn to ask himself why he was wasting precious travel time this way. Plenty of time to wonder why he was suddenly doing what he never, ever did: putting something or someone else ahead of his own agenda. Plenty of time to get frustrated because he couldn't come up with any answers.

At least not any he cared to think about.

This was becoming a pattern, he realized. Here he was putting Sara's crazy wish to eat at some joint he just knew was going to turn dinner into a long, drawn out ordeal ahead of his own need to stay close on Benny's tail. And back there on that deserted road, he'd put the possibility that she might later regret making love with him ahead of the hard-as-steel certainty that he suddenly wanted to make it with Sara McAllister more than he had with any women in a long time. Maybe ever. The reason for that was something else he didn't care to consider right now.

There was no reason to consider it, he reassured himself. Because as soon as possible he was going to have Benny in custody and Sara home where she belonged. He might not be entirely sure why a woman like Sara suddenly held such appeal for him, but he knew exactly what his appeal was for her. Sara was bored, lonely, frustrated…take your pick. In fact, now that he thought about it, she was probably all three.

She was starved for excitement and adventure and she had it in her head that he could provide it. Maybe he could. But he sure as hell couldn't provide everything else a woman like Sara needed to be happy and content. Oh, sure, in the heat of the moment, he could make Sara forget all about things like commitment and happily ever after, but that kind of heat couldn't burn forever. Eventually this trip would end and she was going to have to return to her life and he to his. Then the desire he'd seen flaming in her eyes a while ago would be replaced by regret and self-recriminations, and that wasn't the image of Sara he wanted to carry away with him.

At the Village Inn, which Sara said looked even more impressive than the picture on the billboard, the genial, dark-suited host led them to a corner table in one of numerous cozy dining rooms. The inn was a converted plantation, he explained as he seated them, and just the way his chest expanded as he said it told Flynn it was the kind of place that would expect you to read the menu cover to cover before making up your mind. More wasted time.

"Is something wrong?" asked Sara when the host left them alone.

"Why?"

"Because you've been scowling since we walked in here."

"Sorry. I didn't mean to scowl, I'm just wondering how…" He hesitated as he took note of her expression in the glow from the candle at the center of the table. Candlelight. That tacked another twenty minutes onto the service, guaranteed. Sara, however, seemed oblivious to the fact that this place ran on molasses time. She looked … enchanted, he decided. It wasn't a word that came to him naturally, or often, but it was the only one he knew to describe the look on her face as she gazed around at the room's gleaming dark paneling and period furnishings.

"I was just thinking what a terrific place this is," he concluded finally.

Unbelievably, her expression brightened more. "Oh, I'm so glad you like it. For a minute I thought you were sorry we came."

"Sorry?" he countered as their waitress arrived with a small crock of cheese and a basket—at least a twenty-five-minute basket—of crackers for them to "enjoy while they perused the menus."

"Why on earth would I be sorry we came?" Managing a calm smile, he handed her one of the very heavy, leather-bound menus. "Shall we peruse?"

After their orders were placed, Flynn sat and looked around the room, making a conscious effort not to check his watch or drum his fingers on the white linen tablecloth. Well, maybe one quick look at his watch wouldn't hurt...just so he would know later exactly how long he'd been waiting. As he casually turned his wrist so the watch faced up, he happened to glance across the table and caught Sara's gaze and stopped. There was something expectant about her small smile that made him raise his brows and shoot her a quizzical look.

"I thought maybe we could, you know, talk," she said in response to his look.

"Sure. Okay. What did you want to talk about?"

She shrugged in a way that made the blunt ends of her hair dance against her throat and made Flynn remember how soft her skin was there, especially that small dip right below her ear. He reached for his water glass and took a sip.

"Nothing special," she replied. "Just talk. I've been sort of wondering about what you said about not being close to your family."

He shot her a sardonic look over his still raised glass. "That's your idea of idle chitchat, asking someone about their family relationships?"

"Not usually," she said, looking predictably flustered, "but you did mention it back in Norfolk and I've just been sort of . . . wondering about it."

"First of all, I never said I wasn't close to my family."

Sara frowned. "I distinctly remember you saying—"

"I said," he broke in, "that I don't *have* any family."

"Flynn, everyone has family of some sort . . . no matter how distant or unorthodox."

"Not me. At least, none that I consider family."

"Oh."

He stared at her through the long silence, watching with some amusement as her uneasy gaze fluttered around the room and finally returned to settle on him with a hint of speculation she tried to hide. Was it the candlelight, he wondered, or were her eyes really that intensely blue?

"So now you want to know why, right?" he asked.

"I certainly don't want to pry."

"I know exactly what you want, Sara. You want me to fill in the missing pieces, answer all those questions running through your mind. You want to know what makes a man say the things I said to you out on that road a while ago. What kind of man— in this age of commitment and defensive sex—admits he's only interested in physical relationships of short duration. Right?"

"That's a little sweeping, isn't it? I just wanted to get to know you. I thought we could be . . . friends."

Up to that point he might have shrugged off her questions with a vague non-answer, but not now. Something in her somber, wistful admission prohibited evasion and had him considering doing something else which he never did, talk about himself.

"All right, here it is," he said, "not pretty, but brief. My father was one of this country's first Vietnam casualties. I barely remember him. I do remember my mother crying, a lot, after they came and told us he'd been killed." Recalling those days brought more pain than it had a right to after all this time. Flynn derided himself for being stupid enough to get drawn into this in the first place. So she had amazing eyes, and she wanted to know how a coldhearted bastard like him got that way. That wasn't his problem.

Resolving to make the brief version of his life even briefer, he took another gulp of water, found a safe spot somewhere over Sara's shoulder and talked mostly to that.

"Afterward my mother went to work full-time as a receptionist in a doctor's office. But that didn't quite make ends meet, so she took a job a few nights a week tending bar at a place downtown. Not a dive," he added, not wanting Sara to draw the wrong impression of his mother. "It was..." He shrugged, recalling the Church Street Tavern with more detail than he cared to. "Just a place. They served food and everything. Sometimes, if she knew it would be a slow night, she'd even bring me along and let me wash glasses or sit in the back room and read or do homework."

"How old were you?"

"Thirteen," he said, meeting her eyes briefly and seeing in them a shining concern Flynn told himself *had* to be a trick of the candlelight. She hardly knew him. No one who knew him had even cared that much about him; why should she?

He found that safe spot over her shoulder again. "Anyway, one night when she was scheduled to be off, her boss called and asked her to cover for another bartender who was sick."

"Did she go?" Sara asked when he suddenly dropped into the dark silent whirlpool of memories his words had uncovered. It was a place he didn't visit often, or willingly.

"Yeah. Yeah, she went. She'd never say no. Not to the extra money we could always use, or to someone who needed a hand. She went. When she got outside, her car wouldn't start. It was old and real temperamental in cold weather. I stood in the doorway to wave goodbye, just like I always did. She would always wave back as she got to the end of the driveway and call out, 'Leave a light on, kiddo.' It was..." He stopped and swallowed, his mind reaching frantically for a fast way out of this, and knowing, with a dark suffocating certainty, that there was no fast or easy way out from here. Never had been.

"It was sort of a private joke, you know, something she said, even though she knew I always left a light on anyway." He half-smiled at the image of himself at thirteen. "I was still a little scared being there alone at night."

"I'm still sometimes a little scared of being alone at night, even now," Sara said.

Flynn met her gaze briefly, nodding acknowledgment of her attempt to sympathize. "Anyway, the car wouldn't start and I was hoping she would let that be an excuse not to go to work after all, when the guy next door happened to come out and he offered her a ride. She took it, figuring she'd get a lift home off a friend from work."

He was silent for a long time and Sara didn't say a word. When he finally raised his eyes and looked at her, her expression was open and watchful and...reassuring somehow, crazy as that sounded.

"She didn't need the ride home," he said hurriedly. "Later that night, some guy who had a beef with the owner of the bar walked in carrying a semiautomatic and sprayed the place with bullets. He killed three people. My mother was one of them."

He heard the ocean of shock and sympathy in Sara's sharply indrawn breath.

"Oh, Flynn, how awful for you."

He lifted his water glass and grimaced to discover it empty. Without a word Sara placed hers in front of him. "It wasn't a time I'd care to relive, that's for sure."

"I know how I felt when my parents died," she said. "I can't imagine what my life would have been like if it had happened when I was only thirteen."

"I guess that all depends," he said, aware of the harshness that invaded his tone, "on whether or not you have an Uncle Roger to take you in."

"Is that what happened to you? You went to live with your uncle?"

Flynn nodded, caught in another powerful backwash of emotion, this one without the cushion of love that thoughts of his mother always carried with them.

"Yeah, that's what happened to me. The day after the funeral he and Aunt May came to the house, picked through everything we owned for what they wanted and sold the rest. Just like that. It was bad enough that my mother was gone, but suddenly everything else was gone, too. One day I had a home, things of my own, a place where I belonged. The next I had nothing but a duffel bag full of clothes and a room in the basement where my aunt and uncle *let* me stay . . . and never let me forget it."

"They sold everything?" she asked softly.

Flynn nodded. "Don't get me wrong—we didn't have much. Certainly not much of value. My mother's good dishes and stuff, my bed . . . I asked to keep the bed—they could have let me keep my own damned bed, at least . . . " He made a gesture with his hands as if to hold onto something that weren't there. "You might not think things like dishes and furniture matter to a kid—*they* sure as hell didn't believe it—but they mattered to me. They were . . ." He paused and shrugged, hating this. "Part of my past, part of something that was gone."

"I know those things matter," Sara said, reaching out to cover his knotted fingers with her hand. Her touch promised relief in a way that Flynn had learned not to trust. "And how much they matter. I know because after my father died, we had to sell some personal things, things that had been in my family for years, just to put a dent in the gambling debts he left behind, and I know how much that hurt. It would have been a million times worse to lose everything."

Even though he was staring at the place where their hands touched, Flynn felt the sudden tension in her and looked up.

"Is that why you're in trouble financially now? His gambling debts?"

He noted Sara's inner struggle before she finally nodded.

"And you're thinking about what will happen if you lose everything to Bowers, aren't you?" he asked.

"I'm sorry. I'm sure that must seem pretty selfish compared to what you've just told me, compared to all that's happened to you."

"No, it doesn't. You can't measure your pain against someone else's. Pain is personal. So is the way you deal with it."

She tilted her head and stared at him sadly. "Based on what you told me just now, and earlier, I'd say your way of dealing with it is to close yourself off from any sort of genuine relationship with others."

"The lady scores a knockout. Want some cheese and crackers?"

"No, thank you. Whatever happened to your aunt and uncle?"

"Don't know. Don't care. I left to enlist on my eighteenth birthday and I never looked back."

"And then after the service you became a bounty hunter."

"Not right after. Eventually. Things I'd done both in and out of the service made me a natural for it." He leaned back and stared at her. "I've done some things that you'd probably find as *inappropriate* and offensive as you do the fact that I hunt men for money."

"And also equally high risk?"

He shrugged. "I guess."

"Just for the record, I don't find your work offensive."

"You sure seemed to that first night."

The corners of her mouth lifted in a small, uncertain smile that felt as if it were connected directly to his heart. "I thought a lot of foolish things that first night."

"Things that you don't think now?" countered Flynn, peeved as all get out that it should matter so much to him.

She nodded, then before he could press further, added, "I do find it interesting, however, that you choose to take as much risk as possible in your work and none at all in your personal life."

"Personal being the operative word," he shot back, automatically moving his hand so that they were no longer touching. "And I'd like to keep it that way. I'm not up for being psychoanalyzed tonight, Sara."

"Good, because I'm no analyst, but you don't need to be one to see that you refuse to let anyone get too close to you because you're afraid you might—"

"Lose?" he interjected harshly. "Right again, Sara. I'm afraid I might lose. So before I let myself care about anyone or anything too much, I ask myself if having it is worth losing it. And you know what? So far, with the exception of that overpriced hunk of fiberglass and metal parked outside, which I confess to buying in a moment of pure weakness, the answer has always been no."

"You can't compare people to things," she said, sounding exasperated.

" I can do whatever I want. This is my problem," he reminded her. "People, animals, things...we're all subject to the same whims of fate."

"I'm not sure I believe in fate, at least not in fate alone."

"Well, I do," he declared, leaning forward and lowering his voice to a fierce whisper. "I think of how my mother shouldn't have even been in that place that night, how she wouldn't have been if that other bartender hadn't gotten sick, or if her boss had phoned for another replacement, or if the guy next door hadn't happened to come out when he did. I think about all that, and I believe, damn it."

"You were only thirteen when that happened, Flynn, and..."

He smiled darkly. "Meaning what? I should have outgrown these feelings by now?"

"Of course that's not what I meant. But when it comes to letting someone close, how can you possibly know what you're missing if you never—"

"Can it, Sara," he ordered, holding up a hand to silence her. "You're wasting your breath, believe me. I've been pitched by the best about this, by women with far more experience and fewer scruples than you have, and the result is always the same...no sale. You see, I don't need to have my past explained or interpreted to me. I *know* that I'm afraid. I like being afraid. It's safe. And I think it's pretty damn clever of me to stay this way as long as I have. So you see, Sara, it's not a question of denial or recovery or whatever the latest psychobabble buzzword is. The real reason I don't have a woman or a home or a family is that I just plain don't want them."

"I see," said Sara, even though Flynn knew from the look in her incredible eyes that she didn't see, not really, and that she never would.

But that wasn't his problem, either.

In spite of the fact that dinner at the Village Inn was every bit as wonderful as Sara had anticipated, and that she had also gotten her wish that she and Flynn might talk and get to know each other better, she left the restaurant with a hollow feeling inside that not even her surrender to a piece of the chef's spectacular blueberry cream pie could fill.

For a large part of her life, Sara had mistakenly believed that food could fill any emptiness inside. During the past few years, however, she'd grown to understand that there are different kinds of hunger, some that no amount of sugar in the world can ease. The emptiness inside her now was one of those.

It had to do with her talk with Flynn, she knew. At first he'd been reluctant to talk, but once into it, he'd revealed more of himself than Sara had ever expected he might. And more than he himself had expected to reveal, she suspected, or had wanted to. The only explanation she could think of for that was that, in view of the rather strong physical attraction between them, Flynn wanted to make absolutely certain that she understood his position on the matter and accepted it. Which she now did. What choice did she have?

Not surprisingly, the conversation over dinner afterward had been sparse and very superficial. Now, in the car, Flynn seemed to want to keep things that way. Sara didn't mind. The hours behind the wheel, followed by the trauma of landing in that ditch and then the emotional upheaval of hearing Flynn talk about his past, had left her exhausted. It wasn't long after they had returned to the highway and were finally on the direct route to Miami that she drifted off to sleep.

She woke to a loud grating sound that was only slightly louder than Flynn's reaction.

"What . . ."

"The tail pipe," he told her through gritted teeth. "The perfect end to a perfect day."

Sara wasn't sure what exactly was wrong with the tail pipe and she thought it best at that point not to ask too many questions. As it turned out, she didn't need to. The whole unfortunate situation was revealed in staccato bursts intermingled with Flynn's disparagement of cars in general, the manufacturer of this one in particular and himself for having given in to the impulse to buy it in the first place.

Bottom line: the entire exhaust system had to be replaced. It had something to do with the way it was soldered together, according to the tow truck driver who eventually responded to their call from one of the roadside emergency boxes.

"Of course," the man added as he yawned and scratched at the chest pocket on his shirt where the name Mervin was embroidered in red script, "we'll have to wait for the final verdict till we get y'all towed back to the station, being as I'm not an actual mechanic."

Flynn's smile was deadly. "That figures," he said.

Replacing the exhaust system of a high-performance sports car in a one-filling-station town isn't an impossible feat. But it's darn close. They discovered that fact gradually over the course of the next fourteen or so hours, as they waited first for the actual mechanic to arrive to officially open the station, and then watched as he examined the Corvette's underbelly with much head shaking and clicking of his tongue.

"Flynn?" Sara said at one point.

"Mmm?"

"You don't think that by any chance, you know, that landing in that ditch might have caused—"

"I'm not going to think about it," he broke in. Then to her amazement, he flashed her a reassuring smile. "Don't you, either."

After Billy-Bob, the actual mechanic, finished crawling around under the car, he got on the phone to what seemed like every other station and automotive supply store in the state and finally located the replacement parts he needed for the job. After that it was just a matter of waiting while Mervin got back from towing his brother's Jeep out of a creek and went to pick up the parts so that Billy-Bob could finish the fish-stick sandwich his wife dropped off for his lunch and then finally go about installing them.

Flynn remained outwardly calm throughout. If anything, he seemed to get more laid-back as the day stretched on. It might have been the heat, thought Sara, or that he'd long ago resigned himself to the whims of fate. Whatever it was, one thing didn't change. No matter how nonchalant he appeared, each time she looked into his eyes she had the sensation that she was watching a meter like those in taxis . . . only instead of totaling up dollars and cents, this one kept count of minutes lost.

By the time they were on their way again, Sara was exhausted, and she knew that in spite of his insistence to the contrary, Flynn had to be also. She kept him company for as long as she could, then drifted off to sleep for what felt like hours, waking to the now familiar hum of tires on pavement. Without lifting her head, she slit her eyes open then widened them all the way at the sight of a giant, frosty piña colada coming up fast on the right. "Come and cool off South of the Border," invited the brightly colored billboard.

Sara smiled. Talk about mind over matter, she was suddenly as thirsty as if they'd been crossing the desert in a covered wagon instead of cruising along the interstate in a car that Flynn claimed had state-of-the-art climate control. She was also sticky. Either it was getting much hotter out there as they drove south, or the car's temperature sensors weren't all they were cracked up to be. At that moment, her idea of heaven consisted of a piña colada and a shower.

Not that she would dare broach the subject of either one to Flynn. She had no doubt that he had calculated to the minute what dinner last night and the exhaust-pipe fiasco had cost in travel time and was going to shave minutes off every pit stop they made until he'd recouped it.

Stretching her legs a bit, she stared out the window and tried unsuccessfully to recapture yesterday's feeling of unadulterated joy in the trip. Not that she wasn't still glad she'd insisted on coming along; she was. But what had passed between her and Flynn last night had changed things. Yesterday, with her new clothes and new hair and Flynn in the seat beside her, anything had seemed possible. Not any longer. Now there was a solid steel wall of reality between her and yesterday's wide blue horizon.

A few miles farther along another billboard came into sight. This one boasted that the water was cool and the tamales hot South of The Border. Intrigued, Sara sat up straighter in her seat, paying attention now, and sure enough another billboard soon slid into view. This time she couldn't resist laughing out loud.

"Hey, sleepyhead," Flynn greeted, slanting a lazy smile her way. "I thought maybe you were going to stay zonked out around the clock."

"I feel like I could have," Sara replied, stretching her shoulders, relieved that Flynn seemed to have left behind all the anguish and frustration of the night before.

"What's so funny?" he asked. "Or were you laughing in your sleep?

"No, I've been awake for a while, actually. I was laughing at that billboard back there, the one that said 'Fill up your trunk with Pedro's junk.' Did you see it?"

"How can I miss it? There's a billboard hawking South of the Border every few miles for a fifty-mile stretch on every route approaching the place. Just wait, they get more frequent and less subtle the closer you get to it."

"What is South of the Border?" she asked.

"Originally it was only a small gift shop just south of the border between North and South Carolina. Then they added a motel or two, more shops and restaurants so that now it's a regular honky-tonk extravaganza right out in the middle of nowhere. Which, I suppose is a big part of its appeal. When you've been driving for a long time even a stop at South of the Border sounds good."

"I'm so glad you're the one who said that," countered Sara.

He shot her a sideways look. "Oh, no, don't even think it, Sara."

"Come on, Flynn, we have to make a pit stop soon anyway. Why not make it there?"

"Sara, it's a tourist trap, for Pete's sake. Wall-to-wall with guys in Bermuda shorts snapping pictures of kids wearing beaver tail hats and wives in T-shirts that say 'I survived South of the Border.' "

"Sounds like fun to me."

"Everything sounds like fun to you," he muttered. "That's the problem with this trip."

"I take it you're still peeved about last night."

"No. I refuse to think about last night. I'm just thinking about getting to Miami."

"Good, then if you're not annoyed with me, maybe you'll at least think about making a quick, very quick, I swear, stop at South of the Border."

"What for?"

"Personal reasons," she snapped, rolling her eyes in exasperation.

"You can take care of personal reasons at any rest stop without leaving the highway."

"Maybe. But I can't buy a South of the Border postcard to send to Nancy at a rest stop...or souvenirs to bring home to her kids."

"Souvenirs?" he echoed, sounding as shocked as if she'd suggested bringing home live baby alligators, which, come to think of it, Nancy's kids would probably love.

"Yes, souvenirs—small tokens of remembrance that one brings home from vacation for loved ones."

"But you're not on vacation," he reminded. "This is supposed to be work."

"Oh, right," replied Sara, wondering how on earth she could have forgotten that little fact. "But Nancy and the kids don't know that."

"Then you can fill them in when you get home. It will explain why you didn't buy any souvenirs."

"But Nancy will worry like crazy in the meantime. Come on, Flynn, how long can it take to use the ladies' room and buy a few measly postcards?"

"I don't know. I've never done either."

"Very funny. It won't take long, I promise. Ten minutes. Can we spare ten minutes for a good cause?"

"No," he retorted. He glanced at her and shook his head in defeat. "But as long as you promise me you'll keep it to ten minutes, I'll stop anyway."

"Cross my heart," replied Sara as she settled back to read the signs which were, as Flynn had predicted, coming fast and furious now.

South of the Border was not quite like anything Sara had ever seen. Not that she was a world traveler by any means, but South of the Border wasn't even like anything she'd ever seen in a movie. Covering the space of perhaps a half dozen large city blocks, it was a collection of motels, gift shops and restaurants ranging from food stands to sit-down establishments. Emblazoned everywhere was the likeness and corny quips of the founder and evidently self-appointed czar of South of the Border, Pedro himself.

Subtlety was clearly not Pedro's style, thought Sara, gazing around the neon-lit wonderland where a carnival mood prevailed. With no pretense of sophistication, this was unabashedly a place to have fun, a place where even a guy in a cap adorned with fishing lures and an empty beer can could feel like one of the crowd, and while just days ago Sara might have wrinkled her nose in distaste, at this moment she didn't see anything especially wrong with that.

In fact, she was enjoying herself in an unexpected sort of way, and in spite of the fact that the same could not be said of Flynn. He wandered behind her through the stadium-size main gift shop looking as if he'd rather be somewhere—*anywhere*—else.

Remembering her promise, she resisted the temptation to browse through counter after counter of amazingly tacky doodads and headed directly for the racks of postcards. With the postcards in hand, she quickly grabbed a few kid-size T-shirts with a grinning Pedro on the front and turned to Flynn.

"All set. How did I do?" she asked.

"You're about twenty minutes over the limit," he replied, "but considering the sheer madness of this place, I'd say you did just fine."

They stopped to pay the cashier, then headed to the central lobby of the main building. From the adjacent arcade came the mingled sounds of traditional pinball machines and the electronic serenade of video games. The aroma of fresh popcorn filled the air and as Sara traced the scent to a nearby cart, her stomach clenched, reminding her of how long it had been since lunch.

"Are you hungry?" asked Flynn.

She shook her head, not wanting to pressure him when she knew how anxious he was to get on the road. "Not especially."

"Then how come your stomach's growling?" he inquired, his mouth slanting into a wry smile.

"How can you hear my stomach growling over all this noise?"

"Intuition," he said, his smile growing cocky. "I just have to concentrate and I know what you want, what you're thinking, what you're feeling." His smile faded suddenly as their gazes locked. His voice turned low and rough. "Why is that, Sara?"

"I don't know," she said softly, dazed by the look in his eyes and by what he seemed to be saying. She didn't have time to ponder it the way she'd like to, however. Flynn quickly slid his easygoing mask back in place.

"So then, since it's been established that we're both hungry, what shall we eat?" He took the shopping bag from her and reached for her hand to lead her through the crowd that seemed even thicker now than when they arrived. "Hot dogs, pizza, Mexican."

"Mexican seems appropriate, don't you think?" she asked, savoring the thrill of walking hand in hand with him as casually as if they did this every day, as if he had a right to hold her hand, as if they were more lovers than friends—as if they even were friends.

"*Si,*" replied Flynn, grinning at her.

Sara laughed and shook her head as she tugged him in the opposite direction. "Then come this way, Pedro, follow the sign of the flashing taco."

"You mean the flashing sign of the taco," he corrected. "Wording can be very important when you're following a lead."

"So can timing, I understand. So, just out of curiosity, how come you're not dragging me back to the car right now?"

He shrugged and shouldered his way around a boisterous gathering of tourists. "We have to eat sometime, and you looked like you were having fun and... Oh, how the hell should I know why? I'm just not, okay?"

"It's okay with me, boss." She drew encouragement from the wry look he slanted her. "I was just wondering if, since you're in such an understanding mood, you'd like to take a ride to the stars with me?''

His green eyes narrowed sharply. ''What the hell is that supposed to mean?''

''Nothing to get frantic about. See? Right over there.'' She pointed behind him at a brightly lit spire that carried a glass elevator up to the circular platform high above. Tiny white lights proclaimed it to be a ride to the stars.

''Oh.'' Sara wasn't sure if it were relief or disappointment she heard in his tone. ''Would this flight take place before or after the tacos?'' he asked.

''Your choice.''

''Before,'' he decided with mock seriousness. ''That way I'll have something to look forward to.''

They made their way through the crowd to the ride, reaching the ticket window just as the young women inside slid the grate shut. ''Sorry,'' she said. ''I'm closed.''

''Come on,'' countered Flynn in a wheedling tone as he leaned on the small counter in front of the window and smiled at her. ''As long as you're still here, couldn't you sell me a couple of tickets? We really had our hearts set on taking a ride to the stars tonight.''

''So take it tomorrow, instead,'' she retorted, blowing a bubble with her gum. She pointed to the sign at the front of the booth. ''We open at eight and we close at ten.'' She poked the gum into her mouth and added, ''Sharp.''

''Right,'' he said, turning away from the booth with a grim expression.

''Poor Flynn,'' said Sara. ''I have a feeling you're not used to hearing no from a woman after using that smile.''

He shrugged and had the decency to look uncomfortable. ''One thing's for sure, I don't usually use it on sixteen-year-olds. Sorry about the ride.''

''We could always do as she suggested,'' commented Sara after taking a deep breath.

''What's that?''

''Come back in the morning.''

"That would be a little tough to do, Sara, since by eight o'clock tomorrow morning we'll be a couple of hundred miles from here."

"We don't have to be."

He stopped walking and shot her a warning look. "Don't start. There's no way I'm going to lose a whole night's travel time . . . and even if I was going to lose it, it sure wouldn't be at a joint like this."

"I thought some of the motels across the road looked very nice. One even has a heated indoor pool. Doesn't a swim sound relaxing?"

"Nope. It sounds like another fifty miles between me and Benny."

"But Benny has to sleep, too," she argued. "And he has to do all his own driving. At least you have me to relieve you once in a while."

"Don't remind me."

"Just think, if you get some sleep, you'll be able to go that much longer without having to let me drive again."

He rubbed the back of his hand across his stubbled jaw. "I have to admit, that is sort of a tempting thought."

"And think how much better we'd both feel if we had a chance to take a shower."

"I feel fine as I am."

Sara wasn't surprised to hear that, since he looked pretty darn good, as well. Flynn seemed to be much better than she was at surviving on fifteen-minute pit stops.

"Well, I don't feel fine," she snapped. "I feel gritty and grungy and sticky and . . . and worried."

He frowned at the last. "Worried? About what?"

"About you driving any farther without some decent rest. I mean it, Flynn, it's just plain dangerous. Have you ever thought about what could happen if you fall asleep at the wheel of that car doing eighty—which is how fast you drive most of the time?"

She could tell by the look on his face that it wasn't something he'd invested a whole lot of time thinking about, and that he didn't especially like the images her question had brought to mind.

"No," he said at last. "I don't think about it. Mostly because whatever's going to happen is going to happen, and I know there's not a damn thing I can do to change things."

"That is the most ridiculous, irresponsible—"

"But," he interrupted, his expression stormy, "I've also never had anybody else along whose safety I had to take into consideration. Like it or not, that changes things a little. So I guess we can spend the night here, but we're out of here at the crack of dawn," he added before she could get too excited. "You'll just have to ride to the stars next time through."

"Deal," agreed Sara. "At the moment I'd much rather see a real bed than stars, anyway."

By the time they drove the short distance to the stretch of road where the motels where located, there was a no-vacancy sign at the one advertising the heated indoor pool. The place next door still had the vacancy light on, however, and Sara waited in the car while Flynn went in to register.

He hadn't bothered to ask if he should request one room or two. Sara reasoned that might mean that he simply assumed that since they were traveling together they would share a room, if only to keep expenses down. Whatever the reason, the thought of being alone in a small motel room with Flynn made her pulse quicken with nervous anticipation. Of course, the fact that he hadn't asked might also mean that he had no intention of sharing a room with her. Separate rooms was the safer, saner, *appropriate* approach, to be sure. But it didn't have nearly the same effect on her heartbeat.

The longer she waited for him to return, the more anxious Sara became. She began thinking about what might happen if he did get only a single room. Perhaps with only a single bed. What then? Her skin prickled with possibilities. Is that what she wanted? she thought nervously. Surely not. Sex with a man she hardly knew, a man who was all wrong for her, a man who even if she *hadn't* known was wrong for her had himself taken great pains to explain that fact to her. It was the antithesis of everything she'd been taught and had ever thought she wanted.

Thought she wanted. Why, all of a sudden, did the question of what Sara McAllister wanted seem so important, and so very unclear? While she was still wrestling with that, she suddenly recalled the ploy she'd seen used in dozens of movies, not to mention countless novels, the one where the mismatched couple thrown together by circumstances arrive at the motel only to discover they must share the last available room. What if that happened tonight? Or, she mused, what if Flynn *arranged* for it to happen? She wouldn't put it past him. She wouldn't put anything past him, actually. What would she do then?

Before she'd come up with an answer, he returned, pulling open the driver's door and hunkering down to talk to her. "All set," he announced, "except for one little hitch."

Sara could hardly control her smug smile. "Let me guess. They only had one room left?"

He shook his head. "No, they had two rooms . . . but they're the very last two. One's the first room here on the bottom floor. The other's the last one up there on top. So," he continued, holding up two keys on plastic rings, "lady's choice. Would you prefer to be closer to the parking lot or the ice machine?"

Chapter Eleven

You, thought Sara, the realization bringing with it a sudden rush of desperation. *I don't care about parking lots or ice machines, I just want to be close to you.*

They'd been all but inseparable for days, and the sudden prospect of spending an entire night away from Flynn caused a pain that made Sara wonder what it was going to feel like to say goodbye to him for good.

She shrugged under Flynn's watchful gaze, certain that the very last thing he wanted to hear was that she was growing more emotionally attached to him with each passing moment. "I guess I'll take the top floor."

Later, alone in her room, she turned the shower on full blast and stood under the spray until the hot water ran out. The only nightgown she had with her was the one she'd been wearing the night she left home. Reaching for it automatically, Sara pushed her arms into the sleeves and then suddenly froze as the folds of faded flowered cotton were about to envelope her. Everything inside her rebelled.

"No," she said out loud, ripping her arms free and hurling it across the room. "No, no, no."

It wasn't enough. Circling the double bed, which was covered by a spread in standard motel earth tones, she snatched the nightgown off the floor and stuffed it into the wastebasket.

That made her feel marginally better and the significance of that wasn't lost on Sara. The nightgown symbolized what had come to seem like another lifetime, another world—most of all, another Sara. She wasn't naive enough to think that she'd left all that behind for good, but for the first time in her life she had a reprieve from it and she wasn't ready to crawl back into her shell just yet. Not even symbolically.

So what to wear to sleep? Avoiding her naked reflection in the mirror, she rummaged in her bag for the roomiest of her new shirts, this one an attention-attracting shade of bright yellow, which she usually avoided, and pulled it on. The color suited her, she decided, examining her reflection in the mirror. Lots of things suited her that she had never before dared to try, like short hair and boots and spur-of-the-moment adventure. Humming to herself, she rinsed out her underwear and towel-dried her hair, marveling at how easily the new cut fell into place. She had to admit, Nancy had been right about her hair.

And maybe about a lot of other things as well. Afraid to allow that thought to grow, Sara anxiously paced around the room, taking stock. There wasn't a whole lot to look at. Aside from the bed, a nightstand and two matching club chairs, there was a clock radio and a television with a menu of the available pay-per-view movies bolted to the top. Unfortunately, she didn't want to listen to the radio or watch a movie. With an exasperated sigh, she threw herself into one of the chairs. Why was it that after years of living on automatic pilot, every thought she had lately led to the same thing…the thorny matter of what she did and didn't want?

Stretching her legs, she propped her feet on the bed and crossed her legs at the ankles. Then she uncrossed her feet and dropped them back to the floor before finally curling them onto the seat beside her. She was undeniably restless, and the reason for her restlessness was right downstairs in the room overlooking the parking lot.

What was Flynn doing? she wondered. She'd bet that he'd headed for the shower as quickly as she had, in spite of his insistence that he didn't mind roughing it for as long as he had to. Thoughts of Flynn, wet and soapy, filled her head. She pictured water beaded on his shoulders and arms, and puffs of white foam slathered across his chest ... his hairy chest, she decided, certain that Flynn would have exactly the right amount of dark, curly chest hair. In fact, it was hard for Sara to envision anything about him that might be less than exactly right as she imagined him leaning against the tile wall in the steam-filled shower. His eyes were narrowed and he was smiling ... He was smiling at her, reaching for her. ...

Sara bolted upright in the chair. What was wrong with her that she was thinking such things?

Nothing.

The answer erupted from somewhere deep inside her. There was nothing wrong with what she was thinking. Or, for that matter, with what she wanted. It suddenly occurred to her that she'd been wrong a moment ago when she told herself that Flynn was the cause of her restlessness. He was the inspiration for it, to be sure, but the real cause lay much closer to home ... inside Sara herself. Taking place inside her was the same old tug-of-war between what she wanted to do and what she ought to do.

Resting her head on the back of the chair, she closed her eyes and wished Nancy were there to talk things over with. Instantly her eyes flicked open and found the telephone on the nightstand. Sara was across the room, the receiver in hand and about to push the button for an outside line, when she succumbed to a wry smile and slowly lowered the receiver onto the cradle. It would be great to talk to her friend, but she really didn't need to phone Nancy to know what she would have to say about all this. In her own inimitable style, Nancy would zero right in on the heart of the problem and no doubt cheer raucously to hear Sara finally confess to being what Nancy had for years been telling her she was, a normal, flesh and blood woman.

Sara's smiled broadened as she recalled how easily she had always shrugged off that description. She wasn't shrugging now. Facts were facts, and the fact was that she was interested in... Attracted to... Oh, what the heck, she thought, if Nancy were here she wouldn't let her get away with those wishy-washy pronouncements. The fact was, she wanted Flynn.

That established, Nancy would immediately want to know if he was worth the trouble. He was, Sara was sure of that. Any man who could look her in the eye and tell her she was beautiful and who only yelled a little when she landed his most prized possession in a ditch and who would afterward drive sixty miles out of his way to eat dinner at the restaurant of her choosing was worthy of a high degree of lust, among other things.

Next Nancy would want to know what was she going to do about it? Ah, there was the rub. As always, what she wanted was shadowed by what she'd been told was appropriate or expected. More than once Nancy had teasingly predicted that the inscription on her tombstone was going to read, *Sara McAllister... she always did what was expected.* Suddenly, the awful truth of that outweighed any trace of humor, grating Sara's nerves raw.

Lord knew she was old enough by far to decide for herself about her own expectations and what was appropriate for her, and it suddenly occurred to Sara that perhaps she had been taking the easy way out in that regard for too long. It had been easier to maintain the status quo than to forge a new path, to simply pick up where her parents had left off in preserving and maintaining the good name and pristine image of the McAllister family. Even if that image no longer fit... and maybe never had. It had been easier to follow the path of least resistance than to acknowledge to herself and the whole world her innermost hopes and dreams, and easier by far than going after them—with all the risks and setbacks and disappointments that entailed. Struggling to save the house kept her busy and preoccupied, and it kept her from having to take a chance on herself.

How she envied Flynn for being so certain of what he wanted and did not want out of life, even if she didn't agree with all his choices. How must it feel to be so absolutely sure of yourself? And how did you get to be that way? Flynn was full of advice on the subject, she mused, recalling his rules for getting what you want.

Be very sure of what you want, he had told her. Was she very sure she wanted Flynn? Sara didn't even hesitate. Of that, at least, she was very, very sure. More than anything, she wanted to make love with Flynn. She wanted much more than that, actually, but if that's all there could be, she was prepared to accept it.

The first rule—actually asking for what she wanted—was proving to be the killer. Not that she was afraid that Flynn would refuse her. Even her limited experience qualified her to judge that he'd been every bit as aroused as she was last night, and the looks she caught him giving her when he didn't know she was watching assured her that the same hunger still simmered beneath his devil-may-care charm. She was far more concerned with not measuring up to his expectations than she was with Flynn turning her down. She had always failed to measure up to Stuart's.

Whenever you reached for something, there was always the risk that you could fall short . . . or worse you could freeze up and step outside of yourself and be absolutely unable to save yourself from disaster, like watching a tractor trailer hurtling downhill with no driver inside. Sara had learned the hard way how that felt. Was she ready to take a chance on that kind of failure with Flynn?

Wrapping her arms around herself, she walked to the window and stood peering out into the neon-lit light through a crack in the drawn drapes. Risk taking didn't come naturally to her. Given a choice, she opted for being safe. *Safe*. Wasn't that the same word Flynn had used to describe his policy of never getting emotionally involved? How quick she'd been to criticize his attitude, but when it came right down to it, was her own any different? At least Flynn *had* a policy, a code he lived by, a method of deciding if something was worth taking a chance on.

How had he put it? He'd said that he always asked himself if having something were worth losing it. Sara stared out into the night and asked herself her own version of that same question now. Was loving Flynn worth risking the pain and humiliation of failure?

* * *

Fresh from the shower, Flynn stretched out on the bed with his arms folded behind his head, glared at the ceiling and asked himself what the hell he was doing in a place called the Siesta Motor Lodge. He should have dismissed out of hand the idea of spending the night here and told Sara to do her sleeping in the car. After all, this was still his job, his chase, and he called the shots.

The thought had such a hollow ring that he shook his head in self-disgust. Sure, he was the one calling the shots, but only after careful consideration of Sara's feelings and preferences. Not a conscious consideration, he assured himself. On a conscious level he knew precisely what was going on here . . . he wanted Sara McAllister in his bed. Figuratively speaking, that is, since last night the hood of his car would have done just as well. And because he wanted her so damn badly, his hormones were working overtime to screw up his decision-making process. It was all biological . . . subliminal . . . and a weakness he could not afford to indulge right now. So why was he going out of his way to prolong the agony with fancy dinners and overnight stops at tourist traps?

Flynn took a long gulp from his can of soda, wishing it held something stronger. It would, if not for the fact that he didn't want even a mild hangover in the morning to slow him down or further mess up his thinking. Right now, his desire to find Benny and get Sara out of his life was about equal to his desire for Sara herself, and he knew it wouldn't take very much to tip the scales toward disaster.

Deep in his own thoughts, Flynn barely heard the knock on the door. Then too, it was a pretty quiet knock, almost as if the person knocking was half hoping not to be heard. A wry smile creased his lips as he swung off the bed and yanked on the jeans he'd tossed on a nearby chair. It could have been anyone knocking on his door, a motel maid, someone with the room numbers mixed up, anyone. But Flynn knew even before opening the door that it was Sara.

"Hi," she said.

"Hi." He rested his shoulder on the door frame and let his gaze drift from her wide, anxious eyes to her bare feet.

She was wearing some sort of bright yellow thing that ended midthigh and instantly sent his thoughts scattering like a handful of confetti tossed into the wind. Her hair was loose and soft. He wanted to touch it and he wanted to slam the door before he had the chance to. Inside him, the delicate balance he'd been working on since she climbed into his car teetered dangerously. "What can I do for you?" he asked.

Sara immediately jerked her gaze away from the open snap of his jeans and across his bare chest, to meet his eyes. She swallowed hard before replying. "Sleep with me, Flynn."

Somehow he managed not to let his jaw drop. Maybe he hadn't heard correctly, or she had mis-spoken, or she simply meant that she was afraid to sleep up in that room all alone. Maybe... "What exactly are you trying to say, Sara?"

"I'm not trying to *say* anything. I'm asking... Asking for what I want, just like you said I should."

"And what you want is to sleep with me?" he demanded, eyes narrowed warily.

Her smile, as shaky as it was, surprised him. "Not right away. Eventually we could get around to sleeping."

There was no misinterpreting *that,* or the soft, melting look she gave him. *Oh, damn,* he thought. *Don't do this to me, Sara.* He folded his arms across his chest. "And what happens before we get around to sleeping?"

She shrugged tightly.

"Come on, Sara," he said, grimacing. "I told you how things are with me. How it has to be."

"And I appreciate your honesty. Now I'm following your advice. I decided what I want, and I'm asking for it. What's your answer?"

"My answer is to tell you that what you're really asking for is trouble for both of us."

"Sounds like you're undecided. Do you think if I came in, it might help you to make up your mind?"

"Hell, no. If you come in here right now, I just might *lose* my mind."

This time her smile was less of a surprise and more of a physical sensation, like warm hands running over flesh. Her hands, his flesh. As his mind filled with a searing image of exactly that, Flynn wasn't sure if he actually swayed toward her or simply felt like he had because he wanted to so badly.

"Go back to your room, Sara," he ordered. He saw her flinch at the harshness in his tone, but she didn't leave.

"I should think you'd know by now," she said, "that I don't respond well to direct orders."

"So you want me to say it in a roundabout way? Sort of the way you did when you said you want to *sleep* with me? When we both know that what you're talking about, deep down, is something bigger, something that lasts longer than one night, a damned relationship... with promises and all those other things I already told you I won't—"

"Sex, Flynn, I'm talking about sex." Her directness shut him up fast. "Great sex. That's what you offered me, and that's what I'm asking for. But," she added with an elaborately casual shrug, "if you can't deliver on it, then—"

His hand shot out and curled around her wrist, stopping her as she turned to go. Sara looked back, her chin lifting defiantly until their gazes locked.

"I can deliver, all right."

"Well, then ..."

"You're sure? You're really sure this time?"

"I wouldn't be here if I wasn't."

The conviction in her voice was solid and unmistakable and Flynn wasn't buying it for a second. He didn't care what Sara said she wanted or *thought* she wanted, he knew what women like her always wanted in the end. Just as he knew she wasn't going to be getting it from him.

He could only imagine the physical longing and emotional upheaval and massive dose of courage that must have combined to propel Sara to come knocking on his door tonight. And he understood that if he turned her away now, however noble his reasoning, she would be humiliated by the rejection, and the spirit he'd seen awakening in her these past few days would be broken, maybe beyond repair.

Fate, he thought bitterly. *Even when you kept your guard up all the time, it still found a way to play with your life.* The cards had been dealt the instant she walked into Benny's room and straight into his arms. Sooner or later he was going to hurt Sara. Would it really be any kinder to do it now rather than later?

Sliding his hand down to clasp hers, he drew her into the room and pushed the door shut behind her.

Holding her gaze, he slid his palms up her arms slowly, battling the urge to tumble her onto the bed before one of them came to their senses. She looked soft and fresh and too inviting to resist. Pulling her against him, he opened his mouth over hers and took her into a deep, searching kiss that was equal parts warning and hunger. When he finally drew back to look at her, her blue eyes were smoky and dazed with such undisguised yearning that his heart wrenched inside his chest. What was he doing to her? What was she doing to him?

"Ah, Sara," he groaned. "Don't look at me that way. I'm no good for you, can't you see that?"

She shook her head. "You've already been good for me, very good. Just look at me." Her smile was like a small explosion in the dimly lit room.

"I haven't done anything but look at you for days now," he admitted grudgingly, sweeping his attention over her long bare legs, achingly aware of the soft curves and valleys beneath her shirt, and of how they were going to feel pressed against him. It was a well-worn thought path. "That's a big part of my problem."

"Then you know what I'm talking about, and that I'm right. You *have* been good for me, and I don't expect tonight to change that."

Ah, but what about after tonight? He wasn't self-sacrificing enough to ask it out loud, but he wondered just the same. Would she think so sweetly of him when he was gone and all she had to hold onto was the memory of a long, sleepless night in a motel room?

As his hands moved over her shoulders and neck, her eyes closed briefly and he watched, transfixed, as surprise and pleasure shaped her expression. Not for the first time he was vividly conscious of the fact that Sara wasn't accustomed to being touched and stroked by a man. But she was going to be, he vowed silently. By morning she would be very accustomed to being touched by him. He felt the usual gut-level sexual urge to storm and conquer melting away. If all she was going to walk away with—all *either* of them were going to walk away with— was a memory, he was going to make sure it was a damn good one.

They had no future, but for tonight, he was going to pretend there was also no past, no reason they shouldn't be together. And if he had to hurt her eventually, he was going to take special care not to hurt her in any way tonight. This night was going to be pure pleasure. He was going to spend it worshiping Sara's body with his own, the way she deserved to be worshiped.

Bringing his mouth close to her ear, he told her exactly that in provocative detail, and smiled as he actually felt the heat that flooded her in response.

"Flynn, maybe..."

"Shh." He silenced her by pressing his fingers against her lips at the same time his tongue was gently exploring the curve of her ear. "Don't talk... just feel."

"But..."

This time he used his mouth to make his point, once again claiming hers in a hard kiss that soon had her clinging to his shoulders and making small breathy sounds that pushed Flynn past the point of no return. Still kissing her—her face and throat and her shoulders through the thin fabric of her shirt— he led her the few steps to the bed.

Deliberately seeking and holding her gaze, he smiled and bent to lift her in his arms. She tensed, as she had the first time he'd held her this way. He'd expected her to, just as he expected the look of concern that clouded her face. He watched as she became totally self-focused, reading the now familiar doubts in her beautiful eyes, and he lowered his mouth to hers, determined to drive those particular doubts from her forever.

He kissed her until he felt her muscles relax and she melted against him as if she were sinking into a bath of warm sweet honey, trusting his strength, trusting *him*. Only then did he carry her down with him to the mattress. They lay on their sides, facing. Flynn leaned forward so that he was slightly above her and lifted his hand.

Her shirt had at least a dozen tiny buttons at the neck, so tiny and so potentially delaying that he could easily have ripped them open with a quick pull of his hand. Instead he worked them free one at a time, patiently, greeting each half inch of newly revealed flesh with the warmth of his fingertips and his mouth. When the buttons were undone, he peeled the fabric away from her breasts and ran his fingers over them. Sara's soft gasp of delight merged with his own rougher acclimation, and they faded into shared laughter.

"You're beautiful," he whispered, seeing in her face that she didn't yet believe him, determined that she would before he was finished. "Like something I made up in my head, you're perfect and so soft . . . Look, look how you fit into my hands."

Her small smile was awkward and wistful at once. "You have big hands," she murmured.

"Yeah. Lucky me," he said and bent to taste one tight, rose-colored tip that hardened even more under the rough attention of his tongue. He suckled and caressed her with his lips; he licked her and felt her heart beat against his tongue and was swept with a sudden rush of longing that had nothing to do with the physical culmination of this act.

Still kissing and teasing her with his tongue, he moved his hand over the lush curves of her body, sliding lower, playing his fingers in the dip of her waist and then over the swell of her hip. He'd been aware from the first instant he held her that she wasn't wearing a bra beneath the shirt. Now, as he lost himself in the sensual exploration of her body, his mind jumped with the increasing visceral desire to find out if she were wearing anything else under there.

She was. But far from being disappointed, his excitement quickened at the discovery of panties that were no more than straps across her hips and a skimpy wedge of silk between her legs. He longed to cup that sweet, hot part of her, and explore the mysteries within, but it was too soon.

Breathing deeply in an attempt to calm the pounding demand of his own desire, Flynn reluctantly dragged his hand higher, to slightly safer terrain. Once again he caressed her shoulders and breasts, feeling her wafting between tension and surrender.

"Come here," he said, smiling at her through the shadows and tugging her into a kneeling position on the bed so that he could pull the shirt off over her head, leaving her clad only in the skimpy black panties. He grinned. He knew they would be black, just as he knew Sara had chosen them in exchange for the serviceable white ones he'd bought for her, and he was very, very thankful.

Instinctively, she began to cross her arms in front of her, but he quickly reached out and stopped her, shaking his head as he did. The bed was positioned across from the wide mirror above the dresser and the sudden movement drew their attention to it at the same time. Flynn's response to the image of a nearly naked Sara on her knees in front of him was carnal and instantaneous. The pressure at the front of his jeans grew almost painful.

Drawing a deep breath, he swung around so that he was kneeling behind Sara, both of them facing the mirror. The pale light from the small lamp on a corner table rendered their reflection dusky and intensely erotic. The air seemed charged and potent. Flynn felt passion moving through him in waves so hot and enticing he wanted to hold onto Sara and ride them forever. He sought her gaze in the mirror and held it for a long moment, not yet trusting his control enough to move or speak.

At last he let his hands slip from their resting place on her shoulders, around to her breasts. He circled her nipples gently with his outstretched fingertips, excited to the outer limits of control by seeing as well as feeling her trembling response.

"Are you uncomfortable...watching us this way, I mean?" he asked her.

Sara licked her lips and nodded. "God, yes."

"Don't be. You're beautiful, Sara. *This* is beautiful. The way you make me feel is beautiful, almost too good to be true. Tell me how I make you feel."

"The same ... I mean, good ... Oh, God."

"Uh. Tell me exactly. How does it make you feel when I touch you like this ... " He strummed his thumb hard across the peak of her breast. The tremble that shook her made him dare to draw his caress lower, raking lightly over the patch of black silk between her thighs. "And like this... Tell me, Sara."

"It feels wonderful . . . Beautiful . . . More than— Oh . . ."

"Yeah, oh, yeah."

Her head lolled back. With his chin he nudged her attention back to the mirror. "Look . . . look at us together."

He swept his hands over her, touching all of her, again and again, telling her over and over how good it felt to touch her, how much he wanted her, how many ways he wanted her. With each caress there was a subtle increase in intimacy, with a corresponding increase in the hunger pulsing inside him. Finally the primal urge to claim her at her very core outstripped his careful patience. Slipping his hand inside the front of her panties, he cupped her soft heat the way he longed to . . . needed to. His senses racing closer and closer to combustion, he once more found her gaze in the mirror and exulted in what he saw in her eyes . . . exactly what he wanted to see, a look of pure pleasure and raw need.

This must be what it feels like to drown, thought Sara. She'd read of how at some point when a person is drowning they just give up and surrender totally to a force much stronger than their own will, welcome it even. That's what was happening to her now. She felt as if she were floating on some warm, endless sea, being drawn steadily closer to an invisible whirlpool that was waiting to claim her, body and soul. Only it wasn't water that threatened to drag her under, it was passion. It was Flynn.

How was it possible to feel so dazed and so absolutely awake at the same time? Because that's how she felt, her muscles limp and weak while her senses were wide open and careening wildly. Giving in to the languor, she let her head tilt back until it rested on Flynn's chest. Tantalizing sensations radiated from where his fingers were caressing her with a touch as wispy as butterfly wings. Pleasure made her eyelids heavy, but she couldn't close them. She couldn't look away from the powerful image of their entwined reflections.

In some distant corner of her mind, she was surprised to discover that she wasn't shocked by the sight. She, who habitually tossed a towel over the bathroom mirror when she showered. Amazingly, all the bulges and imperfections that were always so glaringly obvious to her were invisible now. It must be a trick of the light, or a trick of Flynn's, she thought dreamily, because suddenly, seeing her naked body cradled against his bigger, darker, stronger one, she felt beautiful.

Gradually the motion of his fingers against that soft, sensitive part of her became firmer and more concentrated, the strokes deepened and fell into a steady rhythm that was a stark contrast to the absolute chaos within her. Sensations were shooting off in all directions, little fires igniting everywhere his hand roamed, with the hottest blaze of all burning right at her core, edging closer to a fiery explosion with every passing second.

Sara wanted that explosion. The desperate need for it pulsed through every part of her. This was passion like she had never dreamed existed, a steamroller of sensation, a driving, irresistible force that was ignited from outside, but fueled from within. It lifted her out of herself so that she was no longer in control, and didn't want to be. She just wanted the ecstatic tingling at her core to grow and grow. She wanted it so frantically that she whimpered with frustration when Flynn's hand fell still.

She clasped her thighs tightly in instinctive protest as he gently disengaged himself and twisted her around in his arms, the hungry action of his mouth on her throat scant consolation to her reeling senses.

"I'm sorry, I'm sorry," he told her, his mustache and raspy whisper caressing her skin. "I just…this first time…" His gaze sought hers. "I want to be inside you when it happens."

The unabashed eroticism of his admission inflamed Sara beyond belief…beyond inhibition.

"Yes," she whispered, lifting to kiss his face with a hunger that had been building in her for a lifetime. "Oh, yes."

"Help me," he urged, clasping her wrists as she sought to embrace him and bringing her hands down between their bodies, to the open waistband of his faded jeans.

His arousal strained the soft fabric and pressed heavily against her hands. Sara could feel the pulsing of his desire. She fumbled with the zipper, glancing down to watch as she worked it open because she was afraid of hurting him. As she lowered it, the front of his jeans spread in a wide V that filled with swollen male flesh. She glided her fingertips over him, drawing a hiss of pure pleasure from between Flynn's clenched teeth.

Once unzipped, he impatiently worked the jeans off himself, slipping a condom packet from the wallet in his back pocket in the process. He tore it open with his teeth and looked at her with hooded eyes.

"Help me with this," he requested, caressing her arm and the back of her hand as if he couldn't bear to stop touching her even long enough to handle precautions.

"I can't," said Sara, the response automatic. "I never ... I wouldn't know where to begin."

He gave a soft laugh and leaned forward to draw her into a slow deep kiss that made her insides hum.

"Begin here," he said, moving her hand so that it rested along the hard, hot length of him, drawing it slowly up to the velvety tip, helping her to help him. "Slow, and easy, like that ... Yeah, just like that ..."

And then he was pressing her down on the bed and coming down on top of her, the warmth of his skin and the solid, muscled weight of his body adding new dimensions to the devastating assault on her senses. He felt hard and powerful and gloriously masculine and in turn he made Sara feel feminine and giving and beautiful.

She reached up and ran her hand over his biceps, which were clenched and steeled to support some of his weight. That's not what Sara wanted. She wanted to feel all of him, unrestrained, untempered. She wanted to be consumed by him, and she arched restlessly to let him know that.

Flynn obliged by settling his body more firmly against hers, letting her know the burning strength of his need. His fingers sank into her hair, holding her still for the searing exploration of his kiss. Sara gloried in his unleashed ardor, matching it as her body twisted with pent-up excitement and her hands swept across his muscle-rippled back, urging him impossibly closer.

He rubbed against her, the feeling of his hair-roughened flesh tantalizing against her throbbing breasts. His chest was exactly as she imagined it, perfect. His broad shoulders and strong, cradling arms—perfect. The stiff, searching heat of him that probed gently at the juncture of her thighs—perfect. Beneath her silk panties, she was dewy and yielding and hungry for his touch.

At Flynn's silent urging, Sara let her thighs slide apart. He reached down, but instead of removing her panties as Sara expected him to, he impatiently shoved the narrow scrap of silk aside to find the delicate folds beneath. His breathing grew ragged as he stroked her there, and so did Sara's. She was panting helplessly when, with a sudden shifting of his hips, he positioned his manhood and began to slide into her.

Sara gripped his arms for support as he slowly, carefully, but relentlessly sank deeper and deeper. He stopped once to give her body a chance to adjust, then pressed on until he filled her completely. Only then did he lift his head to stare at her. Sara met his gaze, breathless and overwhelmed, and her release started right then, even as the lovely physical torment grew and grew.

She floated free, riding the slow rocking thrusts he initiated. For the first time in her life, feeling transcended thought. She was free of herself, free of the past, free even of the future. That moment was everything; the heat and intensity of it carried her far away, Flynn her only point of reference.

She moaned softly as he increased the tempo, driving unbelievably deep inside her with each savage thrust, pushing her closer and closer to the edge. Then suddenly, without slowing, he lifted higher so that his downward strokes pressed directly on the spot where her pleasure was centered, and Sara cried out loud as passion consumed her.

She heard Flynn's hoarse murmur, felt his arms tighten convulsively, and then he was trembling against her even as she felt another small explosion and another, like circles spreading on a deep, quiet pond.

Flynn was thunderstruck by the force of his climax. It had been fire and ice, surrender and pure, unadulterated triumph. In the aftermath of such sweet violence, he was aware of only one thing…that he never wanted to move away from Sara. And that's why it was imperative that he do exactly that, and fast.

He peeled himself from her body; there was no other word for it. They were both drenched, still breathing heavily, and he suspected he probably looked every bit as bulldozed as she did.

"I need a smoke," he said, fighting the honeyed temptation of Sara in tangled sheets.

"I didn't know you smoked."

"I don't." He ran his fingers through his hair. Even his scalp was sweating. "At least not anymore. I still need a smoke."

And a breather, he thought, time to get his thoughts—not to mention the rest of him—under control. *His* control, not Sara's.

"Think I'll take a walk to the lobby. I saw a cigarette machine there." He reached for his jeans and rolled from the bed to pull them on before turning to look at her. After short-circuiting the afterplay the way he just had, he was braced to have her look at him with annoyance or disappointment, even contempt. He wasn't prepared for amusement.

"What's so damn funny?"

"You." Her smile was gorgeous, but different somehow. Mysterious, he decided, like she knew something he didn't. And he didn't like it. "Will you bring me back a can of soda?" she asked.

"Sure. What kind?"

"Anything cold will do. And Flynn," she said as his hand closed on the doorknob.

He glanced at her.

"I get the feeling you don't want to talk about this," she said, with a sweep of her hand at the tousled sheets that surrounded her, the sight so lushly tempting Flynn had to steel himself not to tumble down beside her for another round. "But I want you to know that what happened was..." That smile again. "I never knew—"

"Yeah," he said, cutting her off before he heard something he didn't want to hear. "Me, either."

Chapter Twelve

*P*oor Flynn. Sara had a feeling this wasn't going to be easy for him. Actually, she thought with a sigh, this probably wasn't going to be easy for either one of them, but it was bound to be rougher on Flynn than on her.

For one thing, men in general weren't as attuned to their emotions as women were...at least that's what she'd read in the women's magazines, and Nancy, for whom dissecting the male psyche had long been a hobby of sorts, agreed. It was, in Nancy's words, "a guy thing." And Flynn seemed to be even more removed from his inner self than most guys.

The realization that he was in love with her was bound to hit him hard. If she had to venture a guess, she'd say the initial impact was going to be something akin to being walloped with a baseball bat wielded by a prizefighter. Sighing commiseratingly at the prospect, she snuggled under the sheets. Poor Flynn.

For Sara, the realization that she was in love with Flynn and that he loved her in return had come more gently. She couldn't even name the exact moment the discovery had begun to unfold. She only knew that at the instant when Flynn had claimed and filled her body and their eyes had met, the feeling that passed from him through her and back again, had been the purest, rarest form of love.

Knowing that had triggered a release in her soul that she now understood had been building for days, and which had preceded—and outlasted—the electrifying series of sexual explosions that followed. She had welcomed the feeling, gloried in it, thrilled by what it portended for the future for her and Flynn. At the same time she understood that he was not going to be nearly as happy... or as receptive to the idea.

First, there was his fear of being in love. There was no doubt that he meant it when he said he didn't want to love anyone or anything ever again. And then there was the fact that if he ever did have the misfortune to fall in love, she'd bet that Flynn wasn't prepared for it to be with a woman like her any more than she had been prepared for him. Not that it mattered. Love clearly had a mind and a will of its own. *Fate,* Flynn would call it, and that would make him like the situation even less.

Fortunately, there wasn't a whole lot he could do to change matters. If Sara didn't believe that with her whole heart and soul, she would be feeling a little frantic right now at the way he had pulled away after making love to her. It was precisely the abruptness of his withdrawal, along with his dazed expression and his absurd craving for a cigarette, that convinced her that in spite of what Flynn might say and what he believed, he had been touched as deeply and irrevocably by her as she had been by him. Knowing that, she found it easy to believe that everything was going to work out in the end.

During the last several days she had discovered that beneath all her old doubts and insecurities beat a very strong, and when the occasion demanded, a surprisingly reckless heart. She had the heart of a fighter, and she going to fight for Flynn. Somehow, some way, she was going to see to it that they stayed together. It was meant to be. In a way, Flynn was right about fate. You couldn't fight it, but you could trust it. And Sara did.

He returned a few moments later with a couple of cans of soda and a pack of cigarettes, which he tossed unopened on the table by the window. Flipping open one of the cans, he handed it to her.

Sara took a sip and waited as Flynn swallowed about half the contents of his own can in a single gulp. When he finally lowered it and glanced at her, she met his quizzical look with a wry smile.

"So," he said, looking more ruffled than she would have imagined possible for the fearless, nonchalant John Flynn. "Did you want to spend the whole night here?"

"Is that what you want?" Sara asked quietly.

"It's up to you. It's *always* been up to you, Sara."

"I know that. In that case, yes, I'd love to spend the rest of the night in your bed... Assuming, of course, that you'll be spending the night here, too."

"Where else would I spend it?" he asked, shooting her a sardonic look.

"I'm not sure. You look edgy, ready to bolt."

He shook his head. "I'm not going anywhere."

"I'm glad." She placed her soda can on the bedside table and deliberately moved to make room for him by her side. When he hesitated, the corded muscles in his throat betraying his tension, she smiled. "You know, Flynn, as you may have already gathered, I'm not all that experienced in this sort of thing, but I have heard it said that regrets belong to the morning after." She lifted the sheet slightly in an unmistakable invitation. "Can't tonight belong to us?"

She was right, thought Flynn, chagrined that he needed to be lectured in matters of this sort by Sara, of all people. Although, he had to admit, the Sara sprawled with such tempting abandon across his bed was different from the wary, rigid woman he had first met. This Sara was confident and enticingly relaxed... and she was waiting. Waiting for him, Flynn thought with something close to amazement.

In spite of everything he'd told her about what a lost cause he was, and all his none too gentle warnings to stay away, she still wanted to be with him. He felt the panic that had begun to take hold of him sliding away, replaced by a fresh urge to possess her. This time, however, the sensation was more liquid than fire, more varied in texture and current, less urgent.

As he slipped into the bed and reached for her, a feeling he couldn't name wound its way through him like a slow moving river, warm and wide and without end. He felt helpless and powerful at the same time, and overlaying it all was the awareness that he wasn't alone in this. Never before, not even in the midst of the greatest physical intimacies, had he ever felt so bound to any woman as he felt to Sara right now. Never had he felt so close to a woman, so attuned to her every desire, so lost in a world that was totally defined by her scent and her heartbeat, so dependent on her for pleasure, for excitement, for comfort.

Comfort wasn't something he usually sought to give or receive when he was making love to a woman. It was only one of the things he wanted to give Sara. He wanted to thrill and heal and soothe her all at the same time. As he slowly kissed his way down the length of her body, bringing his mouth steadily closer to the sheltered cove of her femininity, he sensed from the tension in her muscles that this was also new to her. He slowed up a bit, determined to ride out her resistance, determined to make up to Sara for this and all the other things she had missed out on in her life. Determined, at least for this one night, to fill her with pleasure.

As he moved lower, he gradually eased her panties off and coaxed her legs wider apart, making a place for himself. When at last his mouth found her, soft and damp and smelling of heat and flowers and woman, Sara jumped. He immediately dulled the force of his approach, knowing instinctively that anything more would be too intense, too soon.

Experience rendered him far more knowledgeable about women's bodies than she was, and he used that knowledge now to crumble her weakened defenses. He brought her slowly to the edge of her own desire and kept her balanced there for breathless moments, stringing out the pleasure until it edged toward torment, then plunging her into the fire within. Even then, he employed every trick he knew to prolong it until she was trembling and crying out loud, a broken sound of wonder and joy.

All the while, desire built inside him, rushing, straining, filling him with heat. When he couldn't hold off any longer, he rose up and entered her, his fierce thrusts quickly bringing her back to the edge of fulfillment so that he could tumble over with her this time, leaving both of them stunned, shaken and content.

In the morning, they made love once more, before either one of them had fully come to their senses, thought Flynn, in an effort to diminish the earthshaking impact of their joining. It didn't.

Afterward, they were both quiet. While Sara showered, he went upstairs to retrieve her belongings, then left her alone to dress while he put gas in the car, returned the room keys to the desk and stopped at the coffee shop.

"What's this?" Sara asked when she joined him at the car.

She was dressed much the same as she had been the day before, and Flynn was swept with the urge to take her back to bed. What happened to her *real* clothes, he wondered irritably. He was feeling irrationally irritable this morning, considering. Fatigue, he told himself. It had, after all, been a long, mostly sleepless night.

"Breakfast," he said in reply to her query about the waxed paper bag he'd tossed on top of the car while he arranged two cups of coffee inside.

She reached for the bag and glanced inside, then wrinkled her nose. "Sugar doughnuts?"

"Yours is plain," he told her. "I know how you are about calories."

"Flynn, even without sugar, a doughnut is loaded with calories. And grease. It's an all-around rotten way to start the day."

"But a fast one," he added, "fast being the operative word right now."

"I know you want to make up for lost time, but just think about it. Taking a few minutes to eat a sensible breakfast now will actually save time in the end because we won't have to stop for lunch so soon."

"I bought enough doughnuts for breakfast *and* lunch."

"You're hopeless." She crumpled the bag shut and tossed it to him. "You can eat sugar and grease for breakfast if you want to, but I'm going over to the coffee shop for some cereal."

Flynn slammed his door and stepped to the front of the car to block her path. "Oh, no, you're not."

"Oh, yes, I am."

"Not if you want to ride out of here with me, you're not."

Sara rolled her eyes. "Stop trying to sound like this is Dodge City and you're the big bad bounty hunter."

"I *am* a bounty hunter," he said, his voice rising.

"And I'm hungry."

"Then eat a doughnut."

"I want cereal."

"Cereal takes too long."

"For heaven's sake, Flynn, all I want to do is walk over to the coffee shop and buy a box of cereal and a carton of milk to go."

He hadn't realized she planned to get the cereal to go, but cereal versus doughnuts had ceased to be the point a few minutes back. This had to do with will. His versus hers. Flynn knew the way he wanted things to be. The way they *had* to be. And he didn't want Sara getting any foolish hopes otherwise . . . at least no more than she already had.

"We don't have time," he said firmly.

"How long can it take to buy a box of cereal?" she demanded in exasperation.

"Too long. Get in the car, Sara."

"No."

Flynn squared his shoulders. Now what? It had never occurred to him that Sara might plant herself on the concrete walk and refuse. And it should have, since this was pretty much the same thing that happened the night she'd insisted on tagging along on the search for Benny. And look how that was turning out, he thought, kicking himself for letting things degenerate this far.

Usually, when he issued an order, Sara might grumble and fire disgusted looks at him and take her sweet time, but in the end, she'd get in the car. Something told him that wasn't going to happen this time. Before he could make up his mind whether to give her another chance to get in on her own or simply pick her up and put her in the car, an elderly man who had evidently been standing in the doorway of the next room, taking in the entire scene, approached them.

"Hold it, hold, hold it," he said, making traffic cop motions with his uplifted hands and smiling broadly, as if this were a play being enacted for his enjoyment. "Forty-seven years my wife and I have been married and never once have we argued about breakfast."

"That's nice," Flynn told him, "but this isn't really about breakfast." And it isn't really any of your business, he managed to refrain from adding. Barely.

Evidently sensing his impatience, Sara intervened. "We're sort of in a hurry," she explained. "Actually we're in a big hurry, and Flynn is right, we don't have time for breakfast."

"Nonsense. You never have time, or find time, you *make* time." The man wagged his finger at Flynn. "Your wife is a very smart lady, but if you won't listen to her, at least listen to an old man. Breakfast is the foundation of the whole day. You mess up on breakfast..." He gave a thumbs down signal. "It's downhill from there."

Flynn could have told him that today was going to be downhill from here no matter what he ate. It had nothing to do with breakfast and everything to do with the matter-of-fact way this stranger had assumed that Sara was his wife. What else would the old geezer assume? Sara simply didn't look like a pickup or a one-night stand. She looked honest and caring and exactly as if she ought to be someone's wife. *But not his,* Flynn thought grimly. *Never his.*

Sara's prediction about the morning after was proving to be painfully on target. All at once the regrets he'd managed to hold at bay throughout the night washed over him, leaving him feeling cold and empty. And sorry.

"There you are, Charlie," said a petite woman emerging from the room next to theirs. "I've been looking all over."

Charlie gave Sara a bemused look. "After forty-seven years, she thinks maybe I've taken to hiding under motel room beds?" He smiled as he turned to his wife. "Just waiting for you, my beauty."

The elderly woman preened at the compliment, one Flynn would wager she'd heard at least a thousand times before, and as she gave her husband a pleased smile, she truly *was* a beauty. *The eye of the beholder,* he thought, and for some reason the stupid anger that had prompted him to square off against Sara over a bowl of cereal left him.

"I recommend the oatmeal," their friend Charlie said as he offered his arm to his wife and the two of them walked off toward the coffee shop together.

Flynn gave Sara an awkwardly apologetic shrug. "How about a compromise? You get in the car and I'll drive you over and wait while you get your box of cereal to go."

"*Two* boxes of cereal to go."

He shook his head, surprised and bewildered that she could make him laugh so easily when his heart felt like a hundred-pound weight strapped inside his chest. "Two boxes of cereal sounds good to me."

Sara would forever remember the last leg of their trip as a series of hurried pit stops strung at wide intervals along an endless ribbon of steamy blacktop. They ate in the car and slept in the car, Flynn only rarely acknowledging sufficient fatigue to surrender the wheel to her for a short stretch. She followed his orders not to leave the highway for any reason whatsoever without first waking him to discuss it and thus managed to avoid any new catastrophes.

By the time they arrived in Miami, she was convinced that her sarcastic reference to *riding* out of Dodge City had been prophetic. She *felt* as if she'd ridden a horse most of the way there... complete with saddle sores, stiff muscles and an aching back. Flynn wasn't in much better shape. He was just better at ignoring discomfort. The result of lots of practice, he explained when Sara grumbled that she was the only one grumbling all the time.

The realization that he was so adept at ignoring his own feelings didn't buoy her confidence any. The truth was, in spite of her relief that the long hard drive was over at last, she felt a twinge of trepidation over what might happen next...and how quickly. Once they located Benny, their deal—and their reason for being together—would end.

Given her choice, Sara would prefer to have a few days to spend on a sun-drenched Miami beach with Flynn, burning herself into his heart the way he had quite unintentionally burned his way into hers. She would even settle for a few days of tramping around with him in the tropical heat, following clues to Benny's whereabouts. She was certain that, given enough time, she could make Flynn see how right they were together, how even by his own definition, the love between them was worth taking a chance on. The question was, would she have enough time?

"Is there any place in the country you don't know your way around?" she asked Flynn as he steered through the streets of Miami as easily as a native would.

He shrugged. "A few, I suppose. I've never seen much of Idaho. Or Alaska."

"Much? You mean you've been both places? Have you been to all the states?"

"At least once or twice. Most a lot more often than that."

"And I've never been anywhere."

"You're somewhere now."

"Yes." She glanced at him, thinking that right now she was exactly where she wanted to stay forever. She did her best to keep that thought from glowing on her face. She had no intention of pressuring Flynn into anything, or trying to guilt trip him into it. That wasn't what she wanted. She wanted him to find the truth about himself on his own, the same as he had helped her to do. "Yes, I'm someplace now, all right."

Her dreamy tone drew a sharply curious look from Flynn. The look was indicative of the swiftness with which the most innocuous conversation between them could turn to something heated or tense or misunderstood. Though the overall mood always remained within civil boundaries, something dark and portentous hovered just beneath the surface as Flynn battled private demons, which Sara understood had been with him most of his life.

Hoping to distract him from speculating on the reason for the starry-eyed look he'd just caught her flashing, she said, "I can't imagine how it must feel to be able to just pick up whenever you want and take off wherever you want to go."

"It's not exactly like that, Sara. This is my job, remember? Not a whim or a lark or some crazy impulse to do something to break up the monotony of my life."

"Is that why you think I wanted to come along?"

He glanced at her in spite of the heavy traffic in the commercial district they were in. "Isn't it?"

"I don't know," Sara confessed. "I don't know why I came. It was so unlike me to just push myself on a stranger the way I did."

"I know that."

"But I couldn't stop myself. The urge to go was just so strong, as if getting in this car and driving off with you was meant to be, as if it was..." She reached the logical end of that sentence before she remembered what an emotionally charged word waited there. It was too late. Flynn's sardonic glance told her he knew exactly what she was going to say. So she went ahead and said it. "As if it was fate."

Flynn turned into a parking garage adjacent to a high-rise building that glinted like a tower of mirrors in the midday sun, and punched the button on the ticket dispenser as if it were his arch enemy.

"What do you think about that?" she asked against her better judgment as he carefully scanned the rows for an available parking spot.

"I'm not going to think about it," countered Flynn. "Not now. Not ever."

"Of course not. You'd prefer to think that I came along because of some silly whim on the part of a foolish, lonely woman. That way you can dismiss it and me and—"

That did it, thought Flynn. He spun the car into an opening, slammed the shift into neutral and turned to her, one hand closing on the back of her neck.

"You really want to know what I think? I think you came with me because you were looking for something," he growled, jerking her closer.

His kiss started out hard, intending to punish her for God only knows what...for existing, perhaps, so that he could find her and want her when he knew she couldn't be his—at least not in the impossible, forever kind of way that part of him wanted more with each passing day. It didn't matter why he wanted to hurt her, because it turned out he couldn't do it. Almost as soon as his mouth touched hers, it gentled of its own volition, the initial stabbing thrusts of his tongue melting into one long, hot, seeking caress after another.

When he finally pulled away to look at her, Flynn felt breathless, and afraid. "I just hope to hell that someday you find it," he told her.

The glinting tower of glass was the Seagate Building. Sara struggled to match Flynn's long stride as they walked to it from the garage. She also struggled not to let his flash of temper in the car adversely affect her mood. She told herself that she should be happy that he was miserable. It seemed reasonable to assume that the more irritable he was, the harder a time he was having conquering his feelings toward her, and that was one battle Sara wanted him to lose.

As they approached the Seagate Building, Flynn explained to her that it was one of Miami's two major trade centers for jewelry and fine art. The showrooms, including that of Ivan Mulhouse, the man they were there to see, were posh fortresses on the upper floors, while the first floor housed an array of small shops. A quick glance in the stunningly understated display windows told Sara they were for window-shopping only. A quick glance at her reflection in one of the windows did little for her self-image. Surrounded by such elegance, she felt more tattered and road weary than ever.

"I wish we could have checked into a hotel before we came here to see Mulhouse," she told Flynn. "It would've been nice to at least have a chance to wash my face and comb my hair."

"You'll get one."

"Sometime this millenium?"

"Sooner than you think," he promised, slanting her a wicked threat of a grin.

"What's that supposed . . . What are you doing?" She came to a mulelike stop as he grabbed her hand and began to pull her into a dress shop.

"I decided you need something new to wear," he explained, with a pleasant smile that Sara was certain was entirely for the benefit of the elegantly clad saleswoman eyeing them suspiciously.

Why wouldn't she be suspicious? Their clothes were rumpled, their movements slow and stiff, as if, she thought with a trace of wry amusement, they were both coming off a five-day bender. Flynn was sporting a day and a half's worth of dark stubble, and she probably looked like it had been a while since she'd had any personal contact with a hairbrush.

"Are you crazy?" she demanded in a soft, sharp whisper.

"I'm beginning to think so," he retorted just as sharply, "but that's beside the point."

"Right. The point is that even if I did need something to wear, you don't wear clothes from a place like this . . . you display them."

"Fine. Display this." He had her inside now and with the same forced smile he riffled through the hangers on a circular rack until he came across a wheat-colored linen suit, yanked it out and handed it to her.

"May I help you?" the saleswoman asked, scurrying forward.

"Yes," replied Flynn. "The lady would like to try this on."

The lady, thought Sara, would really like to toss the damn suit over his head and leave him there to face the humiliation alone. But he looked so adorably disheveled, and it really was sweet of him to want to buy her something . . . even if it was something entirely unsuitable in both style and color.

She managed a little smile of her own as she told him exactly how sweet his gesture was.

"There's nothing sweet about it," Flynn replied, one side of his mustache flexed in wry amusement. "It's business. Now try on the suit, Sara."

Business. Of course. Belatedly it dawned on Sara that they probably wouldn't get past Mulhouse's door looking like street people. Adjusting to this more logical, if less romantic, reason for coming in here, she turned and asked the saleswoman where she could try the suit on.

As the obviously reluctant woman showed her to the fitting room, Flynn called after her, "And, Sara, once you get it on . . . wear it."

"What if it doesn't fit?" she asked, always prepared for that possibility.

Flynn's gaze slid over her as relentlessly as a wave rolling to shore.

"Don't worry, it'll fit."

He said it with the supreme confidence of a man who knew intimately of what he spoke.

Sure enough, it fit. And even Sara had to admit that the suit flattered her more than she expected it would. Instead of competing for attention or swaddling her in layers, the tailored lines and neutral shade emphasized the soft curves of her body and made her expressive eyes and her broad smile the focal point of her appearance. This must be what Nancy meant when she said that you should wear your clothes, rather than letting an outfit wear you.

She took advantage of the privacy of the fitting room to comb her hair and make use of the few makeup essentials that were all she had in her purse. She emerged feeling as polished as possible, considering, to find that the suit had already been paid for by Flynn. The saleswoman was a whole lot more friendly to her than she had been earlier, proof that money not only talked, observed Sara dryly, but could also win friends and influence people.

Flynn had left a message that she should wait for him in the lobby, so Sara found a seat on one of the cushioned benches opposite the elevators and watched people come and go. Miami, she observed, had a style all its own...bright and easy and worthy of the city's hot, sassy reputation. Her only doubt about the new suit she was wearing—that the skirt, which ended a good six inches above her knee, might be too short—was dismissed as she saw skirts much shorter and much tighter pass by.

She noted a great many white and pale toned suits on men, and was struck by how the definition of "business attire" varied so greatly from one part of the country to another. She paid scant attention to a tall man approaching in a more traditional dark gray suit until she realized the man was Flynn.

Not the same Flynn who had left her in the dress shop, however, not the easy-going, jeans-clad Flynn she had come to know and love. This man was intimidatingly handsome, and she felt a dreaded bubble of uncertainty begin to swell in the pit of her stomach.

He stopped before her, pulling her lightly to her feet and staring at her for several nerve-racking seconds before unleashing a familiar grin that burst the bubble inside and made it easy for Sara to breathe again. "Not bad, partner, not bad at all."

"I could say the same for you," she replied. "New suit?"

"Nope, just something I keep tucked away in the trunk for emergencies."

"Some day I'm going to have to take a long look inside that trunk of yours."

"Anytime." He lifted his hand and offered her a silver-colored shopping bag she hadn't noticed until then. "These, however, are new. And they're for you."

Smiling with surprise, she peered into the bag. "A purse," she exclaimed. "And shoes . . . to match the suit."

"Sit down and let's see if they fit."

"What size are they?" she asked, sitting.

Flynn tugged one boot off and held the shoe for her to slip her foot into. "Eight and a half. What do you usually take?"

"Eight and a half," she said as her foot settled comfortably into the sexy open-toed pump. "How did you know that?"

"Actually, I didn't. With your height, I figured you had to be somewhere between a seven and a half and a nine...this was the only pair they had left in that range. I guess it was—"

He stopped, and their gazes locked.

"Fate," Sara finished for him.

Ivan Mulhouse's twelfth-floor office was every bit as elegant and finely appointed as the rest of the Seagate Building. Just outside the outer door, Flynn stopped her.

"I almost forgot," he said absently, pulling a pair of over-size tortoiseshell glasses from his inside pocket. "There." He slid them into place on a startled Sara and opened the door before she could protest. "Try to look like an insurance company executive."

"Flynn, what are you . . ."

They were inside the office by then, where the ultra thick carpeting invoked a cushioned silence, which made her startled exclamation seem even louder, and Sara immediately fell silent.

She glanced around as Flynn spoke with the receptionist, taking in the gold-framed oil paintings on the wall and the airily decorated waiting room to her left. Off to the other side was what she deduced must be a display room. There was a massive table in the center and one full wall of brass-handled drawers, which Sara assumed must hold samples of the "Jewelry and Fine Collectibles" that according to the lettering on the door were Mr. Mulhouse's stock and trade. It was obviously a very profitable business . . . unless, as the man back in Norfolk had suggested, Mulhouse was increasing his profits by dealing in rare stolen coins on the side.

Flynn turned to her as the receptionist picked up the telephone.

"She's checking to see if Mulhouse will be able to fit us in before lunch."

"What did you tell her?"

"That we represent the National Insurance Company and that Mulhouse has been recommended to us as someone who might be able to handle appraisals on the large volume of jewelry and valuables policies we're writing in South America. I made sure she understood what a very lucrative proposition it is."

"Okay, now make me understand," she said, turning her back to the desk and speaking softly. "What on earth is going on?"

"It's all part of the job, Sara."

"But how is it going to tell us if Mulhouse is dealing with Benny?"

"It won't . . . but if I told his receptionist I was here to question him about stolen coins, I wouldn't get my foot in the door."

He turned back to the receptionist as she hung up the phone with a brilliant smile. "Mr. Mulhouse will be glad to see you and your associate, Mr. Flynn."

The slender blonde led them to Mulhouse's office and opened the door for them to enter.

Mulhouse rose as they walked in and came around the desk to greet them. He was a tall, trim man with silver hair swept back from a high forehead, and came around the desk to greet

them. Dressed in a pearl gray suit with a sheen almost as glossy
as his black patent leather shoes, he looked to Sara more like a
lawyer, or even a judge, than someone who fenced stolen coins.
Although, as Flynn had explained, this was fencing elevated to
an international art form, with most of his buyers coming from
South America and Europe.

"Mr. Mulhouse," said the receptionist, still standing by the
door.

Mulhouse glanced at her. "Yes, Stephanie?"

"If you won't be needing me for a while, I'll be going to
lunch now."

"Fine, fine, but do be sure to have calls forwarded to the
service while you're gone so that I can give my undivided attention to Mr. Flynn and his lovely associate."

"This is Sara McAllister," Flynn told him. "She's National's appraisal coordinator for the entire eastern seaboard."

As they shook hands, Sara managed to meet Mulhouse's
openly impressed smile with a look she hoped radiated poise
and competence and did not reveal her frantic hope that Mulhouse wouldn't ask her any questions.

"Wonderful, wonderful," he said, graciously leading them
to the cushioned barrel chairs in front of his desk before returning to his own seat. "And who did you say recommended
my services to your firm?"

Uh-oh, thought Sara.

"Vincent Blais," Flynn replied without hesitation, "of
Maxwell, Blais, and Schiffer."

"Of course, of course, a wonderful man Vincent."

"The best," agreed Flynn.

Sara felt her stomach unclench a notch. Flynn knew what he
was doing. He did this all the time, in fact. All she had to do
was sit back and look like she knew what was going on and . . .

"Ms. McAllister?"

She snapped forward in the seat and stared at Mulhouse.
"Yes?"

"I asked what other appraisal services you're currently using?"

"Well—" she glanced at Flynn and saw him wink, looking
not at all worried that she was about to blow the whole thing,

"—at the moment most of the appraisals are being done by our own staff."

Mulhouse frowned. "In-house?"

"That's it . . . in-house."

"But doesn't that create the potential for conflict of interest?"

"Oh, a huge potential," Sara concurred, nodding vigorously. "That's why Mr. Flynn and I are here."

"Exactly," said Flynn, leaning forward in such a way as to take the ball from Sara's court and resume control of it.

Determined not to be caught off guard again, Sara listened intently as he explained to Mulhouse how today's visit was only a preliminary meeting to see if he were interested in handling the appraisal work. And Mulhouse was clearly very interested, even when Flynn quoted a fee that sounded to Sara to be incredibly low for the amount of work that seemed to be involved. She kept waiting for him to slip in a mention of Benny or the stolen Garrett doubloon and was nearly as startled as Mulhouse appeared to be when Flynn abruptly stood and signaled that the meeting was over.

"Our underwriters will be in touch with you within the week," he assured Mulhouse as they shook hands across the desk.

"But what about my licenses and qualifications?" asked a bewildered Mulhouse. "Don't you want to know—"

"The underwriters will handle all that," countered Flynn. "And based on Vincent's recommendation, I'm sure everything will be in order."

"Absolutely," said Mulhouse, his chest puffing with pride. "Ms. McAllister, it's been a pleasure meeting with you, and I hope we'll be able to do business together in the near future."

"I'm sure we will," said Sara, not really sure of anything right then.

Mulhouse started to walk them out, but Flynn deftly positioned himself to close the door behind them. "We'll see ourselves to the elevator," he told Mulhouse. "We've already interrupted your day enough."

"Not at all. New business is always welcome."

"But old business must be attended to as well," countered Flynn, matching the older man's smile. "And I'm sure you take your responsibilities to your clients very seriously."

"Of course, of course," said Mulhouse, clearly seeing that this was the way to impress Flynn. He gestured toward his desk. "In that case, I will let you be on your way and I'll get back to my work."

As soon as the office door was shut, Sara hissed to Flynn, "What's the matter with you? You didn't find out anything."

"Sure I did," he whispered, glancing over his shoulder at the closed door as he pulled her away from it and toward the outer office. "I found out Mulhouse is entirely too eager to get involved in doing appraisals for peanuts."

"But why?"

"Good question. My guess is that Mulhouse sees appraisals as the perfect way to find out what's available out there for the picking. Sort of like shopping at home, in his own personal catalog."

"You mean stealing? You think he actually sets up the robberies?"

"On occasion." He ran a disparaging gaze around the expensively appointed office. "I think old Mulhouse got where he is today by running a multiservice operation."

"But we still don't know if he's involved with Benny."

"And one minute of observing his smooth manners told me we wouldn't be any closer to knowing if I'd asked him outright, and that he wasn't going to be easy to trip up. So," he said as reached the receptionist's desk, "I decided to find out what I wanted to know the old-fashioned way."

Catching Sara's blank look as he stepped behind the desk, Flynn shook his head. "I meant by stealing it, Sara."

She chewed her lip nervously as he flipped through the pages of the appointment book that lay closed on the corner of the desk, moving first forward through the dates, then back.

"Got it," he said at last.

Sliding at least her hundredth anxious glance in a minute's time toward the closed door of Mulhouse's office, Sara asked, "Got what?"

"A phone number for Benny, or rather, for Russell Le-Fleur." He quickly ripped the page from the book and showed her the entry for Russell LeFleur, with a telephone number beside the name.

"He was here to see Mulhouse last week. This must be the number of the place where he stayed."

"And you think that if he's back in Miami, he'll be staying at the same place?"

Flynn hurried her out into the hallway and pushed the button for the elevator. "I think it's the best lead we've got at the moment. In my experience, guys like Benny are creatures of habit. They like the safety of familiar surroundings."

Not until the elevator doors slid closed with them safely inside did Sara's racing pulse slow. "That was horrible, excruciating," she said. "I'm still shaking."

Flynn grinned and gathered her against him, starting her pulse racing for reasons that had nothing to do with fear. "You shouldn't have worried. I would never let anything happen to you. Besides, you did great. You think pretty quick on your feet for a novice."

"I had no idea what to say to him, or where you were going with that appraisal farce."

With her face pressed against his solid chest, she felt him shrug. "To tell you the truth, neither did I at the start. I had no idea how that was going to play out, only that I needed to get a firsthand read on that guy."

"You're crazy," she said, lifting her head to confront him. "What if he caught on to the fact that it was a lie? What if he was dangerous? Or had a gun in his desk drawer?"

"I'm sure he is, and does . . . have a gun on him, that is. But nothing did happen, that's all that counts. I'm just glad his receptionist was at lunch. It would have been hell getting at that appointment book with her sitting there."

"You mean you still would have tried?"

"I would have thought of something," he said offhandedly as the elevator reached the ground floor and the doors opened. "It's just lucky we got there when we did."

"Right, luck," said Sara, tossing him a smug look as he stood holding the door open to let her exit first. "Or something."

Chapter Thirteen

The search for Benny reminded Sara of the Easter egg hunts her father used to devise when she was a little girl, with one clue leading to the next. They stopped at a hamburger place near the Seagate Building, ordered lunch and borrowed the phone book to follow up on Flynn's hunch that the number next to Benny-alias-Russell's name had to belong to the motel or rooming house where he was staying. Sure enough, the number matched the listing for the Ocean Villa Apartments, a short distance away.

The Ocean Villa was a dump by any standards, but luckily the reservation clerk, a potbellied man with sweat stains in the armpits of his nylon shirt, was susceptible to persuasion. A little persistence and a hundred dollars bought them the information that Benny was indeed registered there, but he was not in his room at the moment. An extra fifty got them a bonus, the news that Benny spent his evenings at a popular night spot called BlackJack's.

Flynn decided it was best to wait and try to catch up with him there later, reasoning that staking out his room could backfire if Benny saw them first. It was much less likely that he would spot and recognize them in a crowded public place. To Sara's immense relief, he didn't suggest that they take a room at the Ocean Villa. She would have preferred another night in the car to crawling between the sheets at that place.

Instead, he drove to a motel a short distance away, this time registering for one room without bothering to ask. She took the fact that he assumed they would sleep together again as a good sign. Now all she had to do was make him see that deep down he wanted the same thing she did—to sleep together again and again for the rest of their lives.

Inside the room, which was decorated in a gentle-on-the-eye color scheme of mint green and pale apricot, Sara threw her things on the bed near the door and claimed the shower. She was thrilled to discover that the basket of toiletries included not only shampoo and conditioner, but also a razor and shave cream. She had been prepared to beg Flynn to let her borrow his, even knowing that such intimacies would probably be alien and unwelcome to a man who didn't want a woman in his life long enough that she would need to shave her legs.

Correction, Sara told herself reassuringly, a man who *thought* he didn't want a woman in his life. She'd lived with a lonely hole at her core long enough to recognize the same emptiness inside Flynn. He needed someone to love him in spite of himself, someone who would help him to love in return, and she was determined to be the woman to do just that. Sara's certainty about this surprised her, but it also gave her strength and confidence in unexpected—and unprecedented—ways. For instance, it gave her the confidence to emerge from the shower with a towel wrapped around her wet hair and another knotted loosely, but painstakingly—and she hoped enticingly—around her body.

Holding the small bottle of body lotion also provided by the hotel, she crossed the room to where Flynn was sitting and held it out to him.

"Would you mind rubbing some of this on my back?"

He looked up at her and his entire body stilled, the taut flexing of the cords in his throat telling Sara that either the towel or the stretches of rosy, still damp skin it left exposed were having the desired effect on him. It was at least a full minute before he took the bottle of lotion from her.

"Sure." His voice was tight and unnatural sounding.

"Shall I sit on the bed?" she asked, already heading there.

"No." Flynn caught her wrist from behind. "I don't think that's a good idea, Sara. On second thought I don't think this is a very good idea, either." He tossed the lotion on the dresser.

"My skin will get dry without it," she said, turning to him and trying to surface from the suffocating awkwardness she felt in this new role of would-be seductress. This was so hard for her, but time was running out and she didn't know how else—short of pleading and arguing, both of which she outright refused to resort to—to get through to Flynn.

"You'll live," he retorted with a harshness that seemed self-directed. "And a lot more happily, believe me, if you keep your dry skin and I keep my hands off you."

"You didn't mind putting your hands on me the other night. I didn't mind, either, Flynn."

"Well, maybe you should have, or I should have had more sense, then maybe we wouldn't be where we are now."

She wet her lips, swallowing her pride and reaching for courage to resist the urge to run and hide from this the way she had from most other potential disasters in her life. "And just where are we now, Flynn?"

Flynn's gaze held hers. Sara saw something dark and impenetrable fall across his green eyes, and her heart spasmed painfully.

"We're the same place we've always been, Sara. Nothing's changed for us except the name on the sign out front. Nothing will." He turned and headed for the bathroom. "I'm going to take a shower. If you know what's good for you, you'll be dressed when I get out."

Oh, she knew what was good for her, thought Sara. What's more, she also knew what was good for him. What she didn't know was how to get him to see that. She didn't have near the experience in this sort of thing as most women her age, and she'd never had any female wiles to speak of. Not that she would use them in any case, or believed for a second that scheming or artifice would work on Flynn. He'd said it himself, he'd been pitched by the best.

Sara had no illusions that she was any match for the best, but she knew in her heart—without having any idea *how* she knew—that she was right about this, and that she was right for Flynn. She wasn't going to scheme or grovel; she didn't need to. This was meant to be. If she could just hang onto that thought, she told herself, and make the most of every moment she and Flynn had left together, it would all work out fine. It had to, because she wasn't at all sure she could go back to the way things used to be.

Flynn came out of the bathroom looking clean and smooth-shaven and just about as ornery as he had when he went in. Sara was sitting by the window, dressed in the narrow white leggings she'd bought and a black top belted at the waist.

"I see you took my advice," he remarked, raking his gaze over her, his mouth twisting in a disparaging grin as if she'd failed some secret test of his. The nerve of him. He was the one who'd ordered her to get dressed in the first place. *Fate, do your stuff,* thought Sara bleakly, *because I am no good at all this.*

"I thought I'd better get dressed if we're going to Black-Jack's."

Flynn paused in the act of pulling a black T-shirt over his head and cocked one eyebrow in her direction. "We?"

"That's right . . . partner."

"Sorry, partner, tonight's a solo performance."

"Hold on. If you think I drove all the way down here to sit in some hotel room while you—"

"While I risk my life trying to take down a guy who I know for a fact has used a gun in the past? Is that what you were going to say?"

"While you finish *our* job—"

"*My* job. If you think I'm going to be saddled with watching out for a woman who has already—"

"You're *sadly* mistaken."

"You're out of your mind."

"I'm going."

"You're staying here." He had finished dressing, pulling his leather jacket on over his shoulder holster. Now, with a look of grim determination, he picked up his change and keys from the dresser. "I mean it, Sara."

"So do I," she countered. He could talk about danger all he wanted. Right now, the danger she feared most was letting slip through her fingers the slim chance she had to change Flynn's mind about them being together. She had no intention of spending what might well be her last night with him alone in this room. How could she prove she was indispensable to him if she allowed him to dispense with her so easily? "If you don't bring me with you to BlackJack's, I'll take a taxi."

"With what? Until I split the fee with you, you're broke."

Sara tossed her hair back. "Don't worry. I'll think of something."

"Damn it, Sara. Why does everything have to be so hard with you?"

"Maybe because it's worth having," she said softly. "Don't you know that you have to fight for anything worth having?"

"In that case, you must be worth the whole damn U.S. mint. All right, you can come," he growled, "but make sure you stay well out of whatever happens and do *exactly* as I tell you."

"Of course," replied Sara.

Comparing her to the U.S. mint had to be considered progress, she told herself as Flynn walked beside her to the elevator in stony silence. Even if he had gritted his teeth as he said it.

Sara had never before been inside a place like BlackJack's. Noisy and smoky and dark, it was clearly a spot where men and women came to meet and have a rowdy good time. The action was kept from being too rowdy by the beefy young bouncers stationed at the entrance and at strategic spots throughout the spacious club. While Flynn paid the cover charge for both of them, she glanced at the placard announcing the featured entertainment. On weekends, rock groups took the stage, but on weeknights like tonight, the club featured a pianist by the name of Spinner Cantrell.

Cantrell was good, Sara noted as they moved inside where the clear, tumbling notes of a Scott Joplin tune were audible above the noise of the wall-to-wall crowd. Flynn led the way straight to the bar, another first for Sara, who found herself wedged in between him and what looked like a motorcycle gang.

Taking a deep breath, she balanced one foot on the brass foot rail the way she saw others doing and gazed around, mesmerized by the action on all sides.

"What'll it be?" asked the bartender.

"Draft," replied Flynn, "and . . ."

He trailed off and both men gazed at Sara expectantly. "Oh. I'll have a whiskey s—" The word "sour" caught on her tongue. BlackJack's didn't look like it catered to a whiskey sour crowd. Suddenly Sara didn't want a drink that came with a cherry and a swizzle stick.

"Whiskey," she said. "Straight up." Whatever that meant.

Flynn arched a brow but said nothing.

"Brand?" asked the bartender.

"Brand?" she echoed.

"As in which brand of whiskey do you want?"

"Oh, right." She slid her gaze past him to the row of gleaming bottles stacked opposite. "Jack Daniel's will be fine."

Flynn chuckled as the bartender turned away to get their drinks. "You do think quick," he said, a note of reluctant admiration in his tone.

Sara shrugged and reached for the shot glass full of amber liquid the bartender slapped down before her.

"Just part of the job," she said, as she took a gulp and instantly felt her throat pucker and her eyes water. She glanced sideways to find Flynn watching her and looking exactly as she expected, amused as hell. "So it went down the wrong pipe," she sputtered.

"Right. Yours. You want to switch drinks?"

"I do not. Like I said, it's all part of the job."

"Here's another part, start scanning this place for Benny. I'll start in the corner behind you, you take the half of the place behind me. That way we can pretend we're talking and it won't look so obvious."

"Sure. Now aren't you glad there's two of us here?"

"Tickled pink," he growled. "Start scanning."

Sara began moving her gaze from one person to the next, looking for Benny. Her half of the room contained the entrance and the constant movement of people in and out didn't make her task easy.

When she told Flynn so, he said, "Stop grumbling. And stop squinting. You're making it too obvious that you're looking for someone."

"That's not exactly unusual in a place like this, is it? People will just think I'm looking for likely prospects."

Flynn kept his gaze moving behind her, but the edges of his mustache tipped downward. "See any?"

"As a matter of fact, I do," she said, savoring even such a lukewarm hint of jealousy.

"Where?" He twisted to look where she had been looking.

"Oops," said Sara. "He just left."

"What a shame."

"How about you? See anyone who interests you?"

"Haven't looked. I've decided it's bad form to mix business and pleasure."

"I see. But of course, since we happen to be in business together, at least temporarily, then . . ."

"Hold it. I see him."

"Where?" she said, freezing in response to Flynn's hurried order not to turn around.

"He's standing at the end of the bar," he told her. "Okay, you can take a look but make it quick and don't be obvious."

Sara turned her head slowly and spotted Benny at the far end of the bar, standing alone, staring out over the crowd. Just as she began to swing around, his eyes reached her and stopped. Time slipped into slow motion as she watched a look of bewilderment form on Benny's familiar face, only to be quickly replaced by one of shocked recognition.

His gaze immediately fired past her to Flynn. Sara heard Flynn's muttered epithet and saw Benny whirl away from them and disappear into the crowd.

"Oh, no, not this time, pal," Flynn said as he lunged away from the bar. He strained left, then right in an effort to see over the crowd. "Damn, that must be the back way out of here that he's taking." He shoved his way through the crowd around them with Sara trailing in his wake before coming to a sudden halt.

He glared at Sara. "You wanted a chance to help, well, you got it," he snapped. "I want you to help me get past that wall of testosterone guarding the door."

"How did Benny get by him?"

"He must know Benny. He just stepped aside. Something tells me he won't extend me the same courtesy."

The music had stopped, but it was still hard to be heard over the noise. Sara wasn't sure exactly what Flynn was proposing.

"That guy looks pretty big, Flynn. I'm not sure that even together we—"

"That's not the kind of help I want from you, Sara," he broke in. "I need you to distract him so I can get out that door. Just give me a minute to get over there so that I can make my move as soon as you get him out of the picture. Then you just wait here until I get back."

Sara gaped at him. "But how in the world will I . . ."

He ducked his head and cut short her protest with a quick, hard kiss. "You'll think of something. You always do."

Right, thought Sara as he moved away, *always* being all of two or three times in her whole life. Sure, she had pressed him to let her come along tonight, but she hadn't expected this turn of events. She was no good at this sort of thing, certainly no good at distracting beefy blond Adonis types from their work. Which is what Flynn was expecting her to do. He was expecting the impossible. He was *counting* on her, she realized suddenly.

Through a fleeting opening in the crowd, she glimpsed Flynn standing a short distance from the door, watching her, waiting, as every passing second made his job more difficult and maybe more dangerous as well. That got her juices flowing. Without having any idea what she was going to say or do when she got there, she started toward the back door.

As always when she was nervous, a tune started playing in her head, a sort of subconscious attempt to soothe her nerves. In this case the tune wasn't even all that soothing. It was the last number of Cantrell's set, a classic rocker by Jerry Lee Lewis. As she took the final steps toward her destination, she noticed that the hulk by the door was tapping his foot as if the same song were playing inside his head, and suddenly Sara knew what bait she was going to use to hook him.

"Hi, there," she said, sidling up to him the way she'd observed seemed to be standard operating procedure here.

For an agonizingly long few seconds, he stood with his oversize arms folded across a bulging chest and looked her up and down. Then he grinned. "Hi back at ya."

Sara leaned closer. "I've been watching you all night," she told him.

"Oh, you have, have ya? How come?"

"I happen to think you're very..." Sara groped wildly. "Watchable."

"Oh, yeah?" He seemed pleased enough with that.

"Definitely. What's your name?"

"Todd."

"Todd. Nice name. You know, Todd, I've discovered something we have in common."

"What's that?"

"Music. I can tell that you just love music."

"That's right, I do." He looked as thunderstruck as if she'd guessed his birthday on the first try. "How'd you know that?"

She shrugged. "I'm very, very observant. Now tell me the name of your favorite song."

"That's easy. 'Too Sexy,' you know, it's a rap song by—"

"I don't believe it," she cut in, cognizant of the hurry-up looks that Flynn was flashing her from behind Todd's broad back. "That's my favorite song, too."

"Wow."

She gritted her teeth mentally and reached for his hand. "You've got to come with me."

"Hey, I'm not supposed to—"

"Just for a minute." She pursed her lips and fluttered her lashes. "I just have to play that song for you on the piano."

"You can play the piano?"

"Uh-huh," she said, still pursing and fluttering wildly. This feminine wiles stuff was more work than she expected. "And I want to play that song especially for you."

"Well..." He vacillated as she tugged on his hand. "I guess if it's just for one song I could..."

Sara was already dragging him with her through the crowd. Not until she actually reached the piano did she fully comprehend the position she had gotten herself into. She had led this man—this very big, not too bright and quite possibly none too understanding stranger—to believe that she was going to play the piano for him. This piano. Right here in front of the largest audience she'd faced since that disastrous night fifteen years ago. On that awful night she had frozen and been unable to play a single note, and suddenly the blood running cold through her veins made it seem a real possibility that the same thing was going to happen to her all over again now.

"Well, go ahead," prodded Todd as she stood paralyzed in front of the small platform that held the piano. "You gonna play or not?"

"Of course, I'm going to play! That is, if it's all right? Now that I think of it, perhaps the management might not—"

"Jack don't care," Todd assured her. "Not as long as you're with me."

She tipped her mouth into a smile. "Well, then . . . What am I waiting for?"

Somehow she managed to climb onto the platform and lower herself to the piano stool. Purely as a stalling tactic, she ran her fingers over the keys. It had been days since she'd practiced and her fingers felt stiff and cold. And she wasn't even sure she could fake the song that she'd only heard a few times on a tape one her students had made. And for all she knew, the piano wasn't even tuned properly and . . . and there were a hundred reasons she couldn't go through with this. And one overriding reason she had to.

Brushing her hair aside, she slanted a quick glance toward the back door and was startled to see Flynn still there, staring at her. He was concerned about her, she realized, and he had put that concern ahead of chasing Benny and collecting his fee and everything else that was supposedly all he cared about in life. She shouldn't be so surprised, she told herself. Hadn't he done the same thing time and again on the way here? He may not be able to say "I love you" out loud to her, or even admit it to himself, but he was a master at showing it.

The warm feeling that surged through her spread quickly to her fingertips. This time they danced over the keys with more zest and purpose. She didn't care if there were a thousand people watching; she was determined to play this piano and keep playing it for as long as it would help Flynn for her to do so. She suddenly understood that the only way to get Flynn to see that she loved him—loved him so much that it was worth taking a chance loving her back—was to show him.

The first few notes of the song were cautious and exploratory, but as the melody fell into place inside her head, her fingers automatically translated the notes to keystrokes and the next several bars were stronger and surer, and then she added the chords and the sound she created ripped across Black-Jack's and Sara became lost in her creation.

Watching from his spot near the door, Flynn told himself for the hundredth time to get the hell out of there before Benny got too great a head start. Only this time he finally felt able to actually act on the internal command. As soon as he'd told Sara to distract that hunk of beef guarding the door, he had regretted it. In spite of her pretenses to the contrary, Sara wasn't cut out for any of this... or so he'd thought.

Watching her sidle up to that young bouncer had filled him with all sorts of fears, but she had seemed to handle herself—and the bouncer—like an expert. Then, just as he was about to duck out, he saw her approach the piano and he'd been unable to tear himself away. Belatedly realizing what she intended, he'd understood the gut-wrenching fear Sara had to be feeling, and he felt it with her—for her. It was an unsettling experience.

There was no way he could walk out of there knowing she might panic and need him. Nothing, not Benny nor the reward money nor maintaining his blemish-free record of never losing a runner, mattered to him nearly as much as the fact that Sara might need him. He didn't want it that way, he didn't like it, but it was a fact. And for now he had to live with it. Later, after Sara was gone from his life... Later... Actually, he wasn't sure about later, only that it loomed ahead like an endless black abyss. But he was used to living with that, much more used to it than he was to feeling this constant pull on his heart that called everything he was and everything he believed into question.

The sound of the piano filtered to him above the noise. Sara was sitting at it now, her beautiful hands moving over the keys. He couldn't actually see them from where he was standing, but the details of her hands, of every part of her, were permanently etched in his mind. He listened to the music grow stronger, so attuned to the woman playing it that he could feel her emotions in the sound she was making; he could hear her fear and tension and the exact moment when they gave way to the powerful magic inside her, the same magic he'd witnessed that first night when she played for him alone.

Suddenly he was aware that he wasn't the only one listening. All around him people paused and turned toward the piano, drawn by the sparkling beauty of Sara's playing. She was going to be all right on her own, he thought, reaching at last for the door and pulling it open only enough to slip out undetected.

Safely outside the club, he started down the stairs, taking two at a time. The staircase had solid concrete walls and ended at an equally solid steel door that was chained shut, making it impossible for him to get out. The good news was that Benny couldn't have exited this way either, and since he hadn't returned to BlackJack's, he may have lost time looking for an alternate escape route. If so, it worked to Flynn's advantage. He had allowed Benny too much of a lead, but he was still younger and faster, and anything that worked to slow Benny, lessened the gap between them.

The staircase stretched three stories above BlackJack's. At the top was another door, also bolted, and a small window near the ceiling with the glass broken. Jagged pieces of glass still scattered on the floor suggested to Flynn that it had been broken recently. Benny was shorter than he was and would have had to struggle to reach that window, thought Flynn with satisfaction. That meant more wasted time for him.

He had no difficulty hauling himself onto the ledge beside the window or sliding through it. He positioned himself to look down and spotted Benny on the fire escape below him, cautiously picking his way down.

"You might as well hold it right there, Benny," he shouted. "I've got you covered on the ground."

Benny's head jerked. He glowered up at Flynn. "Covered by who? The broad? Don't make me laugh."

"Laugh all you like," Flynn countered, edging lower all the time. His tone was casual, almost detached. "The fact is this is a done deal, Fortrell."

"Only if you catch me, and so far, you haven't done such a bang-up job in that department in spite of your hot-shot reputation for always getting your man."

"The game's not over yet."

"Oh, no? Think again."

Letting go of the metal ladder that ended a good eight feet above the ground, Benny collapsed in a heap on the concrete.

C'mon, break a leg for me, thought Flynn as he watched. But the wiry older man soon sprang to his feet and took off around the corner of the building. Flynn abandoned the casual approach he'd hoped might enable him to catch Benny off guard and bolted down the rest of the fire escape, leaping to the ground even before he'd reached the bottom rung. He landed on his feet and sprinted around the corner where Benny had disappeared, ending up in a dark alley that ran from the street in front of BlackJack's to the parking lot behind it.

Instinctively he checked for his gun. The alley was not only black, but silent, and for some reason the total absence of sound suddenly made him think of Sara and her music. Or maybe it was simply that thoughts of Sara were never more than a heartbeat or so away from him these days. Whatever the reason, the fracturing of his concentration, brief as it was, resulted in a split-second delay in his response time as Benny got the jump on him from behind a parked car.

Damn, thought Flynn, that was three stupid mistakes he'd made on this job, when he usually never even made one.

"What happened to your backup?" Benny taunted, pressing what could only be the barrel of a gun in the center of his back. "Did she have to make a pit stop to powder her nose?"

"What's the point of this little scene, Benny? You might as well do yourself a favor and hand me that gun, and the coin, too, while you're at it. You're never going to be able to fence it now that I've talked to Mulhouse.''

"You saw Mulhouse?'' he snapped.

"That's right. How do you think I found you here? I offered him a piece of the reward on the coin and he sang like a boys' choir.''

"Reward? Counting your chickens before they're hatched, aren't you? You can't collect a reward for something you don't have.''

"But I will have it—and you along with it, Benny. Sooner or later.''

"Don't start with that *I always get my man* line. Spare me, Flynn, as I told you, I'm not impressed with your reputation.''

Flynn laughed softly. "Not yet, maybe.''

"Not ever. Time's running out. In a few days, that bond on me is forfeited and it won't be worth your time to keep chasing after me.''

"Not financially, perhaps,'' Flynn conceded. "But I never give up on a runner, Benny, never have, never will. Wherever you run to, you think about that.''

He heard Benny sigh.

"That's what I was afraid of, Flynn, and it's really too bad. But if you're going to insist on being so damn pigheaded and dedicated, then there's only one thing I can do.''

He heard Benny cock the revolver.

"Damn shame,'' he muttered, sounding not overly concerned that he was about to rip a whole the size of a fist through Flynn's middle.

Flynn braced himself, doing a split-second review of his options and realizing that none of them were very promising, when the sound of Sara's voice reached him from the opposite end of the alley.

"Flynn?''

"Well, well, well.'' Benny chuckled.

Flynn went cold inside. "Get out of here, Sara. Get the hell back inside.''

"Keep coming or I'll shoot him,'' Benny called out.

"Don't listen to—''

Benny shoved the gun barrel into his side hard enough to make him wince. "Move," he ordered. "Your backup finally shows up, the least we can do is go meet her."

Flynn walked in front of him for about twenty steps before sighting Sara. She was inching her way along, staying close to the building. Even in the darkness, he could see that her expression was pale and stricken, and for the first time that he could recall he felt fear so strong it turned his stomach.

"Listen, Benny," he said, prepared to make any deal, any sacrifice, to get her safely away from there.

"Shut up," Benny said. "I'm doing the talking now. Hello there, Ms. McAllister, fancy meeting you here."

"Hello, Russell . . . I mean, Benny."

"Are you enjoying your stay in Miami, Ms. McAllister?"

"Well, actually, I haven't seen a lot of Miami. We only arrived today and—"

"Now that's a damn shame. Flynn, where are your manners? Dragging a woman all this way and not showing her the sights. But not to worry, Ms. McAllister. You're in very good hands now."

"The hell she is," growled Flynn, desperation and frustration forming a tighter knot in his gut with each passing second.

"Uh-uh," warned Benny, stabbing him again with the gun barrel. "Manners."

"No, please, don't hurt him," pleaded Sara, stepping forward.

Flynn straightened from the instinctive crumbling response to the sudden sharp pain in his side. "For God's sake, Sara, stay back—"

Benny broke in. "Don't listen to him, Ms. McAllister. You saved his life by showing up here a few minutes ago. You want to go on saving it, you do just exactly what I say."

"Don't listen to him, Sara, he's not going to kill me. He's a two-bit thief, not a murderer. I've got his rap sheet. He's never murdered anyone in cold blood."

"Not yet," Benny agreed calmly. "And I certainly don't intend to murder you and leave a witness behind . . . Am I making myself clear?"

Reaching a new level of fear, Flynn had no choice but to nod.

"Good," said Benny. "The fact is, I don't have any real desire to kill anyone, simply to take my leave of this rather awkward situation. And," he added directly to Flynn, "I'll just have to take my chances that common sense will eventually win out over your ridiculous dedication to your work. So then, if everyone gives a little, there may be a much less messy way out of this for all of us. It occurs to me that by taking Ms. McAllister along with me, I can—"

"Forget it," interjected Flynn, twisting around to face Benny, desperation pushing him to the edge of his control.

"Your vote against the motion is duly noted. Your turn, Ms. McAllister. Do you want to come along with me and let your new friend here go on living? Or shall I kill both of you right now?"

"I'll go," Sara blurted out, her trembling tone tearing at Flynn's tenuous control.

"One vote for, one against, and since I vote with the lady, that means she comes. Sorry, old man," he said to Flynn.

"Not as sorry as you're going to be, Fortrell."

"Don't be such a sore loser."

When Flynn made a sudden move, Benny instantly brought the gun up level with Flynn's midsection, his rigid expression signaling that the time for chatter was past. "Take your gun out and drop it on the ground," he ordered.

"I'm not carrying."

Benny fingered the trigger deliberately. "Don't play games that you're not prepared to lose."

Furious, Flynn glanced past him to Sara. She stood with her hands clenched, her eyes imploring him to do as Benny ordered. Every instinct he possessed balked at such complicity. If he were alone here, he would take Benny on regardless of the risk involved. But he was no longer alone in this, and Benny had unwittingly zeroed in the very heart of the matter—Flynn had to do or say whatever necessary to prevent Sara from being hurt in any way.

Without a word, he slowly removed his gun from the shoulder holster under his jacket and dropped it on the ground a short distance away.

"Now kick it over to her," ordered Benny.

When he had kicked it to within a few feet of where Sara was standing, Benny ordered her to pick it up and hand it to him. Once he had Flynn's gun tucked safely in his waistband, he slowly sidestepped until he was close enough to Sara to grasp her by the elbow. Flynn's insides boiled at the sight and at his own inability to do anything about it.

"Now you're finally going to have a chance to see some of this fine city," Benny said to her. "You and I are going to take a little ride. And you," he said to Flynn, "are going to go back to wherever you're staying and wait. I assume you at least found the lady a room somewhere?"

Flynn nodded. "She has the number."

"I'll call you there and let you know where I drop her. A warning, Flynn, one hint that you're not doing what I say and I'll find a quiet little place with no witnesses and let her take the bullet that had your name on it."

"Since we agree it has my name on it, why not take me along and leave her here?"

Benny chuckled. "Because she promises to be a much more obedient hostage . . . and besides, I find myself curious to hear all about this sudden change in Ms. McAllister's appearance and how on earth she got mixed up with the likes of you."

Good question, Flynn thought bitterly, cursing himself for letting it happen to begin with and for each progressively more stupid step he'd taken along the way.

"Shall we go?" Benny said to Sara, shifting his aim from Flynn to her in a way that made it an order, not a request.

Gripping her arm noticeably tighter, he fired a final glance at Flynn, positioning the gun barrel so it was resting against the soft, vulnerable spot at the side of Sara's jaw. Flynn quivered with fury at the obscene sight.

"I know you, Flynn," he said. "And I know you're going to get the urge to come after us. When you do, you just stop and think about this."

Flynn's mouth went absolutely dry as he watched them walk away in the direction of the parking lot. He felt furious and helpless at the same time. There was no way he could do as Benny ordered, return to the hotel room and wait for him to call. *If* he ever called. Benny himself had swept that from the realm of possibility when he said he would never murder anyone and leave witnesses behind. Flynn was icily aware that there would be no witness in that car with Benny and Sara.

Although he had intended mostly to reassure her, he had been telling the truth when he told Sara that Benny had never killed anyone, and he still believed the odds were that he wouldn't do it now. But this wasn't a damn roulette wheel he was spinning or a back-alley crap shoot—this was Sara's life. And there was no way he was going to sit on his hands and take chances with it—especially not when it was his fault she was here in the first place.

Waiting what he hoped was a sufficient amount of time, he followed them toward the parking lot, taking the precaution of stopping at the corner and peering around it in time to see a white midsize sedan pull from the lot with Benny at the wheel. A rental, no doubt. That explained why they hadn't spotted his car when they checked the lot earlier. As soon as they were safely on their way, he bolted for his car, gunning the engine and leaving the lot only seconds behind them.

Instead of coming up behind them at the corner, however, he hung back until he saw Benny turn right and then turned right onto a secondary street that he knew ran parallel to the main route they were on. He couldn't risk trailing Benny too closely or for too long. But he also couldn't risk losing him; the direction he was headed in would take him directly to the highway. In a matter of hours Benny could have Sara out of the state, and there was no way Flynn was going to let that happen.

His mind raced as he tore along the quiet street at an unsafe speed. He was thankful now for the working knowledge of the city that Sara had commented on earlier. He only hoped he could remember which left he needed to take to reach the expressway on-ramp. He was convinced that was his best hope of stopping Benny.

Benny would most likely expect that even if Flynn was following along, he would play it safe for a while. Making his move as Benny tried to get onto the freeway would, he hoped, take Benny by surprise. Flynn figured that if he were lucky, he could cut him off so that he had nowhere to go. The commotion that resulted should draw a crowd of witnesses pretty quickly, and maybe, if he was very lucky, even the Miami police.

He didn't care about the complications that might result from their intervention in the apprehension of a runner. He didn't care about anything except saving Sara, and the gut-wrenching fury with which he cared told him things he didn't want to know about his feelings for her, things that he had been trying to avoid thinking about, things that—when this was over—he was going to have to deal with once and for all.

He took the left turn on two wheels, slowing only slightly as he approached the corner and then jamming on the brakes with a loud screeching sound as he realized he had overshot the on-ramp by one block.

Glancing to the left, he saw the white sedan with Sara inside put on its blinker and begin to veer toward the on-ramp. There were other cars around, too many of them to make what he was about to do even marginally safe. Safety had become relative, however.

If he sat there and let Benny get on that expressway, he would have almost no hope of forcing him to release Sara before he was damn good and ready.

If he shot forward now, with enough speed to propel the car over the low guardrail separating him from the downhill ramp, he would be quite literally getting the jump on Benny.

It was his best hope, thought Flynn. Hell, it was his *only* hope.

First he revved the engine to reassure himself that the power he needed was there waiting, then he jerked on the shift and floored the gas pedal. Thinking only of Sara and not at all of the lethal damage he was about to inflict on the car's underbelly, he left the pavement and sailed onto the Miami interstate.

Chapter Fourteen

Sara watched in disbelief as Flynn's car shot into view before her. That's exactly what it looked like, as if the sleek black vehicle had been fired from a cannon into their path.

At the same instant she realized what was happening, Benny shouted and jammed on the brakes, managing to slow his car slightly. Still, Sara knew intuitively that a collision was unavoidable. Bracing her feet against the front panel, she grabbed onto the door handle and squeezed her eyes shut.

Luckily, Benny had slowed the car as they entered the on-ramp and still hadn't increased speed. Even so the impact was jarring enough to make her teeth rattle.

It was all over in a split second, and Sara opened her eyes, thanking God that she hadn't hit the windshield. Benny wasn't so fortunate. He was still gripping the steering wheel for dear life and shaking his head as if dazed. Blood drizzled from a gash on his forehead. The windshield was a massive web of cracks.

The urge to get out of there rose like a tidal wave inside Sara. Shaking violently, she fumbled with her seat belt and clawed at the door lock, and then suddenly Flynn was there.

"Thank God, you're all right," she cried as he opened the door and pulled her free. "How—"

"I jumped out before you hit," he said hurriedly. "Are you okay?"

Not waiting for her reply, he quickly ran his gaze over her and evidently decided she was. Satisfied, he lurched around and got Benny out of the car as quickly as he had Sara, but with decidedly less care.

Swinging Benny around like a rag doll, Flynn shoved him against the cement wall that bordered the on-ramp. Either he wasn't cognizant of how out of things Benny was at the moment, thought Sara, or he simply wasn't taking any chances.

His chest heaving with deep, frantic breaths, he retrieved his gun from Benny and pointed it at his head while he maneuvered him into handcuffs and stuffed what looked like the bench warrant for his arrest in his chest pocket. Then he rummaged through the rest of Benny's pockets until he found whatever it was he was looking for. The Garrett doubloon, Sara realized as Flynn, smiling triumphantly, tossed it to her for safekeeping.

Finally, he reared back and grabbed Benny by his blood-stained shirtfront, lifting him off the ground until they were at eye level.

"Gotcha," he said.

The police arrived on the scene within minutes. After Flynn explained the situation to them, they were very helpful. And, Sara observed wryly, very impressed by Flynn's skill at flying an automobile.

"Damn shame about the Corvette, though," said one young officer, shaking his head at Flynn's car, which Sara noticed did look a lot flatter than she remembered.

She quickly glanced at Flynn and saw a mixture of grief and resignation in his expression, and she realized that the car was a total loss.

"Yeah, well," he replied, shrugging. "It's only a car."

Only a car? Had she heard Flynn correctly?

"Oh, yeah, right," drawled the officer. "Only a car, he says. That's like saying Air Jordan is *only* a basketball player. That car of yours was a cream puff...and part Lear jet from the looks of what you pulled off here tonight."

Another policeman nodded his head. "You said it. I figure you had to be airborne for a good three seconds. Doesn't sound like much maybe, but try flying it sometime." He grinned at Flynn. "That was one damn risky stunt you pulled."

To her amazement, as she listened to them talk about it, Sara felt even more panicky than she had when it was happening. Maybe because now she had time to fully comprehend the danger that all of them, but especially Flynn, had been in.

Instinctively her gaze was drawn to him and their eyes met. Though he replied to the policeman's comment, he looked only at her.

"Some risks you just have to take," he said.

With Benny secured in the back seat of a police cruiser, it was arranged for them to have a police escort to the hotel to pick up their things and then on to the airport. Flynn wasn't taking any chances on getting Benny back to Boston before the deadline. Separate arrangements were made to have the car towed away, and with a final pat on its rear bumper, Flynn followed her into the police cruiser.

In the room, Sara quickly gathered their clothes and stuffed them into their bags while Flynn phoned the airlines to book seats for the three of them. Him, her and Benny, and most likely with Benny safely ensconced in the seat between them. She did her best not to panic at the thought of how little time they had left alone. Flynn had just risked his life and sacrificed the only thing he acknowledged caring about for her sake. That had to count for something.

Sara just prayed it counted for everything. Because where she and Flynn were concerned, everything is what she wanted.

She emerged from the bathroom with his shaving case in hand, in time to hear him confirming the ticket arrangements with the airline representative. She stopped, staring at him with a growing sense of dread until he hung up the phone.

Flynn turned to her, still sitting on the edge of the bed, his expression fixed and remote.

"Did I hear you say Providence?" she asked.

He nodded.

"Are we flying into Providence instead of Boston?"

"*We're* not," he replied, standing. "You are."

Sara held her head high in spite of the crumbling within. "Why?"

"Because that's where you live," he said impatiently. "It's time to go home, Sara."

"What if I'm not ready to go home yet?"

"Then you better get ready in a hurry. Your flight leaves in ninety minutes."

"I thought maybe I'd fly to Boston with you," she said, anxiety making it an effort to breathe and talk at the same time. "I could stay a few days and..."

She stopped. Flynn was already shaking his head.

"That won't work, Sara. *We* won't work."

"We've been working just fine the past few days," she reminded him with quiet desperation.

"The past few days have been...like a dream, something far removed from reality."

"What's wrong with that?"

"Everything," he said, growing exasperated. "Life's not a dream, Sara. It's real, with real pain and real disasters and real losses."

"I know all that."

"And the best you can do is to avoid as much of that grief as you can... you haven't learned that yet, but you're about to. I just wish I hadn't had anything to do with teaching you."

He stormed past her and into the bathroom. Sara followed.

"You think that's all you taught me? Do you really think that's all I've learned on this trip?"

"No," he said, looking around for his stuff and realizing she had already packed it for him. With nothing else to do, he faced her.

"Unfortunately, you probably saw and learned a lot of things you'd be better off not knowing. I'm sorry about that—about all of this, damn it. But I never wanted it to happen. I didn't want you along in the first place. I didn't want to make all those stupid stops along the way where we had too much time on our hands. I sure as hell didn't want you to..."

"To what?" Sara prompted when he fell into an uncomfortable silence. "Fall in love with you? Is that what you didn't want most? Or were you going to say that you sure as hell didn't want to fall in love with me?"

His jaw came up. "I'm not in love with you."

"Liar."

"Think about it, Sara, if I loved you would I be sending you home alone?"

"Yes. It's because you love me that you're in such a hurry to get rid of me. If you didn't love me, you'd keep me around a while for more great sex and then say goodbye. But you're afraid that if you let this go on too long, you won't be able to send me away. You won't be able to do what you think you have to do...put me out of your life yourself, before someone or something has the chance to do it for you."

His mouth twisted in a disparaging grimace. "That's the stupidest thing I ever heard."

"Yeah, it's the stupidest thing I ever heard, too. I just didn't want to say so and hurt your feelings."

He shot her an impatient look and edged past her. "This wouldn't even be worth discussing if we had time for it, which we don't."

He rummaged in his bag for a minute, then crossed to the desk and hunched over it with his back to her. When he turned, he held out to her the piece of paper he'd been writing on. Curious, Sara stepped forward to take it.

"What's this?" she asked, even as she realized it was a check. A check drawn on Flynn's personal account for an exorbitant amount of money...far more than the share of the reward he'd promised her. She gazed at him suspiciously. "What on earth is this for?"

"Nothing unsavory," he countered dryly, "if that's the conclusion you were ready to jump to."

"Then what—"

"That's your half of the recovery fee, plus the reward the auction house put up for the coin. You earned it."

"You never mentioned that there was a reward offered on the coin."

He shrugged.

"How can you afford to give this to me? I mean now, before you've even collected anything?"

"I don't have to collect the recovery fee on Benny, because I put up the bond in the first place." When she squinted at him in bewilderment, he added, "You see, I'm not just a bounty hunter, I'm a bondsman. In fact, that's the majority of my business. I started out doing this—the bounty hunting—but these days it's more of a . . . hobby."

"Pretty lucrative hobby."

"It's not always this lucrative, believe me. But I've got that check covered."

"Why didn't you tell me any of this before now? I mean about the reward or your work?"

"Never saw any need to. If you recall, when this whole thing started, I was only trying to bribe you into the use of a room. Even I'm not crazy enough to pay that amount of money for a room."

"For this amount you could buy my whole house," she remarked, glancing at the check again.

"That's what I had in mind. The check is good, Sara. I want you to use the money to save your house and put your life back the way it was before you met me."

The sheer absurdity of that swept all other concerns and feelings aside and pushed Sara to the very edge of whatever flimsy barrier was separating her from the storm of despair and desperation gathering within.

"If you really believe that's possible," she said, carefully and quietly so that she wouldn't give in to the screams building inside her, "then you're even crazier than I thought. Don't you know that nothing is ever going to be the way it was? Not for me, or for you."

"Sure it will be," he told her, with a notable lack of conviction. "You were in a slump when I came along, ready for a little change of scenery. When you get home and pay off some of those debts, things will look different. You'll see. In a few weeks, you'll forget all about this. And all about me."

"A little change of scenery? Is that really all you think this has been?"

"That's all it can be, Sara."

"And how about you?" she pressed, banking down on the ache that had risen from her chest to the center of her throat. "Are you just going to forget all about me?"

For a second, Sara thought she saw his mouth tremble, then he shrugged and tossed her that damn self-effacing grin. "I'm sure going to try."

That did it, snapped whatever was holding Sara back from doing what she wanted most to do. A week ago she would have accepted that he could dismiss her so easily; she would have believed it and believed that what she felt and wanted was hopeless. But not now.

Moving closer to Flynn, she reached out and slid her palms across his chest, shoving them under his leather jacket where he felt warm and solid.

"What are you doing?" he asked warily.

"Only what you always accuse me of doing...making things hard for you."

"Sara..."

"If you plan on forgetting me in a hurry," she continued, ignoring the warning in his eyes, "you're going to have your work cut out for you. Because I plan to give you something worth remembering."

Linking her hands at the back of his neck, she pulled his head down until his mouth touched hers. After his initial hesitation, it wasn't much of a battle. Flynn went into the kiss willingly, his mouth opening over hers, his tongue invading with deep, hungry thrusts.

When he abruptly pulled away, Sara got the distinct impression that he did so because he was afraid that very soon he might not be able to stop. Which was exactly what she wanted.

Her arms still wrapped around his neck, she lifted up and caressed his full bottom lip with her tongue. "You call that a goodbye kiss?"

"Come on, Sara," he groaned when she lifted herself against him again, searching for the position where their bodies meshed perfectly, and finding it.

"You really want me to stop?" she murmured, sliding her hands along his spine in the sort of long, slow, kneading caress that made him tremble.

"Yes," he answered as she drew his lip between hers and sucked gently on it. "No... Yes. Ah, Sara, what do you want from me?"

"What do you think?" she whispered against his open mouth.

He pulled back quickly to look at her, surprise and excitement in his eyes. "There are a half dozen policemen and an excon waiting for us downstairs," he reminded her.

"Then we better not waste any more time."

He gazed at her with disbelief and desire. And then he reached for her and pulled her close. He lowered his head, hesitating just before their lips met, as if he felt the need to issue a disclaimer, and muttered, "I don't love you."

"Prove it," said Sara.

He took her quickly, without even making use of the bed that was only a few feet away. Maybe it was because he thought that hard, fast sex was the best way to prove to her, and to himself, that this was about lust and not love, maybe because the adrenaline from the night's activities was still surging in his veins the same as it was in Sara's, and maybe it was simply because he was as hungry for her as she was for him, and even that short detour to the bed was too much of a delay.

They tore at each other's clothes, opening and removing only what was necessary so that their hands and mouths could be where they wanted... needed to be. Sara drank in the pleasure of touching him, of feeling his muscles swell and tighten beneath her fingertips, and the thrill of his hot, soft mouth on her throat and breasts, and his hands, warm and rough and impatient, on her thighs and between them.

Then he was lifting her, impaling her with his heat and strength. Sara was gripped by a deep sensual awareness of how perfectly her body gloved his, awed by the miracle of their joining, as if they were the first man and woman ever to have discovered this incredible gift of passion.

The slippery, rhythmic contact of their bodies moving together sent excitement ripping through her in one white-hot wave after another. Throwing her head back, she clung to his shoulders and wrapped her legs around his waist. The pleasure stirring deep inside her was made sharper by the desperate awareness that this might be the last time she ever held him this way. In spite of her wish to make it last, the sensations coiled tighter and tighter, until they exploded and sent her soaring toward ecstasy. Flynn went with her, his hands clenching her hips almost painfully as his husky moan of pleasure warmed her skin.

Afterward, he slowly lowered her to her feet, and when their gazes locked, everything she wanted to see was there in his sad green eyes. *I love you, Sara. I need you, Sara. I want you with me forever.*

Of course, he didn't say any of it. Sara didn't really expect him to. And she wasn't sure if that made what was happening easier or much, much harder.

"I'm sorry," he said instead. "That was probably a mistake."

"What's one more?" Sara countered in a shaky attempt at humor as they both tended to their clothes.

"Don't," he said, and then at her quizzical glance, shrugged as if even he wasn't sure what he meant, and finished buckling his belt. "Don't worry," he said finally. "You're going to be all right. I mean it. You've changed a lot since I first met you, Sara."

"I know."

"Really changed."

"I know."

"I don't mean just your hair and your clothes," he said with an impatient frown. "I mean *you*. Inside. You're going to be all right on your own."

"I know that, too," Sara replied, meaning it. She reached up to touch his face, her heart coming apart inside her. "But what about you, Flynn?"

Chapter Fifteen

Being back in Sutton Cove made Sara feel like Dorothy returning to Kansas from Oz. By comparison, everything at home seemed black and white, lifeless, Flynnless. And of course, that was the worst part. Sara knew she could have handled black and white, if only Flynn were there with her.

It was, she discovered, hard to maintain the new her when she was surrounded by reminders of the old her. Clearly some fundamental changes had to be made. But, she told herself daily, they would have to wait a while. She still wasn't giving up on Flynn. In fact, she had put her life on hold, waiting for him to call, certain she hadn't imagined or misread his feelings and that sooner or later he would call or come for her. She stayed close to home so she would be there for him, investing in an answering machine for those times she absolutely had to go out and screening her calls so she didn't tie up the line unnecessarily.

That really irked Stuart, who phoned several times a day to find out what she planned to do about the house. Sara finally grabbed the receiver when he called and, in an outburst that took him by surprise, told him that *she* would call *him* when she was ready to discuss it. How could she be expected to tell him what she didn't know herself? And how could she make up her mind what she wanted to do about the house or anything else until she knew for sure what was going to happen with Flynn?

One week of limbo stretched into two, then three. Flynn's uncashed check sat on top of the piano, like some sort of paper monument to her trust in him. Sara kept busy with the yard and her students and all the details of life, while the real essence of it remained a blank slate inside her.

The whole town was buzzing with the story of how nice Sara McAllister had gone off with a bounty hunter. Amazingly Sara didn't particularly care what they said or thought. *She* thought that going off with Flynn had been the smartest thing she'd ever done, and that's what counted.

The only person Sara had bothered explaining things to was Nancy. She'd told Nancy everything about the time she spent on the road with Flynn. Well, almost everything. With Flynn, she had finally discovered emotional bonds and loyalties that were even stronger than those she shared with her old friend. She'd told her enough, however, so that Nancy agreed that Flynn did indeed sound wonderful and worth whatever effort it might take to overcome the fear and pain that was obviously buried inside him.

Predictably, Nancy was thrilled with Sara's haircut and the new clothes she'd bought, declaring that the changes were way overdue. She even persuaded Sara to add to her new wardrobe. It wasn't a hard sell. Anticipating Flynn's arrival any moment, Sara had a reason to want to look gorgeous and sexy, and amazingly enough, she felt that way. The feeling was self-perpetuating, she discovered. Now that she felt different—capable and confident and beautiful—other people, even people who had known her for years, looked at her differently and treated her that way, which in turn made her feel even better about herself.

She truly felt like a new woman. There were at least a hundred ways that she no longer fit into the old life she'd run away from. It wasn't only the old clothes hanging in her closet that no longer seemed right, it was the old routine and habits and compromises. She was through making compromises. The problem was that, although ready to throw off the old, she wasn't yet sure exactly what shape the new would take. She couldn't be sure until she heard from Flynn.

Sara wasn't sure when her new spirit and resolve began coming undone. The changes happened gradually. Or maybe they could best be described as "unchanges." The undoing of all her discoveries. Regression. It was as if while she were standing still, waiting for the future to begin, waiting for Flynn, old habits and insecurities had come out of the woodwork to fill the temporary vacuum inside her.

It wasn't something she was even aware of at first. It was subtle and insidious. Then one morning she threw on an old, oversize pair of sweats when she went out to get the mail, and the mailman grinned and said, "Looks like things are back to normal around here."

Sara smiled obligingly at his little joke, not wanting to hurt his feelings even though he had hurt hers. Was this really normal?

That afternoon while she was sorting through some sheet music for upcoming lessons, she came across the music for a piece she had thought she might play at this year's student recital. Usually she didn't play at all, refusing her students' pleas with the insistence that the recital was strictly a showcase for their talents. There were too many parents and former students in the audience for her to feel comfortable playing, too much pressure, too much potential for embarrassment.

With a shrug, Sara slipped the sheet music into the storage box. Why go looking for trouble?

As she was leaving the room, she glanced, as she always did, at the pictures in frames on top of the piano, searching for a particular one. It wasn't one that held a favorite photo of her parents or friends, but rather the one where she had propped the check from Flynn. And where it was now gathering dust, the sun turning the pale gray paper a little yellow around the edges.

Pretty soon, it would be too late to cash it, she thought. Maybe, subconsciously, that's why she was putting off doing so. Was she hoping for an excuse to contact Flynn? Or maybe hoping that Flynn's conscience would force him to contact her to find out why she wasn't claiming the reward that he himself had said she earned?

Is that what she wanted, Sara wondered, to force Flynn to come to her?

No.

In spite of the indecisiveness that was steadily overtaking the clear, cool confidence she'd developed on the road to Miami, Sara was still sure of that much. She wanted what she had always wanted from Flynn . . . she wanted him to want her the same way she wanted him. She wanted him to want her badly enough to overcome the fear inside him, the same way she'd had to overcome hers. If she let the uncashed check become an excuse for either one of them, that wasn't going to happen.

She had to cash it, Sara decided, and soon.

It wasn't as if she didn't need the money as desperately as she had a few weeks ago. Actually, she needed it even more desperately. The bills were still piling up and Stuart had resumed calling her daily to press for a decision about the house. Evidently pregnancy was making Corrine even more demanding than usual.

Sara had given the matter a great deal of thought, weighing the pros and cons of selling the McAllister house to Stuart and Corrine. It wasn't hard to come up with reasons for the pro side, especially since Nancy was constantly reminding her of them. The house was too big, too expensive to heat and maintain, too much work for one person.

The cons were not as numerous or as easy to tick off. It really all came down to the fact that the house was her heritage, part of her history, part of herself . . . her responsibility as the last McAllister in Sutton Cove. Now that she had the means to save it, it seemed she had an obligation to do so. Try as she would, Sara couldn't seem to shake off that sense of duty.

She couldn't sell the house, she decided finally. At least not right now. With the rest of her life in flux, this wasn't the time to go making major, irrevocable decisions. Now all she had to do was break the news to Stuart.

Sara scheduled the meeting with Stuart for first thing the next morning, eager to get it over with. Stuart graciously cleared his calendar for her, assuming no doubt that she would be coming to the bank to accept his offer on the house. She did nothing over the phone to dispel that assumption. Another of her old tricks coming home to roost . . . postponing the inevitable.

She dressed carefully for their meeting, pushing aside her old suits and dresses in favor of a summery new white jumpsuit that Nancy had suggested she wear.

"After all," said Nancy, "you don't work for the bank, and you sure as heck don't need their money anymore, so why dress like a banker? That jumpsuit will knock Stuart's eyes out."

Sara wasn't so sure. If the jumpsuit was as perfect for the new her as Nancy insisted, how come when she looked in the mirror all she saw was the old her in too tight pants?

Yanking off the jumpsuit, Sara dressed in the first thing she grabbed from the closet. Not until she was on her way out the door did she remember it was the same blue suit she'd worn the last time she went to see him. Shrugging, she slipped the check into her purse and shut the door behind her. Who cared what she was wearing? Who cared what Stuart thought?

That was one change that she knew in her heart was permanent. She finally had all traces of Stuart out of her system for good. Getting to know and love Flynn had made her wonder how she could have ever thought herself in love with such a rigid, small-town bureaucrat as Stuart Bowers.

She opted to walk to town, cutting across the park to stroll along the waterfront because she was still a few minutes early. The sun glinting off the water reminded her of Miami. Of course, lately everything reminded her of Miami. And Flynn.

She felt the ever-present ache near her heart begin to swell. Great. Just what she needed when she wanted to be sharp and focused for her meeting with Stuart.

To distract herself from the pain that grew a little more overwhelming with each empty day that passed, Sara concentrated on the familiar landscape, the boats bobbing at their moorings, the red and white canopy outside Sutton House, the seafood restaurant that survived while other ventures in the area came and went, the weathered gray shingles of the old fish cannery that overlooked the harbor.

Periodically the town council debated the merits of converting the cannery into space for shops and restaurants, similar to what had been done with great success in Boston and Newport. Sutton Cove was ideally located to draw business, but the idea never made it past the talking stage. Before it could become reality, someone had to take a chance and act. Unfortunately for the economy of the town, no one in Sutton Cove was brave enough to do it.

At the bank, Stuart came out to greet her personally and warmly. Ordinarily he remained seated at his desk when his secretary ushered Sara to his office, not even bothering to look up until he'd finished whatever he was working on.

Obviously, the project he was working on this morning was Sara. He nodded approval as he ran his gaze over the suit he'd seen her in at least a half dozen times before, and something about his small smile—maybe the way it bordered on being a smirk—reminded Sara of the time when they had been engaged. Thank you, God, she prayed silently as he held her chair for her and offered her coffee. Funny, thought Sara, she'd never before noticed the way the tip of his nose wiggled when he talked.

"You're sure I can't have Ellen bring you a cup of mocha Java?" he asked as he settled into his own chair, flashing her what Sara was sure he considered a very cosmopolitan smile. "Or a muffin?"

"No, thank you," she replied. "I really don't want to take any more of your time than necessary."

"Sara," he said, "Please. My time is your time. That's not only the bank's philosophy—it's mine."

"Well, fine. Just the same, I'd like to get down to my reason for being here."

"And so would I, believe me. You drive a hard bargain, my old friend," he said, chuckling as he shuffled through the papers neatly arranged in folders on the desk in front of him. "But I just knew my last offer would be too good to resist."

"Stuart, this isn't about money or getting you to up your offer. It never has been."

He regarded her smugly. "Sara, please, everything is about money. Nothing wrong with wanting to make a little profit.

Now, I've taken the liberty of having all the preliminary papers drawn up. Of course, I'll want a house inspection performed, but I don't expect to find anything out of order.''

"Oh, but there is," Sara countered, hoping for an easy way out. "There's tons of things out of order in that house, way out of order. The roof leaks and the furnace made this horrible noise all winter, as if it might explode, and all the bricks in all the fireplaces need—"

"Please, please, Sara," interrupted Stuart with a silky laugh. "I know all about what to expect from an old house, believe me, and I'm prepared for it. A clanking furnace might frighten a woman alone, but I assure you, I'll take care of all that and have that place shipshape in no time." He winked at her. "Corrine wouldn't have it any other way."

Sara smiled, thinking how much she hated that kind of cute little married-folks joke. "No, I suppose not."

"Now, as I was saying, I've had all the papers—"

"Stuart, you really shouldn't have done that."

"Nonsense. After all, Sara, we're more than friends."

Wrong, she thought, we're not *even* friends.

"And that's why I must tell you," he continued, his voice becoming deep and concerned, "that I, for one, was relieved to hear you've put all that nonsense with that Flynn character behind you and come to your senses. Anyone can make a mistake, but..."

Come to her senses.

Of course. She had been searching for the right words to describe what had been happening to her—*in* her—ever since she returned home, and there they were. She had come to her senses.

As Stuart went on in that same sympathetic tone, chronicling her mistakes even as he forgave them, Sara thought about that. She was being sensible once again, doing what was expected of her. Doing what was expected of a *woman alone,* as Stuart put it. This suit was sensible. That's why he had nodded approvingly when she walked in wearing it.

Coming here today was sensible. Oh, Stuart wouldn't like hearing that she'd decided not to sell the house, but that, too, was sensible. Deciding not to play in the recital was sensible.

Cautious always qualified as sensible. The shoes on her feet and the food in her refrigerator and the car in her driveway were all very sensible. She supposed it even made sense to put her life on hold while she waited for Flynn to come to his senses too. She was one sensible lady. And if she kept it up, she would soon be so sensible she'd choke on it.

She couldn't keep it up, Sara realized suddenly, and just that simple, broad-as-a-barn decision brought back to her the feeling of power and energy she had felt sitting at the piano in BlackJack's.

She'd been so full of plans and dreams that night. She had to get on with those dreams. With or without Flynn. That didn't mean she loved him any less, she told herself, or had any less faith that what they shared had been real. But she had lived too long inside an empty shell of a life that was made up of things she felt she had to do or ought to do.

Flynn had taken her outside of that and let her discover the joy of doing what she wanted to do. It would be a shame if, because of him, she lived the rest of her life inside a new shell of her own making.

As for the McAllister house, it suddenly seemed so clear to Sara that her real family heritage had less to do with the house and anything in it than it did with what was inside her. For all their shortcomings, her parents had passed on to her some very important qualities and values. Her father's humor and compassion, her mother's fierce pride and determination... The more she came to know herself, the more she saw signs of them in her. *That* was her real heritage.

"You're right," she said suddenly.

Stuart stopped mid-sentence, looking a bit annoyed that she, of all people, had interrupted him.

"You're right about everything," Sara continued. "About me and my suit and the paperwork."

"Your suit? What about your suit?"

"I meant to say house... my house. I'm glad you had the papers drawn up because I want you and Corrine to have the house as soon as possible. In fact, I can't think of two people who deserve it more."

"Well, that's a very nice thing for you to say. With the baby coming and all, we—"

"Of course. A family needs a home . . . and a pool. It makes perfect sense to me. There is just one small problem," she said, leaning forward in her seat with a brilliant smile that seemed to take poor Stuart by surprise.

"What problem is that?" he asked.

"You're going to have to draw up more papers. You see, Stuart, I'm going to sell you the house contingent on your arranging financing for me to buy the old cannery on the harbor."

"The old cannery?" exclaimed Stuart. "What in God's name would you want with that?"

"I've decided to open a bar in the corner overlooking the water."

"A bar?" Stuart came out of his seat and loomed across the desk toward her.

"That's right. A piano bar. I'm going to have tables with umbrellas on an outside deck in the warm weather and serve food, nothing fancy, and there will be a dance floor, with a band for dancing on weekends. And during the week, I'm going to play myself."

"Listen to me, Sara," said Stuart in the sort of tone used to calm a rabid dog. He had just about as much chance of dissuading her, Sara thought with amusement. Poor Stuart. "I know you've been under a great deal of strain lately. And then there was that bad business with Flynn. Damn him, anyway. This is your nerves talking and—"

"No, this is me talking, Stuart. I'm going to do exactly what I just told you I'm going to do, and I'm also going to see to the renovation of the rest of cannery. I'm willing to bet that when push comes to shove, I'm not the only one who thinks it's time for a few changes in Sutton Cove."

"Oh, that old dinosaur of an idea," scoffed a relieved-looking Stuart. "That's been kicking around for ages. You can't be serious, Sara. You'll never pull it off."

Sara smiled. "Watch me."

"And just how do you propose to get others to join you in this foolish scheme?"

"Simple. I'm going to ask them. That's rule number one, Stuart," she said as she reached for her purse and stood. "You have to ask for what you want."

Chapter Sixteen

White candles lit each window in the McAllister house, and the faint rainbow glow of a Christmas tree shone from the sun room, reminders that Christmas was only a few weeks away. Flynn didn't need any reminders. He'd made it through the summer, Labor Day weekend and Thanksgiving alone, but he just knew he wasn't strong enough to survive Christmas.

He stood outside Sara's front door and wiped his damp palms on the legs of his jeans. Damn, he thought, maybe he should have worn something besides jeans, something that would make a better impression. The corners of his mouth twitched at that. It was a little late to be thinking about making a good impression on Sara.

For better or worse, that had happened eight months ago, when he broke into her house and allowed her to believe he was holding her hostage for a few hours. He grinned at the memory, the fleeting enjoyment quickly giving way to the nervous tension that had been building all the way here. Hell, it had been building for a week, while he was stuck in that no-man's-land between making the decision to come here to see Sara and getting up the courage to actually do it.

Okay, he told himself, this is it. He'd run through every worst-case scenario his imagination could ante up and he was prepared to deal with whatever happened. At least he was as prepared as he ever would be. It had taken him a long time to get his act together enough to come here and lay his heart before the woman he loved ... years, actually, but the last eight lonely, unbearable months in particular. Now it was up to Sara.

He rang the bell, heard the old-fashioned chiming somewhere within, immediately followed by a loud cry of, "What now? Damn it."

A loud *male* cry, Flynn realized, the significance of that imbedding itself in his gut with all the subtlety of a bayonet. There was a man in Sara's house. He swallowed hard, his head near exploding from the pressure of his own stupidity. How, in all his wild conjecturing, could he ever have *not* considered the possibility that Sara might have found someone else?

Always when he imagined this moment, he pictured her being overjoyed or angry or annoyed or just plain uninterested in his belated awakening to the fact that he loved her more than he needed the safety zone he'd been existing in for the past twenty years. He never once pictured her with another man.

The front door swung open and Flynn felt what was left of his composure crack wide open.

"Bowers?" he said, openly incredulous.

"Flynn?" the other man replied, looking about the same.

"What are you doing here?" Flynn demanded rudely. He felt rude, damn it.

"I live here," Stuart Bowers retorted, resting the two-foot-long wrench he was holding on his shoulder, as casually as if it were a golf club and he were about to tee off at the eighteenth hole of the Masters. "The question is, what are *you* doing here?"

He lived here? thought Flynn ignoring the question. He lived here with Sara?

A sound like pans crashing together came from the kitchen. Stuart jumped and grimaced angrily. "Will you keep it down in there, for Pete's sake? You're making enough noise to wake the dead.''

No reply.

The idea that he might be talking to Sara that way—and that she was letting him get away with it—filled Flynn with fury.

"I want to see Sara," he said coldly.

Stuart raised his brows. "About what?"

"None of your business. Just get her."

"Hold on, buddy," he said, flashing an acidic smile. "I'm not the one who came knocking on your door looking for favors."

"I'm not looking for favors. I'm looking for Sara. Is she here or not?" asked Flynn, leaning sideways in an attempt to see past him.

Stuart shifted to block his view. "Look, I've got a leaky pipe I've got to get back to. If you want to tell me what business you have with Sara then maybe—"

"I'll tell you what, Bowers," Flynn said, stepping onto the threshold and taking immense pleasure in the way the other man was forced to retreat a step, "why don't you go screw, or whatever it is you need to do with that thing you're holding, and I'll tell Sara myself what—"

Another loud crash from the direction of the kitchen interrupted him.

"What the hell is going on here?" he said.

Stuart shouted over his shoulder, "Will you please—"

From upstairs the loud cry of a baby added to the racket.

"Great," roared Stuart. He glared at Flynn—who was beginning to fit the pieces of this madness together—as if he were to blame.

As the baby continued to cry, Stuart bellowed, "Corrine."

A woman Flynn vaguely recognized from the day she'd driven past and ignored Sara dashed into the hallway behind Stuart. She looked frazzled and angry.

"Don't just stand there, do something," she screamed at Stuart. "I've filled every damn pot and pan we own and now the water is coming out of the top of the toilet *and* the broken pipe."

"It wasn't a minute ago...I almost had it stopped. What the hell did you do to it?" Stuart demanded.

"Nothing. Can I help it if this place is falling apart?"

"Go get the baby, why don't you?"

"It's your turn."

"How can I fix the pipe and hold the kid at the same time?"

"That's not my problem," retorted Corrine.

They were both screaming now, and the baby was crying louder than ever. Flynn smiled.

Corrine glared at him. "Who are you?"

"My name's Flynn," he explained, doing his best to look simply polite and not amused beyond belief by the scene he'd stumbled into. "I'm looking for Sara McAllister."

"She doesn't live here anymore," snapped Corrine, confirming what Flynn already suspected. "She had too much sense to stay in a dump like this. Only a madman would live here and put up with the leaks and the drafts and the ... Will you get the baby?" she shouted at Stuart.

"All right, all right," he muttered as he headed for the stairs.

Corrine turned to Flynn. "At this time of night you'll probably find Sara at the club."

"Club?"

"Right, her club. Sara's," she drawled icily. "It's on the water." Leaning out the door, she pointed toward the harbor. "You can practically see it from here."

"Thanks," said Flynn, pausing as he turned to leave. "Oh, and tell your husband congratulations on getting this place. I know how much he wanted it."

Sara's was a total shock to Flynn, and at the same time exactly what he would have expected.

The shock came from seeing how far Sara had come and how much she had accomplished since he'd wandered into her life and turned it upside down. During the past months, he'd wondered more than once how she was coping, whether freeing her so briefly from the cage her life had become had proven to be a blessing or a curse. He had his answer.

Sara wasn't *coping* at all. She wasn't barely surviving or struggling to readjust or pining away over him, either, for that matter. Although from time to time he had stroked his ego with the thought that she might be. She was doing exactly what he'd predicted she would do.... She was doing just fine. Spectacularly well, in fact, from the looks of the place that bore her name.

The club itself was also what he would have expected from Sara, simple and straightforward, full of color and life and music and so like Sara that now, walking in for the first time, Flynn had a feeling that he'd been there before, a sense of coming back to a place he loved and knew well.

Then his anxious gaze swept across the room and found Sara where she sat at the same baby grand piano she had once played for him alone. Tonight she was playing for what he judged to be a capacity crowd, and loving it. He could tell from the look of wild abandon on her beautiful face. The only other times he had seen her look close to that excited and alive...

Thinking about that now drove all thoughts and feelings from him except for one... that he loved Sara and wanted her. He wanted to drag her away from that piano and all these people and tell her all the things he had to tell her, explain the things that needed to be explained, say he was sorry for the things that needed to be forgiven.

But he knew that was out of the question. First of all, it would embarrass Sara, and he never wanted to do that. He never wanted to hurt or anger or disappoint her ever again. And secondly, after all his planning and thinking, suddenly he wasn't sure he was ready to say what he wanted to say. He wasn't sure he would ever be ready or that there were even words to tell her how he felt, how much he loved her and needed her. If the right words did exist, he sure didn't feel capable of coming up with them right now.

Seeing the evidence of how fully Sara had come into her own and how ably she had made it without him made all the worries and doubts he'd been battling descend on him with the speed and precision of an enemy army camped out inside him. Sara's old life had had so many holes and gaping needs that even a lost cause like him had looked good to her. Now all that had changed. Would there be room in Sara's new life for him?

While he was gradually sliding into dismay, Sara looked up and their eyes met, and Flynn felt his doubts breaking up like a bad radio transmission.

All at once he knew that no words or explanations or apologies were necessary. He knew there would always be a place for him with Sara, and for her with him. He knew it the way he knew that blue was blue or the earth was round. Because that's just the way it was. A fact. A certainty. That's what it was like with him and Sara . . . this love or need or maybe the best of both. It was a fact.

The earth was round long before explorers discovered that fact, and it would have remained round even if they'd never set sail. He liked thinking it was the same for him and Sara. They were meant to be together. Fate, he thought, finding joy where once there was only bitterness. The idea of fate no longer scared him, Flynn realized, watching as Sara finished the piece she was playing and rose.

His heartbeat like thunder, he stood at the end of the bar and waited for her to excuse herself from the admirers gathered around and weave her way through the tables to his side. He wanted as much privacy as possible for this.

Sara's smile was brilliant, like a beacon homing in on him, warming him as she drew closer. Her eyes never left his face. Flynn wanted to grab her and kiss her until they both ran out of breath, but when she was finally within reach, he found himself afraid to even touch her . . . afraid his hunger was so great he might not be able to stop.

"You're here," she said.

Just as a precaution, Flynn shoved his hands in his jacket pockets. "You don't look very surprised."

He wasn't complaining. She looked happy, thrilled, in fact, and he'd settle for that any day.

"I'm not surprised," she said. "I knew you'd come . . . someday. Oh, Flynn, what took you so long?"

He shrugged self-consciously. "I had a lot to work out."

"And have you? Worked it all out, I mean?"

"Yeah. At least as much as I can alone. I guess the rest is up to you." He caught a drift of her scent, and its sweet familiarity made him crave more of her, all of her. "We need to talk," he said.

Sara nodded eagerly. "Okay."

"When can you leave?"

"Whenever I want," she said, smiling. "Did you happen to notice the name out front?"

"I noticed. Congratulations. When did all this happen?"

"Since Miami and BlackJack's. I got inspired."

"It took a lot more than inspiration to put this place together," he observed, taking a long look around.

Sara saw the mixture of pride and admiration in his expression as he surveyed the place that had been her life, her obsession, her nightmare and her baby for the past eight months, and if it weren't already, every headache, every battle with the construction crew, every frantic call to a supplier, became worth it a hundred times over. She loved Sara's, and she was proud of her success, but seeing her accomplishments reflected in Flynn's eyes was more thrilling to her than all the opening-night hoopla and applauding audiences in the world.

"This is incredible," he said finally, bringing his gaze to her. "You're incredible."

"It helped to keep busy," she said softly. "And in a way, it's still coming together."

She quickly explained her plans for the rest of the long narrow building. "Drew, Nancy's husband, is overseeing the development full-time now that I can afford to pay him what he's worth, and we already have a dozen firm tenants . . . including Nancy's shop."

"How many do you have room for?"

"Thirty, not counting outdoor cart facilities for the warm weather, when we should attract the boating crowd. The city council is finally in my corner, but financing is still a mess."

"Who are you working with?"

"Well, until recently, we've dealt predominantly with Stuart Bowers and—" She broke off at the disgusted look he shot her and they both laughed. "I know, I know. We did approach a Boston bank and it seems like they might be interested, but I'm busy with this place and I can't expect Drew to handle that, too."

"I could help," Flynn offered softly.

Sara stopped breathing. She hadn't realized how nervous she'd been, wondering if Flynn were here for the reason she hoped he was or was simply passing through. His offer told her all she needed to know.

"I mean," he added hurriedly, while she was still savoring the knowledge that he wasn't going anywhere in a hurry, "if you want my help. I don't want you to think I'm trying to jump in on the good thing you've got going all by yourself."

"I would never think anything like that."

"And finance is sort of my field. I have some contacts. We could talk about it and if you trust my instincts . . ."

"I trust everything about you," she said, aware of him with every fiber of her being. "Why are we standing here talking about business and financing?"

"Damned if I know," Flynn countered, looking as restless as she felt. "Let's get out of here."

Sara got her coat and spoke briefly with the bartender, whom, she assured Flynn, she trusted to handle closing for the night. They walked outside.

"Where are you parked?" she asked.

"This way. The parking lot was full, so I took a spot on the street."

"We're going to have to think about adding more parking space."

Keeping his hands still safely confined to his pockets, Flynn led her along the street. "Have you considered buying that old place just on the other side of the building?" he asked. "That would make a good size lot, and it looks about ready to tumble down on its own."

"No, I hadn't thought of that. You're right, it would be perfect . . . if it's for sale, that is, and if I can afford it. I'm sort of maxed out."

He grinned at her. "Sounds familiar."

The reminder of the trip to Miami made them both smile, then quickly look away from each other as other, more intimate memories followed.

"Anyway," he went on, "it so happens I'm not maxed out at the moment, and I'm always interested in a promising investment. I could look into some sort of joint venture, if you like."

"I'd like that very much," Sara told him. She stopped walking because he did, and turned to him, fully expecting him to pull her into his arms and kiss her, afraid that if he didn't touch her soon she would be forced to grab him.

Instead of making a move, however, he pulled one hand from the pocket of his leather jacket and opened the passenger door of the battered Ford Bronco he was standing next to. "Here we are."

"This is yours?" queried Sara, taking in the rust spots and assorted small dents.

"Yeah, it's not much to look at, but it serves the purpose."

Sara climbed in, grateful she was wearing slacks. This looked like the sort of vehicle that chewed up panty hose for amusement.

"Where to?" Flynn asked as he slid behind the wheel.

"I bought a new place. It's on the water, not far from here."

She gave him brief directions and winced as the gears shifted with a sound excruciatingly reminiscent of gnashing teeth.

Flynn slanted her a wry look. "Not quite as smooth as the Corvette."

Sara was curious about that. As long as he'd brought it up, she figured the subject was fair game.

"Knowing the way you felt about that car," she said, "I sort of expected that you would rush right out and buy a replacement."

"I did," he admitted. "At least I tried to. I must have checked out cars at a dozen dealerships, but nothing I sat in felt right. Go ahead, snicker, I know it sounds crazy, but it just wasn't the same. All those others were just flashy, overpriced hunks of metal. My old Corvette had personality, and memories. Lots of memories," he added softly, glancing at her.

"It didn't have memories when you bought it," Sara pointed out.

"No," he conceded. "I told you it was crazy. I *wanted* to buy another, just to prove it *could* be replaced…that anything can be, but…" He shrugged. "It just didn't feel right.

"For a while, that really made me angry," he continued, driving slowly along the route she had specified. "I regretted ever buying the damn thing in the first place. It just seemed to reinforce what I believed all along, that loving something isn't worth losing it."

Sara felt her earlier anxiety curl to life once more in the pit of her stomach. Is this what he'd come here to tell her? That he was right all along? That there was no hope for them?

"But after a while," he continued, as Sara listened in tense silence, "it penetrated my thick skull that even though the car was gone, I still had my memories. A lot of those memories revolve around you, Sara, and I wouldn't give them up for anything. Just like I wouldn't have missed out on the time we had together, no matter what else happens. All of a sudden, a lot of things in my past began to look different to me. I started to think about things I hadn't let myself think about for a long, long time, and it was the same. I kept thinking that, in spite of everything, at least I had the memories."

"What are you saying, Flynn?"

"I'm saying that I was wrong... about a lot of things, but especially about us. I'm saying that I want to be with you, forever, if that's all right with you." His gaze volleyed between her and the quiet road ahead. "I'm trying to say that I need you in my life, and that I... Damn it, Sara, I..."

"Stop the car," she ordered, suddenly realizing where they were.

The Bronco stopped as roughly as it handled.

"What's the matter?" Flynn demanded as they both reached for the dashboard to steady themselves.

Their hands touched, and it was like fireworks going off inside her.

Their eyes met.

"We're here," Sara told him. "This is where I live."

Slowly withdrawing his hand so he could shut off the engine, Flynn peered through the windshield at the house.

"It's much more impressive in the daylight," she told him, "when you can see the deck and the beach out back."

"It's nice," he said. "Small, but nice."

Sara turned to him. "There's plenty of room for two."

"What if—someday—we need room for more than two?" he asked softly, his gaze holding steady on hers.

The question filled Sara with joy. "There's also plenty of room to add on. Someday."

Flynn smiled and moved his hand along the back of the seat.

"Flynn?"

"Yeah?"

"What were you going to say when I yelled at you to stop? You know, right after the 'damn it, Sara' part?"

"Oh, that." His hand caressed her shoulder and curled around the back of her neck. He leaned steadily closer. "I was going to say, 'damn it, Sara, I love you.'"

"Say it," she urged, her head tilting back at his silent urging, her mouth only a whisper away from his . . . and heaven. "Say it now."

"Damn it, Sara, I love you," whispered Flynn, and then he was kissing her, fast and hard and deep, as if it were possible to make up for eight months of lost time with one kiss.

It wasn't, thought Sara, when he finally released her and left her struggling for breath, but Flynn came real close. His hands moved over her urgently, awakening all those feelings she'd put on hold. Desire surged inside her as he began to fumble with the buttons on her coat, leaving her no doubt that he was as aroused and famished as she was, famished enough to make love right there.

But that wasn't going to happen. Not after all the time she had waited in anticipation of this night. Not in a Bronco.

"Come with me," she said, opening her door and sliding out.

Flynn followed behind as she led the way down the tree-lined drive, his impatience almost palpable in the cool night air. She reached into her purse for the automatic garage door opener and aimed it at the door. Flynn stood beside her as it lifted and she felt his shock even before she heard his small cry of excitement as the black Corvette parked in her garage came into full view.

"You bought a Corvette," he exclaimed, instantly abandoning her to check it out.

Sara smiled affectionately, thinking how that response was in Nancy's words, a guy thing.

"It's just like my old one," he said. "The same interior, the same sound system ... everything."

"As close as I could remember," she agreed, joining him inside the garage. She used the opener to close the door behind them, which also put out the overhead light.

"Hey, I can't see."

Sara moved closer until they were touching from shoulder to thigh and pressed the car keys into his hand. "Open the car door, there's plenty of light in there."

He did as she suggested, and the car light gave the interior of the garage a faint yellow glow.

With her still pressed close to his side, Flynn barely glanced at the illuminated interior. Evidently, Sara thought with great satisfaction, some things were even more distracting to a guy then a sports car. He finished unbuttoning her coat and pulled her against him.

"You're full of surprises," he murmured, caressing her throat with his parted lips. "I still can't believe you went and bought yourself a Corvette."

"I didn't," Sara replied, her heartbeat picking up speed. "I bought you one."

Flynn levered back and stared at her, his expression incredulous. "You what?"

"I said I bought—"

"But why?" he broke in impatiently. "Why would you do a thing like that when I ... When you had no way of knowing if I'd ..." He swallowed hard, as if not even wanting to think about what might have been.

"I knew," Sara said, her tone wise and full of confidence.

"How? How could you know when even I didn't?"

"Rule three." In response to his bewildered look, she explained, "Rule three for getting what you want."

His mustache tilted in amused understanding. "Which is?"

"Never give up hope. And I never did."

Flynn shook his head, framing her face with his hands as his mouth sought hers again and again. "You're amazing," he murmured between kisses. "And beautiful ... and sexy ... and ..."

"And I have a great memory," interjected Sara.

He shot her a puzzled look.

"Right now," she went on, "I'm remembering a night when we stood kissing just like this, beside a car just like this, and…"

Flynn grinned and caught her against him so that their hips were wed. "I believe it was more like this, wasn't it?"

"Yes," agreed Sara, short of breath suddenly. "I think so. And I've been wondering ever since if it really is possible for two people to make love in a car this size."

"Oh, I think just about anything is possible if the two people want it badly enough," he replied.

Sara smiled and with her hip bumped the door of the car open wide. "I was hoping you'd say that. Get in the car, Flynn."

* * * * *

A Note from the Author

Sara McAllister just might be my favorite among all the romance heroines I've created. I think it's because she's so real. Sara makes brave plans for her future and dreams about them coming true. She's smart and funny and caring, the kind of friend we'd all love to have. She definitely isn't one of those maddeningly plucky heroines who grabs a flashlight and braves a dark attic alone to investigate a suspicious noise, but when the chips are down, she does manage to find the courage to follow her heart. That's not always easy to do.

In fact, not much is easy about being a woman today, trying to find and hold on to what is right for you while juggling relationships, career and the glossy, glamorous magazine image of all that a woman is ''supposed'' to be. Sara was blessed to find in Flynn a man who loves her just the way she is, and even more blessed to learn to love herself the same way.

I'm proud to be part of Silhouette's That Special Woman! project because it celebrates that same individuality in all women and because it showcases all the wonderful and different ways there are to be special.

Patricia Coughlin

Silhouette SPECIAL EDITION

That SPECIAL Woman!

She's friend, wife, mother—she's you!
And to thank you for being so special to us,
we would like to send you a

FREE
Romantic Journal
in which to record all of *your*
special moments.

To receive your free ROMANTIC JOURNAL, send four proof-of-purchase coupons from any Silhouette Special Edition THAT SPECIAL WOMAN! title from January to June, plus $3.00 for postage and handling (check or money order—please do not send cash) payable to Silhouette Books, to: **In the U.S.:** THAT SPECIAL WOMAN!, Silhouette Books, 3010 Walden Avenue, P.O. Box 1396, Buffalo, NY 14269-1396; **In Canada:** THAT SPECIAL WOMAN!, Silhouette Books, P.O. Box 609, Fort Erie, Ontario L2A 5X3.

087 KAS

NAME: _____

ADDRESS: _____

CITY: _____ STATE/PROV: _____ ZIP/POSTAL: _____

(Please allow 4-6 weeks for delivery. Hurry! Quantities are limited. Offer expires August 31, 1993.)

That SPECIAL Woman!   Proof of Purchase

087 KAS

© 1991 Harlequin Enterprises Limited

INTIMATE MOMENTS
10TH
Anniversary

Celebrate our anniversary with a fabulous collection of firsts....

The first Intimate Moments titles written by three of your favorite authors:

NIGHT MOVES	Heather Graham Pozzessere
LADY OF THE NIGHT	Emilie Richards
A STRANGER'S SMILE	Kathleen Korbel

Silhouette Intimate Moments is proud to present a FREE hardbound collection of our authors' firsts—titles that you will treasure in the years to come from some of the line's founding members.

This collection will not be sold in retail stores and is available only through this exclusive offer. Look for details in Silhouette Intimate Moments titles available in retail stores in May, June and July.

Silhouette®

SPECIAL EDITION®

COMING NEXT MONTH

#805 TRUE BLUE HEARTS—Curtiss Ann Matlock
Rough-and-tumble cowboy Rory Breen and mother of two
Zoe Yarberry knew that getting together was unwise. But
though their heads were telling them no, their hearts...

#806 HARDWORKING MAN—Gina Ferris
Family Found
The first time private investigator Cassie Browning met
Jared Walker, he was in jail. Cassie soon discovered that
clearing Jared's name and reuniting him with his family
were easier tasks than fighting her feelings for him!

#807 YOUR CHILD, MY CHILD—Jennifer Mikels
When confirmed bachelor Pete Hogan opened his door to
Anne LeClare and her child, he thought he was saving them
from a snowstorm. But the forecast quickly changed to sunny
skies when they offered him the chance for love.

#808 LIVE, LAUGH, LOVE—Ada Steward
Jesse Carder had traveled far to rekindle the flames of an old
love—until she met sexy Dillon Ruiz. Dillon brought Jesse's
thoughts back to the present, but was their future possible?

#809 MAN OF THE FAMILY—Andrea Edwards
Tough cop Mike Minelli had seen Angie Hartman on the screen as
a former horror movie queen! Now he sensed vulnerable Angie
was hiding more than bad acting in her past!

#810 FALLING FOR RACHEL—Nora Roberts
That Special Woman!
Career-minded Rachel Stanislaski had little time for matters of the
heart. But when handsome Zackary Muldoon entered her life,
Rachel's pulse went into overtime!